Book 4
Seasons
of
Destiny

Winter
Skye

SUSAN
AYLWORTH

Published Internationally by Susan Aylworth
Chico, CA USA
susanaylworth.com

Exclusive cover © 2022 Bright Book Media
Inside design and formatting by Teri Barnett, indiebookdesigner.com

PRINT ISBN 978-1-7340443-0-0
EBOOK ISBN 978-1-955056-13-7

Like Susan's Facebook Page
Follow Susan on Twitter: @SusanAylworth
Follow Susan on BookBub
Follow Susan on GoodReads

For my mother,
Anonna Perkins Hubbard
1925 – 2018
I miss you, Mom.

With special thanks to Becca, Pat, Liza, Lorena, Judy,
Sue, Tabitha, Kathy, JoJo, and Gail.
My friends, you're the best!

CONTENTS

Chapter One

Spring

The old church looked just as she'd remembered. When she'd first started coming here as a child, dragged along by her aunt and uncle, the place seemed intimidating, the services strange, the minister a man to watch with suspicion—the way she watched all men. But Skye had realized over time that this place was different. It was good. The minister and others who were part of this church were good. Now the old stone walls welcomed her, inviting her home. Destiny, California was home. It was good to be back.

Silver Skye Ray parked behind the building and stepped into the crisp spring morning, reminding herself to look cheerful. She was here for a happy occasion, after all. Just because things weren't going as she'd planned… She stopped the thought. This was Amber's day—well, Max and Amber's. It wasn't their fault that men had let her down. Again. That had been the story of her life. Men always let Skye down. Her inner voice challenged, *Uncle Enrique was the perfect substitute dad.* Well yes, that was true, but there'd been so many others.

Ryan jumped to mind. They'd met at an NA meeting and agreed to support one another in sobriety. They began dating and Skye thought they could become serious. She invited him to join her for her family Thanksgiving in Destiny. Then, when she arrived to pick him up, he was as high as a set of birthday balloons. "You can't expect me to meet your family without a little help," he'd slurred. She'd been warned at NA not to get involved with guys who were newly sober, and especially not with others in the group. But she fell for Ryan's cute smile and blue eyes, and with his apparent empathy for her situation as a recovering addict.

At least Doug had disappointed her early. He'd given her a week to get used to not having a date for today's wedding. Doug had been another disastrous relationship, also met through NA. What part of "sobriety is a requirement" did these guys not understand? She couldn't afford to be around people who drank or used. She shook her head, hoping to clear it. Today she needed to be here for Amber, the cousin who'd been like a sister to her and her sister, Sunny. She wanted Amber's day to be perfect, even if their relationship had not always been.

She couldn't forget strangers who mistook Sunny and Amber for sisters, or even twins, while asking if she, Skye, was adopted. She really couldn't blame them. Sunny and Amber were the same age. Both had straight, dark brown hair, dark eyes, and light olive complexions, which made sense since both had one Hispanic and one Anglo parent. Meanwhile, Sunny and Skye shared a mother but had different dads. With her full lips, darker complexion, and wildly curly black hair that required constant conditioning and taming, Skye didn't look like anyone in the family. Lachlan, the owner of the Tahoe gallery where she'd had her last show, had compared her to Meghan Markle, only with curlier hair more like Zendaya's. No wonder she'd never fit in!

Skye pasted on a cheerful expression and hurried into the church. She'd been here when her sister Sunny was married, though she'd missed the wedding of their friend Paris. She might have made it if she hadn't been locked up at the time, the result of her third DUI, this one while driving without a license. Months of forced sobriety had helped her get clean. Now she had to stay clean, and that meant staying away from people who used, especially in the men she dated.

Skye needed someone who could understand what she'd been through, and the only people who could truly empathize were those who'd been there. To make it more difficult, she needed a partner who could accept the unpredictable life of an artist, which could be erratic, as well as emotionally and physically taxing. Would there ever be a guy for her?

She forced a smile as she entered the room where the women of the bridal party were primping and chattering. Sunny and Paris helped one another with the zippers on their attendants' dresses. Amber stood placidly while her mother, Skye's Aunt Olivia, worked on the long row of buttons up the back of her bridal gown.

"Whew! Somebody's gone heavy on the hairspray," Skye said, waving her hand in front of her face as she entered. She cracked a grin. "Hi, everyone."

"There you are!" Olivia said. "Was the traffic heavy coming up from the valley?"

"Not too bad. Why?"

"You're a bit later than we expected, but don't worry. There's still time."

"Good! I wouldn't want to be late to my cousin-sister's wedding." Skye carefully hung her dress and turned to share hugs with the others —big hugs for Sunny, Amber, and Olivia; a small side hug for Paris.

Cousin-sister. Amber resisted the label, but to Skye, it seemed perfect for the relationship they shared. They'd grown up as siblings after Aunt Olivia rescued Skye and Sunny from the Children of Rah compound, taking them from their loving but addicted and neglectful mother when Skye was barely nine. She moved closer. "What can I help with?"

"Paris has things under control," Amber said, looking to her matron of honor, her best buddy since girlhood. "You might want to take a look at the chapel, just to see how pretty it is."

"I'll do that. See you in a few." Skye stepped into the hall and let her face and thoughts fall again. Why was she having such a hard time being positive?

The chapel was lovely, just as Amber had said. Floral arrangements filled the small space with the rich scents of roses and stargazer lilies, Amber's favorite. A riot of flowers in pinks, dark reds, and burgundies accented a base of white roses and carnations with dark green foliage. Ribbons in bright navy, the same color the bridesmaids wore, matched the ribbons on the ends of the pews. It surprised Skye that Paris had done such a good job, given she'd always been such a flake, and given she had to work with an entirely different color scheme than the one she'd chosen. Paris had her own definite likes and dislikes. To create something so lovely in colors not her own? That wasn't the Paris Skye remembered. Instead she recalled times Paris's spaciness had hurt her. Then she gave herself a sharp mental kick.

She'd been through her Twelve Step manuals enough to have them memorized. The one thing she'd never fully embraced about Step Nine now stood out as if written in neon. Her group leader put it plainly: "Step Nine isn't just about seeking forgiveness from those you've wronged. You have to be willing to forgive too. Other people are only human, and they make mistakes just as you have. Be like that princess in *Frozen*. Let it go!"

He was right. Skye needed to put all those old wounds behind her. In that moment, she resolved to let go. To stop wishing her mother had never started drug use and hadn't given birth inside a cult compound, unable to identify her children's fathers. To stop thinking about Ryan and Doug and think instead of meeting a good man, someone who might one day give her the family she'd always wanted but thought she'd never have. To forgive people who'd asked if she was adopted and focus on how Enrique and Olivia had rescued her and her sister from the Children of Rah. Even knowing it might take time and effort, she resolved to let it all go. Now if only she could make that happen...

Closing her eyes, she took in five deep, cleansing breaths, letting each out slowly, breathing out the injuries of the past. Eight minutes after leaving the dressing room, she reentered it. This time, her smile was genuine.

THE CHURCH ORGAN signaled the wedding processional. Skye watched as Olivia entered first, pleased and proud, the mother of the bride escorted by her son and Skye's cousin, Tyler. Skye was close behind followed by Sunny and then Paris. Then came the groom's seven-year-old daughter Kate, adorable in an ankle length replica of the bridesmaids' dresses, her coppery hair in tight French braids.

Kate carried a basket of rose petals that she scattered liberally. Being Kate, she smiled at everyone and waved at people she knew. When she saw her teacher, she called out, "Hi, Mrs. Nguyen!" to the amusement of the guests.

With the groom and his attendants on one side of the altar and the bride's attendants on the other, the stage was set for Amber's entrance. The organ began the bride's theme and Amber swept in on the arm of her father, Skye's *Tío* Rico, the first man to restore some of Skye's faith in men. She looked at Amber, then at Enrique, and then at Max, the man who stood, joyous and starstruck, awaiting his bride. Skye hoped someday a guy would smile like that at her.

As they reached the altar, Enrique placed his daughter's hand in Max's and whispered, "Take care of her, Son. Love her as we do."

Max whispered back, "I will. I promise."

The minister welcomed everyone and invited Max's father forward to offer an invocation. Then he shared a few thoughts about the importance of marriage and how this ceremony created a tighter bond, not only for the couple involved, but for communities and societies as well. He invited Max's brother Keith to offer the scriptural reading the couple had chosen. Keith read from First Corinthians: "Love suffers long and is kind; love does not envy…"

As the familiar words echoed around the congregation, Skye watched Amber and Max become a family. They stood side by side, holding hands. Kate snuggled close by Amber while her twin brother, Will, grasped his father's pant leg.

Skye couldn't help but be amused at the seriousness of Will's expression. Max had been wise to make Will his best man. She'd heard the stories of Max and Amber's stop-and-go courtship. Will had opposed the union, and his animosity had come close to keeping the couple apart. He was all in now and the group—Amber, Max, Will, and Kate—made an adorable family.

For a moment, Skye wondered if she'd ever have a family of her own. She'd wanted that, then feared it was impossible. Recently she'd learned it could happen; doctors said she was healthy enough to bear a child. Now the question was would she? Her inner voice shouted, *Let it go! Don't worry now.* The mantra didn't always work, but in the face of the moment's joy, her negative thoughts diminished.

The minister announced that the couple had written their own vows. Max took a notepad from the pocket of his suit coat and glanced briefly at it. Then he shook his head and put the notes back in his pocket. "I'm going to shoot from the hip with this," he announced. Good-natured laughter flowed around the room.

"Sunny and Evan reminded us that love is a choice." He paused as a wave of assent rippled through the audience. "We agree that love *is* a choice, so some of this may sound familiar." He began reciting: "Today I choose you, Amber Eleanor Reyes, to be my wife, my life partner, and my heart's companion. I promise I will continue to choose you every day for the rest of our lives and even beyond. Even when we disagree or struggle with difficult decisions, I will never again let differences divide us. And I promise to keep choosing you, Amber, each and every day, forever and always."

The audience responded with expressions of assent. When all was silent, Amber began.

"I also took a page from Sunny and asked the Daughters of Destiny to sing as they did at Evan and Sunny's wedding." A murmur ran through the audience at the mention of the town's big success story, the five sisters and cousins who had begun singing together in school talent shows and now had original songs at the top of the country/pop charts.

"They're touring on the East coast this week and couldn't be here..." Amber paused for the disappointed sigh, "but they volunteered their mothers, the women who taught them to sing. I am privileged to have Giselle and Caroline Reed sing the beginning of my vows."

Skye applauded with the audience as the duo, well known to the residents of Destiny, stepped to the front of the church. Giselle picked up a guitar. They sang the words written by Sunny and her friend, Camille Reed, one of the primary songwriters for the Daughters of Destiny:

Today I choose to pledge to you to make your life my own.
Today I choose to love you and to make your heart my home.
I choose to live close by your side each day throughout my life,
To take you as my husband and I'll be your wedded wife.
I choose you. I choose you.

The women sang the song just as the Daughters of Destiny had sung it for Sunny and Evan. Then Caroline announced, "Amber has added a verse for today." The women sang:

Today I pledge to celebrate your children as my own.
Dear Will and Kate, I promise you to make a loving home.
The four of us will grow together, honoring each day,
Loving one another in a tender family way.
I choose you, sweet children, I choose you.

Few dry eyes remained as the wedding guests applauded, the singers took their seats, and Amber began her vows: "Today I choose you, Max Raymond Burnett, to be my husband. I promise I will continue to choose you every day for the rest of our lives and even beyond."

Skye watched her cousin's face fill with joy and peace. A warm tear trickled down Skye's cheek as Amber came to the end of her speech: "I promise to keep choosing you, each and every day, forever and always."

The minister said. "You two have written heartfelt vows, and I'm touched by what you've shared." He waited while the audience settled. "Max Raymond Burnett, do you take Amber Eleanor Reyes to be your wedded wife?"

Max answered, "I do."

"Amber Eleanor Reyes, do you take Max Raymond Burnett to be your wedded husband?"

"I do!" Amber spoke so eagerly that the audience chuckled.

The minister looked to the two red-haired children. "Kate Isabel Burnett and Will Max Burnett, do you take this woman, Amber Eleanor Reyes, to be your mother?"

Both children shouted, "We do!" to the delight of the guests.

"Do you have the rings?" the minister asked. Will, instantly sobered by the weight of his duty, reached into his coat pocket and pulled out a ring box.

"Thank you, Will." The minister picked up one band and held it for the congregation to see. "This ring has no beginning and no end. Let it stand as a symbol of your lasting love." He handed the bands to the couple and watched as they put them on each other's fingers.

"Now that Amber and Max have pledged their commitment in the presence of this company and have formalized it with an exchange of promises and rings, I am pleased to announce they are husband and wife, legally and lawfully wedded. Max and Amber, you may now share the first kiss of your married life."

Skye held her breath as the newly wedded couple stood gazing at one another. They stood at the altar, paused on the brink of a kiss. Max moved slowly, carefully taking Amber's face into his hands and smiling into her eyes before placing a tender kiss on her lips. Amber surprised him by pulling him in for a second, more robust, kiss. The audience laughed and applauded.

The minister announced, "Ladies and gentlemen, I give you Max and Amber Burnett!" The crowd stood, cheering and applauding as the new family led the way down the aisle. Following with the rest of the wedding party, Skye imprinted the image of her perfect, beautiful man—the man she wanted—upon her heart. He was out there some-where, and when the time was right, she would find him.

Chapter Two

Summer

Skye rented studio space in an old, repurposed warehouse near the university. Her floor area, marked off from the others with painted lines, welcomed her home, its scent of paint, canvas, and old concrete cheering her. The success of her one-woman show in Tahoe would have provided enough to pay her studio rent for the coming months, cover her fall tuition, and keep up her daily expenses for some time—if not for the fines and court costs resulting from her DUI.

Her parole would not officially end until she'd paid off all those costs, not to mention the substantial damages awarded to the other party, the people whose car she'd wrecked. She could cover legal fees or fall term tuition, but if she wanted to do both, which she very much did, she needed to succeed dramatically. Again.

That was why she felt so frustrated as she stood, paints and brushes and tools at the ready, staring at a blank canvas with an equally blank mind. She had only a few weeks until the next big show in San Francisco, and she needed to come up with brilliant work. With luck, this show could cover the rest of her expenses—if she stuck to a tight budget—corset-tight, with almost no breathing room. Today she had only three hours to paint before she had to report for work, and here she was, stuck for a subject and not knowing where to begin. She sighed as she tucked her tightly curly hair behind her ears.

Focusing on the time pressure was not the best way to bring creativity to the surface. Instead, she focused on breathing, trying to release tension. Her new AA leader had reminded the group that when they're stuck and want a hit to boost creativity, they need to look at problems that may be getting in the way.

Skye thought back over her efforts to seek and give forgiveness.

After Amber's wedding, she'd returned to the same AA group just once. She took Doug aside and asked his forgiveness for the way she'd treated him when she found him drunk. She also offered her forgiveness.

"Does that mean we can go out again?"

His hopeful look almost tweaked her conscience. Almost. "No, Doug. We're through, but I hope you achieve full sobriety and learn how to maintain it, and I wish you all good things in life." She blew a kiss and left him there.

When she found Ryan, she repeated almost the same conversation she'd had with Doug, except that Ryan had begged a little more. Seeing him grovel helped her realize he wasn't ready for sobriety or for a mature relationship. She politely but firmly told him, "We're through."

She'd gone through Step Nine so many times. Her mother had died as had many of the adults who were involved with the Children of Rah. She'd tried to forgive them all, at least to forgive her memories of them. It had been more difficult to forgive those older kids for all they did, but she kept reminding herself they were just kids and didn't have anyone to teach them better. At this point, Skye didn't know what more she could do.

She was still standing trapped in memory, trying to forgive the ghosts of the past, when Molly, the student artist who rented the space next to hers, asked, "Sorry to bother, but I'm hoping you can help with this painting. It's due for class next week and I—"

"No, I really don't have the time." Realizing she'd snapped, Skye added, "Sorry if I'm abrupt. I'm under a lot of pressure today." She saw Molly's face fall, but determinedly turned back to her blank canvas, guilt weighing heavily on her conscience. Then, contrite, she looked at Molly's painting. "What kind of help do you need?"

Molly gave Skye a better view. "I'm trying to paint a huge flower. Georgia O'Keeffe style, ya know? But I can't seem to get the curve of the petals right. I'm going for an orchid and what I've got here looks more like a daisy."

Sighing, Skye put down her brush and went to help Molly. Twenty minutes later, Molly's orchid had the proper curve to its petals and

Skye stood in front of her own blank canvas again. Molly thanked her profusely and Skye answered, "No problem." Funny how she felt so much better now, even though she'd used a big chunk of time. She still couldn't think of anyth—

Wait! She picked up her brush and began to paint, beginning with dark, jagged shapes near the bottom right of the canvas to portray her former frustration. The colors grew lighter and brighter, the shapes more fluid, as they moved upward toward a shimmering white in the top left. Between, she painted a lightning-strike strip of yellow, the same color as Molly's shirt.

She became so involved in the creation of emotion on canvas that she forgot to check her time. When she suddenly remembered, she had a scant few minutes to dash to work at her part-time campus job assisting in the office that scheduled art exhibitions. She didn't much like this part of the art world, but if she meant to support herself as an independent artist, she should at least understand how it worked, and she was grateful for the income. Catching her breath, she rushed from the building.

Later that evening, Skye ran her memory tape of the afternoon, pausing to consider what had happened. She'd been worried that if she took minutes out to help Molly, she'd lose the time on her own project, but helping Molly had turned her attention away from her own worries and given her the mental space to find a new idea.

A scene from years ago popped into her mind. She and Sunny had taken a long road trip to southern California with their Uncle Enrique and Aunt Olivia. *Abuela* Reyes was mom to Enrique and Donna Reyes —Skye's mother, who changed her name to Dawn Ray when she joined the Children of Rah. *Abuela* moved slowly and spoke with a gravelly voice, but she filled the room with love. In a rare moment alone with her, Skye asked, "*Abuela*, sometimes I remember bad things that happened, and I start feeling like maybe nobody should love me."

"Ah, *chiquita mia*." Her *abuela* stroked her hair. "Everybody feels like that sometimes. You have to tell that feeling to go away. Do something that makes you happy. Sing a happy song, say a jolly rhyme, whatever lifts you up."

"I tried that yesterday in the car." Skye stroked her grandmother's wrinkled hand. "Everybody was talking, but nobody was talking to me, so I tried singing a song to myself."

"*Qué pasó?*"

"Sunny told me to stop singing 'cause I was out of tune."

Her *abuela* chuckled. "I don't guess that made you feel better."

"It made everything worse."

"Hear me, dear one. I have something important to tell you." She took Skye's face in her hands and leaned close. "When you are feeling bad, so bad that you don't think you can feel much worse, that's when you need to help somebody else."

Skye wrinkled her nose. "That doesn't make sense."

"Maybe not. But it works. Try it."

"But you can't always do that. What about yesterday in the car?"

"Maybe you could have offered people a drink and passed the water around. There is always a way to help someone, and it will make you feel better."

"I guess I can try." Skye snuggled against her grandmother, one person who always made her feel loved. Visits were few and *Abuela* Reyes passed not long after, but Skye remembered her grandmother's loving expression when she shared her advice.

She was coming to understand how it worked. When she showed Molly a skill that was difficult for her but which Skye found easy, she was reminded of the skills she had developed. Showing Molly how to get the curve she wanted in those petals took Skye out of her own thoughts so she could return to her canvas with fresh eyes, and that fresh view had given her a new emotion she could convey, something brighter than her earlier frustration.

She smiled. *Abuela* knew what she was talking about. Helping someone else was empowering. She realized that's why it's part of Step Twelve in the AA or NA program. "*Gracias, Abuela.*" Skye looked heavenward as calm settled over her.

THE NEXT DAY was turmoil from the start. Skye must have hit the snooze button without realizing, so she woke twenty minutes late.

Then her toaster sputtered and fried itself, leaving her running down the steps from her apartment with a slice of untoasted bread for breakfast. The professor in her only summer class came up with a huge assignment, due in two weeks, that she hadn't mentioned before. When everyone complained, she drew their attention to page eight of her dry-

as-tinder syllabus.

If that wasn't enough, Skye got a text just before leaving class to grab lunch. With no explanation, her internship supervisor sent the message:

We need you here right away.

So much for lunch. Skye rushed to the office only to find that the emergency was a going-away party for the receptionist, who had a family situation that caused her to leave her job. Skye forced a smile and tried to be cheerful. Maybe she could get lunch here. People were getting out refreshments. That hope faded as the supervisor carried in a stack of pizza boxes.

"Help yourself, Skye," the supervisor said as others stepped up to do just that.

"I think I'll pass. Thanks."

Her supervisor looked more critical than concerned. "Not in a party mood?"

"My stomach is uneasy. Not up to pizza, I'm afraid." In fact, the pizza smelled marvelous and Skye had a hard time not drooling. But part of her effort toward full sobriety was staying away from foods that triggered a desire to drink or use. Pizza had always been her go-to food after a drug binge. Unfortunately, that meant avoiding it now. "In fact," she added, "if the celebration is mostly over, I'd like to get something to settle my stomach before I come back to work this afternoon. Is that okay with you?"

The supervisor, her mouth full of pizza, nodded.

Skye said her goodbyes to the departing employee, although the two worked in different spaces and hardly knew each other. Then she took herself away from the delicious pizza aroma as quickly as possible. She hadn't lied about her upset stomach. It was empty and aching. She needed to eat.

Thinking of her nearly empty fridge and the fact that she'd procrastinated grocery shopping, she chose to grab lunch on the street before going home to change. It wasn't in the budget, but she needed food. Thank goodness the taco truck was here. Skye waited in a long line to order her favorite burrito only to find that the price had gone up and she didn't have enough to cover her meal, even after counting out all her change. She'd cut up her credit cards months ago after her last disastrous, liquor-fueled spending binge, and she'd also killed the quick-pay apps on her phone, a move she now regretted.

Glancing at that phone, Skye saw she was still more or less on schedule but would need to get moving if she wanted to get home, eat, and return to work on time. She jogged to her apartment. As soon as she opened the door, she knew something was off. It only took a moment to realize her roommate was gone, as in permanently gone, all of her things moved out.

Over the last few months, Lila had been living with her boyfriend but lying to her parents about it and letting them pay half the rent on Skye's apartment. Although Skye didn't approve of Lila's behavior and even said so ("If you're going to make this choice, why not accept the responsibility for it?"), she'd actually had little to do with Lila, which meant she mostly had the apartment to herself with only half the cost of rent, not a bad situation.

She found the letter on top of the dresser in Lila's room: "Micky and I rented a house together. My parents found out, and they're cutting me off, but it's okay. Micky has money."

Skye shook her head as she read the letter. Now Lila was separating from her family to become fully dependent on this guy. What if things went wrong with Micky? Realizing she'd begun to worry over something outside her sphere of influence, Skye repeated the Serenity Prayer: "God grant me the serenity to accept the things I cannot change, courage to change the things I can, and wisdom to know the difference." Then she took a deep breath and let her worry over Lila disappear as she exhaled.

"Good luck, Lila." She said it aloud, wishing Lila well although she never expected to see her again. Now she had to find another roommate or she couldn't afford to live here. And the hits just kept on coming. What a day this had been! She threw Lila's letter into the waste basket, grabbed another slice of bread—well, half a slice, since that was all she had left—and rode her bike as fast as she could to get back to work, arriving only three minutes late.

Four long, dull hours later, she rode to the studio space. That's where she found Molly sobbing beside her picture of an orchid that was actually beginning to look like one. Remembering yesterday, Skye resolved to help if she could. Maybe that would help make this awful day look better. "Hey there, Rembrandt." She squatted beside Molly's stool. "I'm guessing this tear-storm isn't about a poor angle on a flower."

Molly turned into Skye's embrace, sobbing onto her shoulder. "My dad lost his job! My parents have money to pay my fall tuition, but not to keep up my rent, and I'm on my own after that. I don't know what to do!"

Skye took a deep breath. Helping Molly could take a while this time. "First, you need to stop crying. You can't come up with answers while you're in a panic."

"Oh. Yeah. Okay."

Skye waited while Molly calmed. Then she said, "Sweetie, lots of people go to school, even when their parents can't pay for any of it. I don't have parents, but I'm managing."

"You don't have parents?" Molly's eyes went wide.

"No, but that's a long story and we're not talking about me today. I've been scraping by as an artist, selling my work to get along." She looked at the almost-an-orchid. "You're not there yet, but in the meantime, lots of us earn our way with part-time jobs. Have you held jobs before?" Molly nodded. "What have you done?"

Still sniffing, Molly answered. "My dad is an accountant. He worked in a firm with two other guys. I answered phones for all three of them last summer."

"You worked as a receptionist."

Molly nodded. "Um-hm."

It would be perfect if Molly could work as the receptionist at the scheduling office. Just like that, the pieces of Skye's terrible day came together, and the picture they created made her smile.

Chapter Three

Autumn

Everything was finally going well. Skye waved at Molly as they crossed trails at the scheduling office. Molly had slipped easily into the receptionist's position. Neither Skye nor Molly would ever get rich on what they earned working for the school, but Skye found it adequate for the present, and Molly's salary covered groceries and the rent on her half of Skye's apartment. "Now I just have to figure out how to save for tuition," Molly had said over hot tea that morning.

"Be glad your folks already covered the first term." Skye skipped the sugar but passed it to Molly. "If you end up having to borrow, that's not the Apocalypse, zombie or otherwise. Most people borrow at least part of their college expenses."

"And graduate with a mountain of debt." Molly sighed.

"Speaking of mountains, my friend, you need to learn to climb only one peak at a time. Right now, your tuition is paid and you're earning enough to cover expenses. You're trying to climb Everest when you've barely made it to base camp."

Molly set down her cup. "How'd you get so smart?"

"Practice." Skye wiggled her eyebrows for emphasis.

Molly left for class minutes later, looking happier than she had in days.

Right behind her, Skye reviewed the last few weeks as she power walked to class. Not only had the departure of her former roomie, Lila, turned out to be a blessing, but so had the vacancy in the scheduling office—the vacancy she would not have known about before it could be listed if she hadn't gone to the impromptu goodbye party.

Even the huge assignment turned out to be no big deal, not for Skye anyway. The project required her to turn in quality photographs of ten original pieces. She had to write two pages on the genesis of each piece, other than the one she considered her masterwork; that one required a five-page discussion. Some of her classmates had scrambled to come up with ten pieces. Others had suffered over what to write. Skye had a portfolio with professional shots of more than sixty pieces, and she had a story for each of them.

The only hang-up was which piece to call her masterwork. In the end, she chose the photo of the painting *Change of Heart*, the one she started that day in the studio when she helped Molly. Writing about it was easy: two pages to explain the work's genesis and three more to analyze why she'd made the choices she did when it came to colors and shapes. She could have gone on for three more, if that had been permitted.

Three days later, she went by the professor's office to pick up her graded project only to find the project, but no grade. Instead, the professor's note said, "See me." Taking a deep breath, Skye knocked on the door. She didn't know whether to be worried or relieved when Dr. Weems opened immediately. "Skye, come in. Have a seat." The look on her face gave away nothing.

"I notice my project isn't graded and I wondered—"

"Oh, it's graded. I've already turned in my grades for the summer course. You should be getting your report soon."

"But—"

Dr. Weems leaned forward. "Skye, I've been giving this assignment for several years. Most students struggle with it. You seemed to find it easy."

Skye shrugged. "It *was* easy—for me, anyway."

"I thought so. It was also brilliant, the best project I've seen. How many pieces did you have to choose from?"

The next half hour turned into a pleasant and productive discussion as Dr. Weems, treating Skye as a colleague, asked her questions about her work and where she'd exhibited. "What exhibit did you consider your best so far?"

Skye considered. "It's kind of a tie. The only one-artist show I've ever done was in Tahoe roughly a year ago. I suspect I got the single-artist opportunity because the gallery owner wanted me to date him."

The professor raised a brow. "Did it work?"

"No!" Skye laughed at the idea. "Not my type. He was good to work with, though."

"What's the other show tied for first?"

"Just a couple of weeks ago, I exhibited at a big gallery in San Francisco." Skye pulled out the gallery's business card, glad she hadn't cleaned her purse yet.

"Impressive. I know this place."

"I felt privileged to show there." For a second, Skye relived the moment she'd first seen their invitation. "I tied it with Tahoe only because I was one of twelve artists they showcased. I got the spotlight in Tahoe and the take-a-number routine in the city. Of course, the San Francisco gallery is larger and so much more prestigious, but being one of twelve?"

"Still impressive. Did you do well in sales?"

"I sold every piece I took—both shows. The piece I picked for your assignment as my masterwork, *Change of Heart*? Three buyers got into a bidding war. It went for more than I could have imagined." Skye had even begun to imagine breathing room in her budget.

The professor asked how much the painting sold for and gave a long, low whistle when Skye answered. "You have definitely reached the professional ranks." She took off her reading glasses and looked Skye in the face. "What are you still doing here? Here at school, I mean."

"I want the degree, and I only have this term and one more to go."

"You don't need a degree to make a good living with your art."

"I know, but I've had a few naysayers in my life. I want to show them I can do this. More importantly, I want to prove it to myself."

Her professor nodded. "That I understand. Go for it, Skye. And come to me if I can ever do anything to help your career along. I have quite a few contacts in the art world and my husband has even more."

"Thank you. I'll remember that." Skye stood, shook her new mentor's hand, and started for the door. "Oh, the grade?"

"An A, of course. I wish I could have given something higher."

"Thank you."

"No, Skye. Thank *you*. One day I'll brag that I once had you as a student."

Skye buzzed all the way home. As she looked back over the tumultuous day she'd had weeks before and what had become of it, she recognized a life lesson learned: *Don't obsess over a bad day. It could be just what you need to set up a series of good ones.*

SKYE NEEDED that reminder when Thursday came and with it, a summons to Small Claims Court. The people whose car she'd hit were suing for additional damages. Skye spent part of the afternoon searching her records and another part on the phone with her court-appointed attorney. Her attorney assured her this could be handled with an out-of-court settlement but would probably require several thousand dollars. So much for room in the budget.

Skye always hit an AA or NA meeting on Thursday evenings and she needed it more than ever after the day she'd just had. But since leaving the group Doug attended, she hadn't found one she liked. One group was mostly women about her age. That would have been perfect, except it was in El Dorado Hills, half an hour's drive each way, even without rush hour traffic. Since her job in the scheduling office didn't end until five, and the meeting started at five-thirty, Skye was always caught in the five o'clock rush and always late, once by forty minutes. She saw no point in going if she got there as the meeting ended.

A friend mentioned a new group starting at 5:30 a few blocks from campus and Skye decided to give it a try. At quitting time, she was among the first to reach the door, arriving at the meeting site just eleven minutes later. She followed the "AA here" signs to a basement room in an old church. It smelled of aging building and fresh coffee.

A middle-aged man approached. "Hi, I'm Ron, the group leader. Looks like you're the first one here." He offered his hand and they shook.

"I hope this group works out." Skye looked around. This is perfect for me."

Ron answered, "Me too. Let's hope."

Four others trickled in and Ron greeted each. Minutes later, the meeting began with Ron giving the usual speech and adding a few words about trying to get this new group going strong. Then they went around the circle with introductions. Skye answered as she always did: "Hi, I'm Skye. I'm an addict and alcoholic."

The group responded, "Hi, Skye."

They moved into Step One. The first step for any addict came when she or he recognized the addiction and admitted the habit had spun out of control, making life unmanageable. Skye smiled to herself, knowing she'd have something to say when it came time to share.

That's when *he* walked in—taller than most of the men she knew, six-three at least; brawny and wonderfully fit; black hair, mustache, and beard, all neatly trimmed; equally black eyes; and a tawny complexion, maybe of Middle Eastern descent. He rang every bell in Skye's awareness and caused every cell in her body to buzz. She couldn't have been more starstruck if an A-list movie star had entered the room. In fact, the star would have attracted her less. "Sorry I'm late," he said as he sat.

The leader said, "No worries. We're just getting started; please introduce yourself."

Mr. Beautiful nodded. "Hi, I'm Pete. I'm an alcoholic."

Skye joined the group in greeting. "Hi, Pete!" Her thoughts took off in a different direction: *Even his voice is beautiful.*

Through the next half-hour, while the group worked through Step One, Skye struggled to keep from staring, but her eyes always found their way back to Pete. Good thing she knew the steps by heart! She'd hardly heard a word, but she couldn't stop watching him. Once or twice, Pete looked up, caught her staring, and gave her a vague, uncomfortable smile. Okay, so he wasn't interested. Not yet. She'd need to make him change his mind.

Skye tried to focus as they came to the sharing portion of the meeting. She wanted to share her experience with her arrest and how jail time had forced her to recognize the addiction. Mostly, she hoped Pete would share; she wanted to hear his voice again. She'd need to watch herself carefully around that one. She hadn't even officially met him, and already she was putty. Or maybe clay. That was an easy comparison. Her sculptures were eventually cast in bronze, but she always began shaping her designs in potter's clay. At this moment, that gorgeous man could mold her any way he wanted.

The woman next to her started the sharing. A tiny little thing, probably in her forties, she told a story of abuse, first by her parents and then by her husband. Self-medicating to shut down the angst, she had become addicted. When she finished, others in the group were nodding. The story was familiar to them all.

Feeling both energized and cautioned, Skye began sharing the lesson she'd learned from her arrest, promising herself to keep it both concise and meaningful. She'd barely begun when Mr. Gorgeous checked his watch, said "Excuse me," got up, and left.

Disappointment washed over Skye like ice water thrown from a bucket, and it felt strongly like rejection. She tried to laugh it off. "Was it something I said?" The group chuckled. She finished her story, but she lacked the focus she'd hoped for. Did he really have someplace he had to be? Or had he left because of her?

Skye pretended to listen through the rest of the sharing, but in her mind, she repeated the Serenity Prayer, reminding herself that she could control her actions toward him but not his responses to her. As the meeting ended, she sucked in deep breaths, mentally repeating the mantra, *let it go, let it go, let it go.*

THE FOLLOWING day required her to remember Step Seven: Humility. It shouldn't be so hard to ask for help, especially when Dr. Weems had already offered it. She managed a smile as she knocked on the professor's door.

"Skye! Come in." Dr. Weems gestured toward a seat. "What can I do for you?"

Skye sat, composing herself. "I'm afraid I have a rather large favor to ask." Skye reminded herself to smile, or to at least look pleasant.

"Ask away. The worst I can say is no."

Her mentor's casual attitude helped, so Skye plunged ahead. "I haven't paid my fall tuition yet. I've been saving for it and I have most of what I need, but the school's already added the late fee, and I'm a couple of hundred dollars short. I have to pay in full within the next week or I'll be dropped from all my fall classes."

"Skye, are you asking me for money?"

"No! I wouldn't do that. For various reasons, I'm not a good candidate for a student loan, but I'm willing to work You've helped many students over the years. I'm hoping you can come up with a bright idea I haven't already thought of."

"Hmmm." Dr. Weems pursed her lips. She seemed to be concentrating. Then she stood. "Come with me. We'll go chat with my husband."

"I don't have much time, and I can't leave campus. I need to get to my office job in forty-five minutes."

The professor's face clouded. "What office job?"

"I work part-time in the office that schedules art exhibits for the school."

"No." Dr. Weems shook her head decisively. "Someone with your talent shouldn't be working an office job. You need to give notice today. Get out of there as soon as you're able."

"But—"

"You want my help? No buts." The professor opened the door and gestured for Skye to step out first. Dr. Weems followed her and locked the door. Then she said, "You don't happen to have any pictures of your recent work, do you?"

"Yes. In fact, I have them with me. I picked them up from the printer on the way here."

"Great. Bring them along."

Skye hesitated. "I don't want to be late—"

"For heaven's sake, Skye. Trust me, okay?"

Reminding herself of the lesson on humility, Skye responded meekly, "Yes, ma'am," and followed Dr. Weems down the hall.

They walked a few yards. Then Dr. Weems opened the door of the department office and asked the secretary, "Is Tom in?"

"Yes, he just arrived," the woman answered. "I'll let him know you're here."

"Don't bother. I'll knock." Dr. Weems led the way to the inner office. She raised her hand to knock, but Skye interrupted her.

"Your husband is Tom Felix, head of the art department?" To her own ears, her voice sounded as breathless as she felt.

The professor smiled. "Come on in and let me introduce you." Dr. Weems opened the door. "Tom? Do you have a minute?"

The distinguished looking man behind the desk turned with a smile. "Sure. Come on in."

Chapter Four

Over the next few minutes, Dr. Weems did most of the talking while her husband listened, then asked questions, then heard Skye's answers. The two professors examined Skye's pictures and asked a few more questions. When Skye looked at her cell phone to check the time, Dr. Weems explained to her husband about Skye's office job. "I told her to quit it immediately."

"I agree," Dr. Felix said. "An artist of this caliber shouldn't be working in an office, not when she could be painting or sculpting." He addressed Skye. "Go on to your job so you aren't late," he said. "While you're there, give your notice—"

"But—"

"Trust me." Dr. Felix echoed his wife. "You finish your shift when?"

"Five o'clock."

"All right. I usually leave around five, but I'll wait for you here. Come back when you leave the office and I'll have some answers for you."

Dr. Weems spoke up. "I'll do some work at my end and meet you both here."

Skye nodded. "Okay. I'll do that." She reached for her pictures.

"Let me keep these for a while." Dr. Felix pulled them out of her reach. "You can pick them up when you come back."

She nodded again. "All right. I can do that."

"One other thing," Dr. Felix said. "I believe I may have buyers for some of your work. Do I have your permission to act as an agent?"

"Yeah. Sure! That'd be great." Skye said a quick goodbye and left, jogging toward the scheduling office. While her feet covered the yards, her mind churned. She didn't know what had happened there, but she hoped it turned out to be as good as it sounded.

SKYE WORKED through most of the afternoon, procrastinating the talk she'd promised to have with her supervisor. The two professors had said she should trust them, but this job was all she had. Of course, if she didn't pay the tuition, she would not be a student anymore, and since this job was just for students, she'd lose it anyway. Reminding herself of the way she'd stayed afloat the previous year, even without the job, she pulled together her courage. Of course, she hadn't had a pending lawsuit then either. A few minutes before five, she asked her supervisor, Lucy, if she could speak to her alone.

"Sure." Lucy led her into a conference room and closed the door. "What's up?"

Skye started with, "I want to give notice" and ended minutes later by describing the scene in Dr. Felix's office.

Lucy listened with skepticism, but by the time Skye had finished, she was nodding along. "I should have known we couldn't keep you. I've seen your work, and they're right. Someone with your talent should be painting and sculpting and whatever else you do. You're good."

"Thank you, Lucy." Skye felt relief wash over her. "That's kind of you to say."

"Were you planning to give us two weeks?"

"Yes, though I can stay a little longer if you need me."

"Oh, we need you. Don't think otherwise. But we can get along without you, too." She looked at the calendar. "Do you think you can stay through this Friday?"

"That's only three more days!"

"Right. Friday is also the end of the pay period. I should be able to find a sub by then, and we'll work with the substitute until we can fill the vacancy. We're not officially part of the university, although we're an affiliate, so we don't have to go through all the regular channels. I'll never *replace* you." Lucy smiled. "But I'll be able to fill the vacancy. You get out there and do your thing and we'll wish you well."

"That's wonderful! Thanks, Lucy." Then, needing something to do with her glut of emotion, she asked, "Can I give you a hug?"

"It's against protocol, but if you don't tell, I won't." Lucy grinned and held out her arms.

Skye hugged her hard. "Thank you so much!"

"Don't mention it." Then Lucy pinned her with a teasing look. "Seriously, Skye, don't mention it. I'd be besieged by people wanting hugs." She winked.

Skye drew her fingers across tightly closed lips. "Our little secret."

"Good." Lucy opened the office door, aware of the many pairs of curious ears waiting for them when they stepped out. "That's it for today, then." She spoke up more than was necessary. "We'll see you for your regular shift tomorrow."

"Yes, ma'am." Skye fell into the same speech pattern. "Thanks again, and I'll see you tomorrow."

Disappointed at the lack of juicy gossip, others in the office began to gather their things. The clock ticked five, and Skye joined the exodus. She would do this only three more times. Then she remembered where she was going and why. She could only hope her professors knew what they were doing.

BOTH PROFESSORS WERE WAITING when she reached the department office. Dr. Weems ushered her in. "Did you give your notice?" she asked as Skye entered.

Skye explained what had happened and that she had only three shifts left to work.

"Wonderful!" Dr. Weems looked at Dr. Felix. Both were grinning like Happy Face posters.

Dr. Felix pulled out a chair. "Sit down, young lady. We have news."

Skye listened as the two professors detailed their efforts of the last four hours: the people with whom they'd spoken, the pieces they'd already sold on her behalf, and the prices they'd been promised for each. When they added up the total, Dr. Weems asked, "Will that be enough to cover tuition?"

Skye, her voice choked with emotion, answered, "I can barely believe it! That will cover my tuition, the late fee, and the rent on my studio space for the rest of this term." She didn't add it would also cover half or more of the out-of-court settlement her attorney had proposed.

"We hoped you'd say that." Dr. Weems practically bounced in her chair.

"Dr. Weems, you look as stoked as I feel."

"That's not all," her mentor responded. "We arranged a space for you in the art exhibition the Soho does in conjunction with Oktoberfest."

"I can't thank you enough. That is so kind."

Then Dr. Felix smiled that same secretive grin. "We've saved the best for last." He took a deep breath and settled in his chair, obviously pleased with the announcement he was about to make. "Do you know of the Jardin de la Vie?"

Skye felt her eyes widen. She swallowed. "That's the very exclusive art gallery and sculpture garden in St. Helena, in the Napa Valley."

"The same." Dr. Felix turned to his wife. "You tell her, Vickie. You arranged it."

Skye had to focus to hear what Dr. Weems had to say. "They have their permanent collection, but they also have one large room they dedicate to works available for purchase, only by northern California artists. They have additional space in the sculpture garden as well." She paused. "We did a video call with the curator there—Filene, we know her well—and I texted her the photos of some of your work."

She paused, sent a twinkly grin toward her husband, and said, "She'd like you to do a one-woman show in both spaces. I calculate you'll need roughly twenty paintings, depending on their size, and maybe fifteen sculpture pieces."

Skye blinked. Hard. "I...I don't know what to say. I don't—"

Dr. Weems cut her off. "Can you be ready by November fifteenth? Installation begins on the seventeenth."

That was less than three months! All that work...in that short a time? And that's after her professors sold most of the pieces she had ready. Skye swallowed hard. "Yes, ma'am. I can. I will. If I'm working in the studio during the time I was working in the scheduling office, I should be able to do that, except. . .."

Dr. Felix cut her off, a frown spreading across his face. "Except what?"

Skye had one panicky moment, thinking of all she still owed from the lawsuit. What if the other party didn't accept her attorney's low-ball offer. "I still have other expenses—"

Both professors glanced at each other and grinned again. Dr. Weems said, "No problem. We're building up to the good stuff."

"Okay." Skye waited.

"Filene—that's the curator," Dr. Weems continued, "wants to buy your big painting, the one you call *Random Thoughts*. She says you 'simply must' show it in her gallery, but she'll mark it sold as soon as you arrive. She wants it for her permanent collection, and the price she's offering should easily cover all your living expenses from now until you graduate. At least."

Skye fought tears. Her professors' intervention came as a timely rescue, another in Skye's life. "Thank you both so very much. I-I don't...know what to say."

Dr. Felix answered. "Say you can be ready by November fifteenth. We all have a lot riding on this."

Skye nodded. "I'll do it," she said, silently promising herself that whatever it took, she'd be ready.

TWO DAYS PASSED. Skye shared her news with Molly, who declared she'd miss her at the office, but agreed Skye couldn't pass up the opportunity. Skye also did her work in the scheduling office, all the while planning in the back of her mind how she would go about prepping for the biggest opportunity of her life coming up so quickly. She began developing plans for smaller pieces for the Oktoberfest show, as well as some ambitious efforts that might impress the cultured crowd at the Jardin de la Vie. Her fingers itched for a brush or sculpting tool, but commitments to work and classes kept her out of the studio until Saturday.

That wasn't all that preoccupied her. This much emotion, this much stress, put on serious pressure to use again—just a little something to take the edge off. She knew better, but the urge was strong. She needed another AA meeting. Not normally a clock watcher, Skye couldn't keep from looking up every few minutes, counting down the time until she could rush to the second gathering of the new AA group. She hoped she'd see Pete there, and this time she'd find a moment to speak to him directly. But whether he showed up or not, she needed the calming influence of the Serenity Prayer, the strength of the group. She needed reminders why using anything again, even a little, would sabotage rather than help.

When five o'clock arrived, Skye sprinted for the door, unlocked her bike, and pumped toward the old church, arriving even before the group leader. She helped set up, greeted people as they came in, and watched the door as Ron, the leader, prepared to start. They began in the usual way and Skye waited and watched as the group began to work through Step Two: "Come to believe that a power greater than yourself can restore you to sanity."

Any time someone shuffled or made a sound, she looked up, expecting to see Pete at the door, but he didn't come. Not at all. At the end of the meeting, she had reinforced her sobriety with another strong reminder and the sharing of others. She had also come to believe she would never see Mr. Beautiful again.

On Friday, Skye's last day at work, Lucy and the others chipped in to buy pizza and a chocolate cake, two foods Skye diligently avoided. Both were triggers since she associated both with using. Saying no would seem ungracious, so she helped herself to small pieces. Then she carried them with her, using her fork to move bits around on her plate, until she could slip the whole thing into the trash can unnoticed. She hated the waste, but she didn't dare eat foods that would trigger more of the urge to use—not when she was already feeling so close to the edge.

Her coworkers, happy to have an excuse for a party even if they didn't know Skye well, made short work of the rest of the food. Skye thanked everyone and breathed a sigh of relief when five o'clock came and she could finally get out of there. She hadn't realized how unsuited she felt for this position until now, when leaving it. She waved her goodbyes, hopped on her bike, and rushed to her studio.

"I've been keeping it safe for you." Molly welcomed Skye.

Enjoying the joke, Skye said, "So much for the guard at the door and the heavy locks all around."

"I'm last defense back-up." Molly adopted a fierce expression, brandishing a putty knife like a weapon. Then she stepped into Skye's space and gave her a hug. "Good to have you back."

"Good to be back. I have a lot to do!" Skye went to work quickly. She'd already envisioned what she wanted for the smaller show in October. She'd been saving a batch of twelve-by-sixteen pre-stretched and paint ready canvases, just for a project like this. She got out all eight, placing them on side by side easels.

"What are you working on?" Molly stepped into Skye's space again.

Remembering the lessons of the past, Skye swallowed her irritation. "I have two shows coming up. The big one, in mid-November, is for a sophisticated crowd of art lovers and serious collectors. I'll need to be highly disciplined and thoughtful in creating the work I take there. But the first show is for a different crowd. Do you know the Soho Gallery?"

"Near Old Town. Yeah, I know it."

"They're staging an exhibit to coincide with Oktoberfest. I guess they're hoping to bring in some of the tourist crowd who might be coming to town for the beer and partying."

Molly snickered. "A different crowd indeed. Do they really expect much crossover?"

"The theory is that the art lovers may drag along with the beer lovers. Regardless of how it works, the Soho expects increased foot traffic for a couple of weeks. At least, they hope so."

"So, you're working on something for them now."

Skye nodded. "The people who come to this exhibit probably won't be looking for 'sophisticated' art or conversation pieces. They'll want something pretty and interesting that they can put up in their living rooms."

Molly's forehead furrowed. "Don't tell me you're doing realism."

"Nope. Not my thing. But I had an idea for a garden series. I can paint them side by side and exhibit them the same way."

"What are you putting in them? Ooh. I see lots of green paint."

"The idea is eight paintings that are similar, but each a little different. The abstract patterns aren't grasses or vines or flowers, but they hint at those shapes. I'm thinking most of the paintings will be covered in greens, like tall grasses, with bits of color peeking through here and there. I want to give nuance and depth to the greens. The dimensional effect should—"

Molly pulled back, cutting her off. "Whoa, Sister! You clearly know what you have in mind. I'll let you go and give you space to paint, but I'll be interested to see how this develops."

Skye chuckled. "Yeah, me too. I always talk a good fight in the beginning. Making it happen is something else."

Molly patted her arm. "If anyone can do it, you can. Happy painting!" She moved back into her space and began working on her own canvas.

Empowering. Skye nodded to herself, thinking back over the events of the last few days. So many people had voiced faith in her ability. It wasn't just talk, either. Dr. Weems and Dr. Felix had gone to plenty of trouble to line up opportunities; they put their own reputations on the line in the process. Lucy, in the scheduling office, was bringing in a temporary clerk to cover what Skye had been doing there; otherwise, Skye would still be stuck with the office schedule and too little time for her art. Even Molly supported her. Many good people were in her corner.

Skye picked up a palette and began mixing greens. It was time for Skye to start believing in herself. She took one deep breath and went to work.

Chapter Five

During the weeks that followed, Skye struggled to find time to sleep. Eating became a catch-as-catch-can effort. Often, she swallowed a breakfast bar as she hurried to class or took a couple of apples to munch on while she painted. Dinner typically involved something else she could eat in snatches while she painted in the evening. Though she tried to keep the foods nutritionally balanced, she knew she wasn't eating well, so she promised herself she'd make time for a sit-down meal every other day. Sometimes she kept that promise.

In the second week of Skye's new schedule, Dr. Weems took her to see the space at the Soho Gallery that had been reserved for her work. Skye wasn't certain whether she felt more disappointment or relief at if small size.

"They'll have six total artists exhibiting at the same time," her professor explained. "All sorts of art." She dropped her voice and stood nearer when she added, "Frankly, I think some of it is trash. Literally. One supposed artist digs in the landfill and makes shapes out of what he finds. Suffice to say, I did not recommend him." She spoke louder. "Don't get me wrong. That sort of thing can be well done, but —well, when you see it, you'll know what I mean."

"I'll watch for that. But I believe you. You clearly have excellent taste since you like my work." Skye winked.

"I *love* your work." Professor Weems patted her arm. "You have a fine future ahead of you, my friend."

"With your help, maybe I do. And I'm deeply grateful."

She returned to her studio still disturbed by the small size of her exhibition space, but by the time Molly came in, Skye was invigorated. "I don't have time to cast anything new before the October show," she reported, "but the sculptural pieces I haven't sold yet will fit nicely.

The garden series and maybe two of the other paintings will fill the space."

"Then you have everything you need for the Soho."

"Yes, I do, and I can begin focusing on the big show in November."

The next day, Skye bought a fifty-pound block of sculpting clay and plopped a chunk on her wheel. The audience at the Jardin de la Vie would be looking for statement pieces. Thinking of those potential clients, she had already made several sketches for possible sculptures, most created in the middle of the night when she awoke suddenly and couldn't go back to sleep. She planned a series about women.

The pressure to perform, both in her art and in her classes, kept her constantly on edge, constantly working. She slept little and ate on the run, barely noticing when the summer heat faded into comfortable autumn temperatures and leaves began to turn. One day, she smelled autumn in the air, but the reminder of the changing seasons only pressured her to increase her pace. She still had too much to do, and she was running out of time.

Skye sculpted a series of four pieces for the November show. Like her other work, these were more suggestions than realistic portrayals and each made a statement about the status of women. On the day she went to the Soho gallery to approve the spacing, she stopped at the school's foundry first, taking in her kiln-dried clay sculptures and arranging for the next steps in bronze casting. Turning her work over to Yusef, the shop foreman, she said, "You and the students do your thing. These pieces have to be right, but they also need to be done quickly."

"We'll give you our best, Skye." Yusef, who looked powerful enough to carry the statue *David* on his shoulder, gently moved her small pieces to a clean table. "It'll be good."

"I trust you!" she called over her shoulder as she left.

Minutes later, she arrived at the Soho Gallery and rushed straight to the place where Dr. Weems's students had agreed to help set up her art. "Not like that," she said when she saw the garden series. "Put them in this order and give each one a little more space." She showed the students what she wanted, relieved when they didn't complain but seemed eager to please.

"Dr. Weems bragged about you," one of the women confessed. "We're all eager to make you happy. She says you're the finest artist she's met in years."

"That's...very gratifying." Skye wondered what to say next, but before she could regroup, someone called the students away to help in another area.

Skye got out the labels she'd prepared, each featuring the title and asking price for one piece. She knew she couldn't expect the crowd at Soho to pay the way people in Tahoe had, so she'd dropped the prices appropriately.

Finished placing the labels, she started for the front door...and saw *him* again. At first, she couldn't believe her eyes, but how many men could there be who looked like *that*? Mr. Gorgeous was definitely standing there in the gallery, directing traffic with the students who already worked near him.

Remembering how he left the AA meeting, and fearing she was the reason for his abrupt departure, Skye hesitated. But if the cosmos saw fit to put him directly in front of her, who was she to complain? She stiffened both her spine and her resolve, put on a flirtatious smile, and flounced up beside him. "Hi there, Pete. Good to see you again."

He turned, the look in his eyes something like shock...and maybe... disappointment? Disgust? No, that couldn't be right.

She stepped closer. "Do you come here often?" Even as she spoke, she knew it was a dumb thing to say.

"I...uh, you must have me confused with someone else."

"No way." Skye shook her head. "Unless you have an identical twin, you're Pete, the guy I met at the...uh, the meeting." Skye remembered the anonymity promised to all who attended AA or NA. What she saw and heard in the meetings stayed there. "It's been a few weeks, but I'm sure you're the guy I met."

He leaned away and took a step back. "No. You're mistaken. If you'll excuse—"

Skye let her skepticism show. "There can't be two like you, my friend." She looked around, dropping her voice. "What's the problem? Ears that may hear? Or is it me?"

He seemed to be gathering his faculties. "I believe you've confused me with someone else. I'm Jamison Peters, glass artist."

Skye reluctantly took her focus off the man to look at his work: a dozen exquisite pieces, sculpted in delicately colored glass, arrayed around her. "Impressive."

"Thanks." He looked around as if scoping out an exit.

A buxom blonde interrupted, simpering, "Mr. Peters, are we finished here?"

"Yes. Thanks, Janae. The setup looks good."

"I, um…" The blonde turned a withering stare on Skye, then glimmered at Pete. "I can still help more if you need me."

Pete turned his hard look on Janae. "No. That will be all."

Janae threw one last wilting look at Skye as she left.

Skye stepped closer and dropped her voice. "Look, Pete, no need for pretense. It's just you and me here. I'm not planning to blow your cover, but, if you don't have something particular against me, I think we should talk. You're Pete. I met you at a Thursday night meeting."

He looked at her for a long moment, as if weighing a decision. Then he said, "No, I'm sorry. You've got the wrong person." Turning on his heel, he hurried away.

Was this guy some odd brand of weird, or was she a plague to be avoided? Confusion and a sense of rejection warred for dominance. Because she was also exhausted, both manifested as tears, but crying was the last thing she wanted. She squared her shoulders. Mr. Jamison Peters, glass artist, might be beautiful, but he was also rude. Deceitful, too. She didn't want to complicate her life with someone like that. A second inner voice countered, *Too bad. He looks absolutely perfect.*

Watching him walk away, Skye spoke aloud, "Too bad. Really too bad."

PETER JAMES KOURY—A.K.A. Jamison Peters, glass artist—hurried to the university's glass lab to complete another project. He had another big exhibition coming up soon and he needed to do well. He was already developing a reputation among certain art aficionados, but he knew how transient that could be. Success with this next big show could keep him in the attention and good graces of collectors with the money to pay well. Strong sales and a few rich commissions could keep him afloat financially until he had solidified his place in the art world.

That wasn't all he needed.

"Oh Peeee-eete..." A fit but figure-enhanced brunette sang his name. He thought this one called herself Tiffy. Short for Tiffany? She'd told him once. He hadn't been paying attention.

Pete gave little attention to most of the students who came on to him—and that included the other dark-haired pixie who 'accidentally' swept by him, offering a sultry, come-hither look as her ample breast grazed his arm. They were legal adults, but still children in his view and in their lack of sophistication. They were too young, too obvious, and far too easy to interest him.

A thin wave of sadness overcame him as he thought of the pretty woman he'd first seen at the AA meeting, the one who recognized him at the Soho this afternoon. How disappointed he'd been to discover she was just another simpering student, throwing herself at him.

What he needed was a partner who appreciated him for his mind, his creativity, his *art,* a woman of sophistication and experience, someone who could understand him at his core. It would help if she also had some empathy for his situation, for the mess he'd made of his life during recent years, the mess from which he was only now recovering.

Pete used his minimal power as a teaching assistant to give Tiffy and the pixie each an errand to run, hoping to get a moment's reprieve from their clumsy attempts to reel him in. The woman he wanted, needed, was out there somewhere. When the time was right, he would find her. Until then, he probably needed to find a different AA meeting.

EVERY ONE OF Skye's pieces at the Soho show sold, with all eight of the garden series going to a gallery owner in Santa Barbara who intended to resell them at a markup. "I'm incensed," Dr. Weems told her. "At the least, you deserve to sell to real customers."

"I don't mind. As long as the work sells, I'm happy."

"Well, I wanted better for you." The professor visibly calmed herself. "Maybe you'll get a little down time now?"

"Maybe," Skye answered, though she frankly doubted it.

If anything, the work became more intense. Skye knew, when she sculpted clay in early September, that she'd have to rush the process to get any pieces ready for St. Helena. For a large sculpture, the plastic mold wouldn't have time to dry in the weeks she had left.

She stopped at the Soho Gallery when the show ended to thank the gallery owner for including her.

"You can join us any time," Winston, the owner, said. "That reminds me, I have something for you. I was going to send it through Dr. Weems, but since you're here…" He stepped into his office and handed her a check for her sales, minus his fee. "We took all six of the artists the school recommended, but, as you can see, not everything sold." He gestured toward the "sculptures" Dr. Weems had labeled as trash. "Those, for example."

Skye chose not to disrespect another artist publicly, even if she privately hoped the guy would take up plumbing. "It takes all kinds." She shrugged, wondering which professor had recommended the trash artist. Then she realized that shared a boundary with the space where Jamison Peters displayed. "How did the glass artist do?"

"Peters? He's another one we'll have back any time. Every one of his pieces sold—and they brought good prices."

"That's good." Then something else occurred to her. "Wait. Did you say all the artists in this show were students recommended by the school?"

"Yeah. We do that at least once a year, just to give your school program a boost."

"Then Jamison Peters is a student, too?"

Winston drew his brows together. "A grad student, I think. We had him exhibit here as an undergrad. Then he was out for a while. I believe we have him scheduled to display the first part of his master's project just before Christmas. That's a preview for the full exhibit in the spring."

Skye knew she shouldn't care, but she couldn't seem to stop. "Great. I'm glad for him. He does good work."

"He sure does."

Skye considered whether she should go home for a real dinner or go back to the studio to work. Instead, she hit an ATM to deposit her check. Then she stopped at the metals foundry to check the progress on her sculpted pieces.

A familiar scent hit her when she entered, a combination of heat, metal, plaster, acid, and other industrial odors she couldn't identify. To her, the foundry smelled like home. She found Yusef and asked about her pieces. He showed her what the students had accomplished.

Each baked clay sculpture had been carefully cut into manageable pieces. The lab's crew—including hired professionals and a team of students—had then made the molds from a modern, flexible, rubber-like material the local crew called "goop." Just before Skye arrived, they poured molten wax into the 3-D shapes to make a wax pattern.

"Looks good, Yusef," Skye said to the foreman. "Do you think I can still make a November fifteenth deadline? Installation begins on the seventeenth. If I don't have these pieces ready two days before, there'll be no time to get them to St. Helena."

Yusef pushed back his hard hat and wiped his brow. "That's pushing it." He paused, apparently calculating. "If the pieces were any larger, I'd say you're stuck on a roof without a ladder. As it is, we may just make it. That is, if you're here every time we need you."

"When do you think the wax will be dry?"

"You can check next Tuesday. If not then, probably the day after."

"I'll be here."

A student interrupted to ask if she could leave to go to her work in the glass blowing lab.

"Yeah. You're done here," Yusef said. The student began removing her helmet and other safety equipment.

Skye told Yusef, "I'll check Tuesday." Then she hurried to catch the student.

"Hi," Skye said, reaching the woman at the door. "This may be a crazy question, but do you happen to know a glass artist named Jamison Peters?"

"You mean Pete? Ooh yeah!" The student's eyes lit up. "He's one of the stars in the glass program, not to mention sweet eye candy. If I could sculpt *him* in glass, I'd make a fortune."

Skye felt the same way. "Might he be working in the school's glass factory?"

"Yeah. He's a grad assistant this term. He teaches a theory class, I think, but he's in the Hot Shop this time of day."

"Perfect. Mind if I walk along?"

"No problem, but I need to hurry."

"I'll keep up."

The student's pace was slower than Skye's usual rush. Sensing she had a willing audience, the young woman chattered at length about her own artistic interests— "I like the other media and all, but mostly I'm into glass" —and how she felt about various professors— "Dr. Weems is my favorite. Well, besides Jamison Peters, of course." They reached the door labeled Hot Shop. The student left her and hurried to suit up so she could get to the forge.

Skye stepped into a scene out of Dante's *Inferno*. Multiple forges, each baking inside to more than two thousand degrees, emanated heat like Death Valley in August and served a host of aproned and goggled artists and helpers. The artisans worked at a variety of projects with varying degrees of skill. The room even *smelled* hot, with a combination of industrial odors creating a unique plaster-acid-glass-heat scent, like that in the metals foundry, but with its own twist.

The heat hit her, spinning her head and causing her to sway in her steps, and she realized it was late afternoon and she hadn't eaten. *Mental note: Get food.*

She scanned the space, amazed at the scene. And that's when she saw *him* again. Pete, or Jamison Peters—the mystery man who'd been haunting her dreams—worked at a glory hole, a smaller version of the forge at his own station, used for reheating glass as the artist shaped it.

He stood in front of the small opening, turning a rod. When he withdrew the ball of glass, its small size surprised her. Skye drew nearer, crossing the room, careful not to attract his attention, and watched as he gently blew into the rod, elongating the shape. Then he put it onto his worktable and began using paddles and punties to fashion a sort of tube that came to a pointed end. That done, he added the piece to a group of similar shapes at the end of the table.

Drawing still nearer, she examined his work. Like hers, his vision was more abstract than real, yet the unfinished piece clearly suggested fire. Small pieces resembled individual flames in variegated shades of red, orange, and imperial yellow.

A deep voice boomed. "What are you doing here, young lady?"

Skye turned to see an older man bearing down on her.

"You aren't supposed to be on the floor without proper safety equipment."

"I…uh…"

"Look around you," the man said. "We work with *glass*. The floor is covered with broken bits and pieces and you're here in sandals? Out." He made a shooing gesture. "Get out. Don't come back until you're properly attired."

"I…uh, yeah, sure. I'll go. I just. . .." She turned to find Pete glowering, his eyes boring into hers, his face—already florid from the heat—reddening further.

"I'll take it from here, Sam," Pete said, stepping toward her.

With the older man—Sam, apparently—still shooing her and Pete bearing down like some avenging angel, Skye made a dash for the door, heavy footsteps close behind. She hoped the steps were from Sam, not *him*. She turned once to look. *No such luck.* When she reached the outer hallway, she turned again, prepared to take her medicine from the gorgeous glass artist.

"Are you stalking me?" He looked ready to chew some of that glass he'd been making.

"No! That is. . .." Skye stopped, stuck for words and dreadfully afraid she was about to burst into tears. How could she explain this? Especially since she probably *was* stalking him.

She considered trying to come up with something about his work or the Soho Gallery or anything to explain her presence. Instead, she let her body take the lead. She fainted.

Chapter Six

First there were voices—sounds, really, with no individual words. Then she began hearing people call to her, but everything around her remained dark. Gradually even the darkness cleared, and she saw faces in a circle around her head: the student who walked over with her, the man who shooed her out, a couple of others she didn't recognize, and Pete. "Ohhhh," she moaned, putting a hand to her forehead. "What happened?"

Everyone tried to explain at once. Then she heard Pete say, "You fainted."

"That's ridiculous," she said, although she didn't recall thinking it. "I never faint."

"Well, you did this time," the older man said. "If you just lie still, we'll get an ambulance—"

"No!" The strength of Skye's voice surprised her. "I don't need an ambulance. I promise I'll be just fine." To prove it, she forced herself into a sitting position. The action caused her to feel woozy again, but she persisted. Slowly, her fuzziness cleared. "It was just a combination of the heat and hunger. I...I skipped lunch." And breakfast. Had she eaten last night? She couldn't remember. "Just give me a minute to clear my head and I'll be on my way."

The older man said, "Well, I don't—"

He was interrupted by the student who walked with her. "I got the water you wanted."

The man took the paper cup and offered it to Skye. "Here. Drink up. We'll see how you're feeling in a few."

Skye drank, at first just a few swallows. Then she realized how desperate her thirst was. The only water she could recall drinking since leaving home that morning had been a sip here and there from a water fountain. She made a mental note to try to remember both food and water. She finished the water and thanked everyone around her. Then she stood, reassuring the group that she'd be fine on her own.

"Are you certain?" the older man asked.

"Yes, I'm sure."

She heard Pete say, "I'll stay with her until she's stable."

"I'll take care of your station," the student offered.

"Thanks, Emily," Pete said. He gave the student a few quick instructions.

"Will do," Emily answered, beaming at Pete as if the king had granted her a boon by allowing her to clean up after him. "You take care," she said to Skye as she left.

The older man asked Pete, "You sure you can handle this?"

Pete, or Jamison, or whoever he was, answered, "Don't worry, Sam. I've got this."

"Okay then." Sam, still sounding doubtful, left them standing in the hall.

Pete said, "Come on, stalker. I'll drive you home."

Skye let Pete lead her behind the Hot Shop to a small, sleek pickup. He opened a door. "Get in."

Meekly, Skye obeyed.

He closed his door, turned on the A/C, and said, "Explain yourself. What was that all about?"

With a few conscious minutes behind her to consider the possibilities, Skye offered the best explanation she had. "I guess I *was* stalking you, but not in any negative kind of way."

He frowned, his expression skeptical.

"What I mean is, I was…curious. Since I saw you at that AA meeting, I've wondered why you didn't come back. Then, when I saw you again at the Soho show, I also saw your work. One artist to another, I'm impressed. When the student in the metals forge mentioned she thought you might be working in the Hot Shop, I followed along. I wanted to see what you do." She offered a pleading look.

"So it's my *work* that interests you." He practically sneered as he drew out the word *work*. What was going on with this guy?

"Well, yeah. I saw you at the Soho Gallery at the show we both did—"

His expression changed completely. "Wait. You had work there, too?"

She frowned. Hard. "Of course. What did you think I was doing?"

"I assumed you were one of the student helpers."

Now she was the one to sneer. "Oh, that's truly flattering."

He had the grace to look embarrassed. "I know you weren't the trash artist," he said. "He had the space right next to mine."

Skye, who'd tried to control her amusement at "trash artist," allowed a smile. "No, I'm not the trash artist. Incidentally, I feel the same way about his work."

"Not much to brag about, is there? I wonder why the professors included him?"

"Dr. Weems suggested they wanted to include multiple media. Maybe the prof who recommended him thought this guy's work might interest someone. Do you know if he sold a single piece?"

"I think maybe one or two. Not much, though. But you weren't me and you weren't the trash dude. That leaves four possibilities. Which are you?"

"I had the space in the room on the south, back corner."

He closed his eyes, apparently visualizing the space. "You had the garden paintings? And the sculptures?"

"Yes. That's my work."

His expression changed again, much more open now. "You're Skye."

She sat straighter, surprised he knew her name. "Yes. Guilty as charged."

"Vickie is one of your top advocates."

Did he mean Professor Weems? "You call her Vickie?"

He smiled. "When I first came back to grad school, it wasn't easy. I kept calling her Dr. Weems, just as I always had. After the first couple of weeks, she said, 'You're a teacher and colleague now, Pete. Call me Vickie.'"

"Then you're Pete here, too. Not Jamison Peters, but Pete."

His cheeks reddened slightly and he dropped his eyes before meeting hers again. "My name is Peter James Koury. Professionally, I'm Jamison Peters."

"But you're Pete at AA meetings."

He acknowledged that with a twist of his lip. "Yep. There, too."

"Then why did you lie to me about it? You were so insistent—"

"I know. I'm sorry. There were, um, other things going on." He started the ignition. "So is it true you haven't eaten all day?"

"Honestly, I've been working like crazy to meet a big deadline and I don't remember the last time I ate—at least, not more than a breakfast bar or an apple."

"I can fix that." He maneuvered the truck out of the parking lot and into traffic.

"I haven't told you where I live. Where are we going?"

"Don't worry. I'll see you get safely home. In the meantime..." He grinned. "In the meantime, I'm taking you to dinner."

MR. GORGEOUS WAS TAKING Skye out for a meal, and she didn't even remember what she was wearing. She examined her ensemble: strategically distressed denim jeans and a linen blouse in a rich salmon pink that highlighted her dark complexion. Had she put on earrings? She touched her lobes and fingered the tiny pearl drops, one of her go-to pairs. She sighed, brushing a stray curl behind her ear. She could look worse. Good thing she'd stopped at the forge when coming from the gallery and not from the studio. She imagined having these same conversations while splattered in various colors of paint. She'd lucked out with that one!

Pete stopped at a local place that catered to students. It offered house-made gourmet pizza, a huge taco bar, and a wide variety of deep-fried chicken and vegetables. It further specialized in artisan coffees and a tea bar featuring kombucha.

"Trendy," Skye said when Pete opened her door.

"Very trendy," he answered. Then, with a shrug, "I just like the food."

"Good enough reason to come here." She swayed slightly.

He caught her arm to steady her. His brow furrowed in concern. "You okay?"

She nodded. "I will be. I just need to eat."

"Then let's get you something." He took a step, preparing to lead the way.

She tried to follow him but swayed again.

"That's it," he said. "Don't get the wrong impression here, Skye, but I don't want to pick you up off the floor again." He put his arm around her waist. "Lean into my shoulder."

She leaned in and instantly felt a full-body buzz, reveling in the warmth of his touch. Maybe it was the combination of the lack of food, the heat, and the nearness of a very desirable man. Whatever it was, Skye felt herself losing consciousness again. "You smell like glass," she heard herself say, her voice far away as she sagged against his side.

Chapter Seven

T he next time Skye opened her eyes, she was sitting up—sort of. As the scene around her cleared, she looked into the eyes of none other than Mr. Gorgeous. He held her across his lap, her upper body resting against his left arm. With his right hand, he held a cup of orange juice to her lips. "Hey, Skye." His voice was insistent. "Are you in there?"

She blinked. Once. Twice. And looked at him again. She thought she must be dreaming; she'd had this dream before. "Whoa," she said, almost reverently. "This is a really cool dream."

He laughed. "No, I'm afraid not. Here." He touched the glass to her lips again. "It's orange juice. It'll raise your blood sugar so you don't pass out again. Twice in one afternoon is a bit showy, don't you think?"

Obediently, she drank. "How long have I been—?"

"A few minutes," he answered. "When I got you inside, I told the manager we needed orange juice immediately. He wants to call an ambulance, but I asked him to please wait until we see what this juice does. If it revives you, we'll get something solid into you."

Skye leaned forward, sitting up straight, and drained the glass. Then, embarrassed by their closeness and her eager response to it, she slid away. "I'm feeling stronger already."

"Good." He nodded to a man standing nearby, maybe the manager. The man frowned but walked away. "Do you think you can sit in a chair?"

Skye nodded, and then realized her voice would serve better. "Yeah. Sure." She stood on shaky legs and moved to the chair across the table from him. Then she picked up the menu and tried to pull herself together enough to read it. "What..." Her vision blurred. "What kind of food do they..." She lost the rest of the words.

"Would you like me to order for you?" he asked. "Their fried chicken is excellent. If we also get you some sweet potato fries, that might give you the mix of carbs and proteins you need to start feeling better."

Relieved she didn't have to make a decision, Skye put down her menu. "Sounds good."

"I'll get you a cup of something warm to go with it. Do you like kombucha?"

She held up her hand. "No, thanks. The food will be plenty, and I can drink water."

He obviously disagreed. She could tell by his tone when he said, "Okay." Then he added, "But if you need more, say so. We want to get you fully conscious again." He gave her a long look. "Will you be okay if I'm gone long enough to place an order at the counter?"

The manager, still within hearing distance, said, "Just tell me what you want. I'll order for you."

Pete thanked him and gave his own order. Then he added her food and ordered a cola to go with it. The manager nodded. "We'll have that right out."

Skye wondered if she'd heard him correctly. "You ordered me a Coke?"

"Not really." Pete hesitated. "This place has its own soft drink brand, but it's similar."

"Why? I just had orange juice. I'll be fine with a glass of water."

"I have a frat brother who's an EMT. He once told me that orange juice is about the fastest way there is to raise someone's blood sugar. Then he said, 'But when you need both kinds of electrolytes, sugars and salts, try Coke or Pepsi.' After what I've seen in the last hour, I'm guessing you need a good dose of both."

"Oh. Thank you." Then she paused. "You were in a fraternity?"

"Oh yeah! I graduated with a degree and acceptable grades, but my real major was partying."

She nodded. "That's a popular major. It also explains why I saw you at that Thursday night meeting."

"You got it." He looked around. "But this isn't the right place for that conversation."

"Oh. Yeah. Sorry. I didn't think."

"You aren't doing much thinking right now. You'll do better when you've eaten."

The manager and a server arrived with trays of food and drink. Pete thanked them and pulled out his wallet, but the manager said, "You're a regular, Pete. Keep your money. This one's on the house." He nodded toward Skye. "Let's just get your friend here feeling better."

Pete thanked them and Skye did the same. Then Pete looked at her and said, "Eat."

Skye obediently bit into the chicken. Pete scrutinized each bite and swallow until he seemed content she could manage. Then he finally began his own meal.

They talked little at first. Skye had forgotten how good it could feel to eat when she was hungry. It surprised her how quickly her food disappeared. Awakened from a slumber of disuse, her stomach begged for more. Pete obliged, going to the counter for a salad and returning for a bowl of thick, creamy soup. Finally he asked, "Think you've had enough?"

Skye leaned back, patting her belly. "That feels good!"

"I know how it can be when you're trying to meet a deadline, but really, Skye. You have to take care of yourself along the way."

"I have ADHD," she said, blurting it out. "People think that attention deficit means you can't focus, and that's true for much of the time, but it also means hyperfocus on projects that really interest me. I can get so into a painting, I almost forget there are people around me or that my body needs basic self-care."

She half expected him to make some polite, forced comment and get her out of there. Instead he nodded thoughtfully, tapping his index finger against his chin. "My aunt, my mom's sister, has ADHD. I've seen that in her." Then a light went on. "She also started self-medicating with over the counter drugs. I'm guessing that you..." He looked around again and stopped.

"You've got it. Lots of self-medicating happening here, which is why I was at that meeting."

He nodded, lowering his voice. "I get that. I'll bet the temptation to use again gets worse when you're under pressure. You said you have a deadline coming up?"

"Yes, and it's soon," she answered. She continued by telling him about the huge opportunity in November.

When she finished, he whistled, long and low. For several seconds, he said nothing. Then, "I don't know whether to be impressed or jealous. That's quite a gig!"

"I hardly believe it myself."

"What are you working on?"

She told him about the paintings she had ready, the ones she hadn't taken to the Soho show, and about *Random Thoughts* and how it had already sold to the curator. Then she described the four pieces she had at the foundry, all in the process of being cast in bronze.

"It'll be cutting it close to get those done by November fifteenth," she said. "The foreman thinks the wax pattern should be cooled by Tuesday or maybe Wednesday. After that, we'll need to remove the wax from the mold. Then I'll have to be there to do my thing, refining the pattern with dental tools, making it exactly the way I want it. Then come the gates and sprues before the whole thing can be dipped into the slurry. Who knows if that will dry in time to cast the bronze? That can take days." She drew a deep breath. "It'll be tight."

He nodded. "I can see that, and I also see your passion for the work." His admiring glance warmed her. Then his gaze seemed to turn inward. "In some ways, glass is a more forgiving medium. I know right away whether it's working or not. Of course, I can often spend hours on a piece, think I'm there, and have the thing shatter at the very end, when it's nearly perfect."

"I know what you mean," Skye responded. "I've broken more than one sculpture piece just taking the clay out of the kiln. My great fear now is that I'll break one or more of these pieces before it can be poured and finished, and I won't have enough for the show. As it is, I'll only have eleven, and Dr. Weems thinks I'll need fifteen."

"I expect you'll make it," he said. "Strategic placement can help you fill more space."

"True."

They talked shop for another hour while the dinner crowd swirled around them. Eventually, Skye checked the time and gasped. "Look how late it's getting! And I need to get back to the studio." She moved to stand.

Pete stopped her, laying his hand over hers. "Are you sure that's a good idea? I know you're worried about your deadline, but you passed out twice today. Your body is trying to tell you it won't keep carrying you through the kind of days you've been having. You might be wise to go home and get some rest. Tackle your work again when you're feeling fresh in the morning."

"But I—" As she tried to stand, exhaustion knocked her down.

Pete jumped up. "Are you going to faint again?"

"No." Then her conscience reminded her that she had neither intended nor expected to pass out the two times it had already happened. "That is, I don't think so. I'm just...tired."

"Exhausted, I'm guessing. You've been putting it all into the work. It's one thing to leave it all on the field when the game is over, but you can't afford to do that when you're tied in the fourth quarter."

She cocked her head, pursing her lips. "Football analogies?"

"I think you get the point." He came around beside her. When she stood, Pete stooped. Then in a move so quick she didn't see it coming, he put one arm behind her knees, the other behind her back, and lifted her off the chair.

"Hey!"

In several long strides, he reached the front door. The manager saw him and opened it before he got there. While Pete walked, he kept talking, ignoring Skye's objections. "The guys in the fraternity were always sharing tips on how to pick up girls. I told them it's easy, but you do have to lift with your legs." When he reached the passenger side of his truck, he put her on her feet long enough to open the door. "Will you need help getting in? Or can you manage?"

"I'm much stronger since I ate, thank you." Skye proved it by climbing into the cab.

"Well done," he said, as if cheering on a major athletic feat. "I'm still not going to let you overdo it. If I take you straight home, will you promise to get some rest? And eat breakfast before you go out in the morning?"

She gave him a long look, eyes narrowing. "Why do you care?"

He paused, as if the answer took some thought. "You know how we're always telling the local community to support the arts?"

She nodded.

"Call this my way of supporting the arts. I can't snag a show at the Jardin de la Vie for my own work, but I can do my best to make sure yours goes as well as possible. That's not going to happen if you work yourself into the hospital." He paused before adding, "And I do feel bad about calling you a stalker."

"That's it, huh?" She twinkled at him. "Guilt and support for the arts."

He nodded. "Plain and simple. Are you clear of the door?"

"Yep, I am."

"Then let's get going." He closed the door and walked around, climbed in, and started the ignition. As he backed out, he asked, "I'm going to need your address."

She told him. "I live on the second floor…and you are *forbidden* from carrying me up the stairs."

"What? You're afraid the neighbors will be jealous?"

She snickered. She couldn't help it. "I'll make it on my own two feet."

"Okay, but I'll follow close behind, just in case. If you fall, you'll land on me."

"You really are going all out, aren't you? I don't think it's necessary. Honestly, I'm doing much better. "

He sobered. "You scared me, Skye. You scared everyone in the Hot Shop and all the people at that restaurant, especially the manager. I know we've barely met, and I hardly know you, but I've been hearing good things about your work for a while now. Vickie thinks you're brilliant."

"That's kind of her."

He shook his head. "Not kind. Smart. She wants to see you burst into the heavens as the newest star on the art scene. When you do, she'll be able to tell everyone she was your teacher."

Skye nodded. "That's how it works, isn't it? But I'm no prodigy and I very much doubt she'll brag about teaching me."

"Are you kidding? She already does. Her husband brags about

having you in the Art Department, and the department drops your name to increase donations. You're already a force to be reckoned with."

"Whew." Skye let that settle. "I hardly know what to do with that."

"I'll tell you what *not* to do with it. Don't make yourself a casualty to be added to that long list of brilliant, budding artists who died too young."

"Don't you think you're overstating? I fainted. I haven't come close to dying."

"How long will it take if you keep forgetting to eat?" Pete stopped at the curb in front of Skye's apartment. "Okay, enough. The lecture is over and I'm not going to harangue you any further tonight. But I am going to make sure you get safely into your apartment and I am going to beg you to stay there until morning. Get some sleep. Eat a good breakfast. Then you can get back to your grueling schedule, but along the way, you'll need to pause here and there for basic self-care, like eating, sleeping, staying hydrated. Will you do that?"

She pulled her brows together. "I thought you said the lecture was over?"

"I'll check up on you from time to time to ask you if you're eating. Remember I've seen ADHD before. I know it can be destructive if you aren't compensating. It destroyed any relationship my family once had with my aunt. You will take care of yourself, right?"

"Yes, sir."

He dropped his head to his chin. "You're right. I'm being pushy and it's none of my business. I don't want to see a promising artist fizzle out, okay?" He grinned. "Maybe I'm hoping to hitch my wagon to your rising star, just like everyone else."

"Little chance of it doing you any good." She opened her door and stumbled out.

"Hey! Let me play the part of the chivalrous hero even if it's out of my league." He jogged to her side. "Come on. I'll follow you up the stairs."

"If you really must." Skye knew she sounded whiny, but she breathed more easily knowing he'd be there if she stumbled. He saw her safely inside and waved goodbye as he left.

Half an hour later, after a quick shower, Skye crawled into bed just as Pete had advised. and allowed herself to consider how grateful she was that Pete had been there when she'd hit bottom, ready to help her rise again. Even before she began to dream, she knew where those dreams would take her and who would be there to catch her when she fell.

Chapter Eight

Pete Koury sat in the living room of his apartment. The room had long since grown dark. Still he sat, arguing with himself, his usually cautious inner voice warring with him.

What are you doing, man? His inner voice could be really annoying.

Maybe talking with an actual human could help him work through this. Internal arguments weren't getting him anywhere. He checked the time—not too late yet—and called Sam. Besides being a great foreman in the Hot Shop, Sam had become a kind of father-confessor and substitute sponsor after Neil, his original sponsor, left the area. Sam, with an AA background of his own, was the only person on campus who knew Pete's whole story. When the man answered, Pete filled him in on all that had happened since the scene Sam had witnessed in the Hot Shop.

"Are you serious?" Sam asked. "A few hours ago, you were throwing her out of the Hot Shop like she was just another art groupie. Now you've appointed yourself her guardian angel. What's going on with you?"

"She scared me." Peter's thoughts were swirling. "I've had women in my classes pull the 'I'm about to swoon' routine and it looks nothing like this. She was really out of it."

"And that's reason for you to abandon all healthy self-interest? You're losing it, Pete."

Maybe I'm actually finding *it,* Pete thought, and he knew he'd lose sleep over that idea. "I don't know, Sam," he said. "Maybe this is…you know, someone I can care about."

"You've gotta be kidding. You remember where you first saw her, right? You told me about that AA meeting…"

"Yep. I remember." Though right now, he wished Sam didn't.

"And you swore you'd never date another recovering addict.

Remember what happened with the last two—well, really three if you count Natalie."

"I don't count Natalie. Let's not bring up Natalie."

"Hey, you're the guy who called her the biggest mistake of your life."

"Sam—"

"But even without Natalie, Sissy and Laurel should have taught you your lesson. If you date alcoholics or addicts, you're in for disappointment. Remember how they both fell off the wagon? And you were right in the middle of it, both times. I know. I got to see how those experiences left you wrung out dry as one of our furnaces."

"That's all true, buddy, but Skye is different. She has too much going for her to do that."

"How do you know? You keep telling me how a recovering addict is more tempted to use when the pressure gets heavy. We both know many people we've met at AA who've fallen off that wagon and tumbled under the wheels. You're right about how pressure kills recovery."

"So what if I am? Skye's a talented artist. Now she has an amazing opportunity and she can use some help to get there. Besides, no one says we're dating. I'm just keeping an eye on her. You know, helping out the cause of great art."

Sam snorted. "Lie to yourself all you want, kiddo. I saw how you looked at her when she fell into your arms. That lady rings all your chimes."

Pete sighed. "Okay. True. You can't blame me for being attracted. I'm a red-blooded male, after all, and she's gorgeous. Beautiful. Those huge dark eyes, and her long, long legs…"

"See what I mean?"

"Score one for you. Sam, what should I do about it?"

"Tell her you'll be busy for the rest of your life and you wish her well."

"Not a chance. Sorry, but I can't do that. I've already made promises."

"Then don't blame me when you get your heart broken."

"I'll remember that. 'Night, Sam."

Pete cut off the call, but the ping pong match in his head went on until after midnight. That's when he realized he had work in the morning and a little self-care might be in order. As he started his bedtime routine, he tabled the internal argument for another day. For now, at least, he'd follow through with what he'd promised.

In the back of his mind, he heard a vague response: *You've been warned.*

He disregarded the thought, knowing he'd already made up his mind.

IN CLASS THE NEXT MORNING, Dr. Randolph asked his students to turn in their short essays on methods of self-motivation. "Essay?" To her embarrassment, Skye realized she'd said it aloud.

"Yes, Ms. Ray. The three-page essay assigned last class?"

"I don't...I didn't hear..." She shrank at the knowing looks of the other students.

"I'm sure you didn't." Dr. Randolph's disapproving glare made her squirm. "We probably discussed it during your nap. It's in the syllabus that we'll have two short essays assigned at random during the term."

"I...I'm sorry. I didn't mean—" Her embarrassment only intensified when she realized she was beginning to tear up.

"See me after class." Dr. Randolph turned away and collected the work from the other students. He dismissed the class minutes later. Skye remained seated, waiting for the other shoe to drop, possibly on her head. "Well now, Ms. Ray." Her professor sat in the desk next to hers. He said nothing more, clearly waiting for her explanation.

She blurted it all out, about working to make a tight deadline and spending so many hours in the studio and at the forge; about having trouble remembering to eat and fainting—twice—during a brief visit to the glass Hot Shop the day before. She concluded her spiel with, "I know I have to put more into my studies, but this opportunity is too important to miss. It isn't every day I get invited to do a one-woman show at the Jardin de la Vie."

"The Jardin..." Dr. Randolph whistled. "Well then." He tapped his chin, seeming to consider his options. He cleared his throat. "You've been a great student until now, and it clearly doesn't sound like you're having problems with self-motivation nor with working hard." His face hardened. "But you do need this class to graduate, so I suggest you find balance in your schedule so that you can get everything done." He admitted he'd assigned the surprise essay as a knee-jerk response when he spotted her sleeping in class the week before. "But if you can bring that three-page essay to my office tomorrow, and stay awake in class, you should do just fine."

Relieved, Skye promised she'd have the paper turned in before she went to the studio. "Oh, and does it have to be a print copy? Can I email it?"

"I don't like to read on the computer screen," he said, "but okay. I'll take it by email. Oh, and don't short yourself on meals or sleep in order to do it."

"No promises there," Skye said. Then, seeing the warning in his eyes, she hastily added, "It shouldn't take me long to put this essay together. Like you said, I'm highly self-motivated. All I have to do is write about it."

"Sounds good," he said, and offered his hand. They solemnly shook on the deal.

As Skye left the building, she told herself, *I can't forget this assignment. How will I remember?* Pulling a marker from her bag, she wrote *essay* in large letters on her left forearm. Then she pushed that concern to the back burner and hurried to the studio.

PETE HAD PROMISED himself he wouldn't see Skye, not today. He'd let her get over what happened yesterday while he got on with his own work. Despite his own wise counsel, he found himself fretting, wondering if she'd rested, if she'd eaten, if she was feeling better. In the middle of the afternoon, when everything seemed to be progressing well in the Hot Shop, he excused himself to get lunch, and told them not to expect him back for a while. Then he drove to his favorite café, picked up two orders, and drove to the studio where he expected to find Skye.

He knew where it was. She'd pointed out the street when they passed the intersection the night before. From her description, he recognized the building, which impressed him all over again. Only serious artists, or ones with lots of daddy's money, could afford that space—and that kind of security.

Security was heavily on his mind when he pulled up to the kiosk at the gate and gave the guard his name. "I'm here to see Skye."

The guard gave him a narrow-eyed stare. "Is she expecting you?"

Peter sat up straighter and smiled. "This is a surprise visit."

"Hmmm." The guard picked up the phone. "I'll call her to see if you're welcome." He dialed and replied to Skye's hello. "Miss Ray, there's a man here. Says he's come to surprise you."

"What's his name?" Her voice wasn't loud, but it carried.

The guard leaned out. "Your name?"

"Pete Koury." He listened while the guard repeated it into the phone.

Pete could hear a long pause. Then, "Okay, sure. Let him in."

The guard gave Pete another once-over. "Just this one time? Or is he always cleared?"

Pete heard Skye's voice ringing clearly. "Let's just say he's okay until further notice."

The guard nodded, said goodbye, and hung up the phone. "You can go back."

"Thank you." Pete rewarded the guard with a grin. "I appreciate it!" Maybe if he came here again, he could bring doughnuts, the way he'd take dog biscuits if he expected to encounter a snarler. The guard looked about as smart as a Rottweiler and every bit as protective.

MORE ANXIOUS THAN she wanted to admit, Skye kept working, putting details on the canvas she called *Nightmare*. Anyone trying to find realism in those shapes and colors would have a hard time making sense of it, but she felt the horror and the terror as she stabbed and swirled the colors—most were dark, but there were also vivid blood reds and oranges in small, spiky streaks.

What am I feeling now? It was a question she often asked herself when she painted. Flicking the brush and scattering bloody drops near the painting's center, she gave the painting a critical study. What she felt right now was neither terror nor horror, but more like irritation.

She realized it had nothing to do with the painting but with the man who would be there any moment. Was she flattered that Pete showed so much attention or annoyed by his hovering? Maybe a little of each. Pete was acting more like a worried big brother than a guy who was attracted to her, and she'd prefer the shared attraction.

The door at the far end of the studio opened, and Pete came striding through. He wore jeans and western boots—not fancy, urban cowboy boots decked out in embroidery, but plain brown ones, the sort that would be highly practical in the Hot Shop. He came toward her, waving when he saw her looking his way.

"Who's the stalker now?" she asked with a lift to her eyebrow.

"Brought you lunch," he announced as he drew near.

"Thank you." She smiled despite herself. He grinned as he handed her the bag. The scent reached her first and she drew in another long breath. "Mmm…more chicken. As it happens, I'm hungry, so you're forgiven. This time."

"I promise I won't do this every day," he said, "but maybe now and then—just to make sure you're eating."

She rolled her eyes. "Are you suddenly my knight errant sworn to protect and defend?" She unwrapped the chicken and took a bite. "Mmmmm! That's good!" She swallowed before adding, "Pull out that folding chair and have a seat. Where's your shining armor?"

"No shining armor here. Metal isn't my preferred medium, as you know." He pulled the chair closer. "I work in glass."

She gave him a grudging nod and took another bite. "This is so good!"

He rummaged through his bag and handed her a cola.

"Thank you," she mumbled around a mouthful of chicken. She took a few sips and said it again, more clearly. "Thank you. Really."

"You're welcome." He cleared his throat and unwrapped his own meal. "How are you?"

"Good!" she answered. "I took your advice and got a great night's rest. Then I scrambled two eggs for breakfast and washed them down with a glass of almond milk. I'm doing well."

"You certainly look healthier than you did." He sat back with a sigh. "I'm relieved. I told you this yesterday, but it's worth repeating. You really had me worried."

"Yeah, well…I'll admit I was not at my best."

"I believe that's safe to say."

They finished their meal, talking about current art projects.

"Speaking of," Skye said with a grin, "Want to see what I'm working on now?"

"You bet!"

"I don't have all my work here," she said as she led him to her works in progress. "I've taken some of the smaller pieces home and lined them up against the wall of my bedroom. I didn't want them to be in the way if I accidentally spilled paint."

"Makes sense."

She showed him *Seascape* with its sea green swirls of color and small, half-seen shapes that might suggest sea creatures, but nothing that looked like a wave or a skyline. *Audio Visual* was an experiment, swirling lines of music curling out of bright, flashy shapes. *Harvest* included some shapes that resembled falling leaves and others that might have been fruits or vegetables, just picked from the garden or plucked from a tree. She showed him two more before saying, "This is the one I've been working on today. I call it *Nightmare*."

Pete whistled. "I can see why. It almost scares me to look at it."

She gave the painting a studied look. "I was worried about that too. Will anyone want a painting that conjures such a feeling?"

"Someone will," Pete said, "if only to hang in a gallery somewhere."

"You think so? I worry when I do something this…stark."

"Honestly?" he dropped his voice. "To me, it looks like a three-day drunk that ends in *delirium tremens*."

"The DTs," she said, nodding. "Been there." She examined the painting again. "Or a bad trip, maybe?"

"Either way, a good reason to hit the AA meeting tonight."

"Oh!" She looked up as though the idea had only now occurred. "It *is* Thursday, isn't it?"

"It is. Would you like me to give you a lift? We could leave from here and I can bring you back when the meeting's over."

"I'll be going to the one in the church basement. You know, the one where I first…where you came that night…"

"I know the one. I decided to go back there too."

"Oh. Okay then." She checked her cell phone. "It isn't for another three hours, right? I should probably get back to painting until the meeting."

"No problem. I'll be back in two and a half."

"Good." Then she asked, "Pete? Why did you leave the meeting that first night?"

He dropped his gaze. Then he said, "Maybe I'll tell you when we know each other better."

She nodded. "Okay. I'll ask again…another time." He watched as she set an alarm and set her phone on a high shelf, away from the paint. The sleeve of her painter's smock slipped back, revealing inked writing on her arm.

"What's that?" Pete stepped close. His voice rose. "Someone's marking you?"

"I did that myself. I didn't want to forget an assignment." She told him about falling asleep in class and the assignment she'd missed.

Pete said he wasn't surprised, given her double fainting spells.

"The prof is giving me a second chance, and I can't afford to blow it."

"Reasonable," he said. "What's the topic?" Skye described the self-motivation essay and Pete made a scoffing sound. "You could do that in your sleep."

"Possibly. I've written a number of assignments that way."

"Huh. I'll bet." He paused, and then said, "I have my laptop in the truck. I'll go get it."

"Uh…why?"

"If you can compose an essay while sleeping, you can do it while painting. You dictate the words you want while you work, and I'll key them into the laptop. When we have it finished, you can take a few minutes to proof it and make sure it says what you mean. Then I'll send it off to Dr. Randolph's email and you'll be golden."

"You'd do that?"

He grinned. "Call it my support of the arts."

Chapter Nine

Skye started a new work, one she called *Missed Goal*, painting the emotions she felt when she realized she'd slept through an assignment and blown a deadline. She used a long canvas—nearly four feet long, but only fourteen inches wide, a symbol of her attempt to show a timeline in the paint. She began on the left, painting her shock and distress. As she moved to the right, she thought about melding shapes and colors, working toward the relief she experienced at getting a second chance. As she worked, she couldn't help but think about Peter. He was certainly an attractive distraction, but she wasn't sure *why* he was going out of his way like this.

While she painted, she talked aloud, working on the essay. First, she shared with Pete the concepts that motivated her work. When she finished, he said, "Sounds great. I recommend you start with your joy in creating. That's something Professor Randolph should relate to. Then you can work through the other ideas you discussed and end with what you said about proving to yourself that you can do hard things, like earning a living as a professional artist. That should easily give you three full pages, probably more."

"Great," she said, and began dictating. She had to go slowly, giving Pete time to key in each sentence before moving to the next, but, to her astonishment, she found that discussing her motivations didn't interfere with her painting. Paradoxically, it helped, and she found herself working faster as she composed her ideas.

She was still on a roll when Pete said, "You've got nearly a thousand words here already. That's more like four pages. Shall we go back through and edit?"

For another half hour, they worked on the essay while Skye painted. By the time they finished the assignment, she had the left third of the canvas nearly complete, missing only the small details she'd add when the first layer of paint dried. "Read it back?" she asked, this time holding her brush still and concentrating on the words as he read.

"Ready to call it good?" he asked as he finished.

"I think so. If you'll send it to me, I can send it to Randolph's email when I get home."

"I have Randolph's email. Do you want me to send it from here?"

She paused. "As long as you let him know it's from me and is actually my work."

"No problem."

"Then let me proofread. Not that I don't trust you, but I've never seen how you write. Maybe you spell like my cousin, Tyler."

He laughed. "Maybe I don't, but you're welcome to read it. That's only reasonable."

She read it through. "Looks like you spell just fine. Punctuation's good too." She gave him a flirty wink. "Yep, it's ready."

"Then off it goes." He started playing with his keyboard as Skye went back to painting. A couple of minutes later, he announced, "You want to come sign in to your account? I've sent the paper to you and all you'll have to do is send it on." She took a moment and signed in. Then he said, "All done. Your essay is submitted."

Skye turned and beamed a grateful smile. "Thank you, Pete. I teased you about the knight in shining armor thing, and frankly, I'm still not sure how I feel about…all of this." She gestured toward him, the food wrappings, the laptop. "But I wouldn't have had a meal if you hadn't brought that sandwich, and I would have been up 'til the early, pre-dawn hours if you hadn't helped me work through that assignment. I'm grateful."

"You're welcome." He stood and began packing his computer. Then he gestured toward her work in progress. "Want to tell me about your painting before I go?"

She stepped away from the canvas. "First, tell me what you see."

He studied the finished portion, roughly the left third of the full canvas. "I see confusion. Maybe some panic. Distress. It's harsh to begin with but mellowing as you move to the right. I'm guessing it will be mellower, softer as you fill in the rest."

"You've got it." She glowed at his assessment. "I'm pleased."

"You do brilliant work. Really, you do. I'm happy to say I helped." He picked up his bag. "Now I'm out of here so you can do some more brilliant work and I can change out of this dirty shirt. I'll be back to pick you up for the meeting in—" he glanced at his cell phone— "in about thirty minutes. Work for you?"

She sharpened her voice. "Yes, boss."

"Okay, okay! I'm going." He started toward the door but stopped and looked over his shoulder with one last smile.

She watched him go, feeling both appreciative and resentful. Was he hanging around only to support the arts, as he said? No less confused than she had been, she went back to her painting. Minutes later, Skye cleaned up, ready to go when Pete returned in a fresh, clean shirt. They entered the AA meeting together, prompting a few raised eyebrows and speculative looks. An hour later, they left together with almost everyone staring after them. At her request, he drove her straight to the studio. She waved him off when he asked if she needed anything.

Skye didn't see Pete on Friday or Saturday, though she found herself watching for him, half grateful he hadn't come, half hoping he would. He didn't show up on Sunday, either, but he picked her up after class on Monday and drove her to her studio, putting her bike in the back of his truck and stopping to pick up lunch on the way.

"You're spoiling me," Skye said when he returned with her burrito bowl and acai shake.

"I want you to succeed at this show." Then he frowned. "Even if I am jealous."

"I will succeed." Skye answered, beginning to believe she just might. Then she added, "And you can be jealous all you like." She winked. "You're cute when you're jealous."

On Tuesday, Skye returned to the forge, only to find Yusef, the foreman, unwilling to remove the wax pattern from the mold. "I'm afraid it isn't fully dry yet. Can you check again tomorrow?"

"My time is getting short."

"Which is why I don't want to mess up the wax," he answered. "Come back tomorrow."

Her anxiety mounting, she agreed to come back. The next day she was relieved to find the wax pattern ready to go. For nearly two hours, she worked carefully, using tiny tools to shape the details that would make her sculpture perfect. Then she turned the work back to Yusef and his crew, who were mostly students filling their lab requirements. "It's ready to go."

"Good. We'll put the individual pieces together into sheets and add the gates and sprues. By tomorrow, Friday at latest, we can dip it in the slurry. Do you want to be here for that?"

Skye considered. "I don't want to slow the process. Why don't you text me when you're ready? If I can get here in time, I will. If not, I'll ask you to go ahead without me."

"Sounds good."

Skye left the forge believing they might just make her deadline.

Yusef sent a text the next day, and Skye arrived at the forge to check the prepared wax pattern before it was dipped. Students had carefully added sprues—wax rods that would become channels when the bronze was poured, and gates—more rods that would allow the bronze to be poured into the mold. Other students had prepared the slurry—a mixture of silica sand and liquid colloidal silicone. Everything was set. "Let's do it," Skye said, and she watched with satisfaction as the wax patterns were dipped.

"Looks great," she told the foreman as the process continued.

"I have a bunch of good students this term." Then he stepped away to make certain the smaller parts of the sculptures were completely covered.

Skye left when Yusef assured her that, once dried, the plaster molds would be placed into the superheated autoclave kept for that purpose, melting away all the wax. "We'll steam it out when that's done," he assured her. "By the time we're ready to pour the bronze, the molds will be in pristine condition. I'll inspect them myself."

"I trust they'll be great." She thanked Yusef and the students and left.

Skye counted to herself as she pedaled her bike toward the studio. The paintings were coming along well. Twelve were finished or just needed detailing, and three more were in process. She still had five more to do, but she had ideas for them, and more than two weeks left to paint. Her thoughts soured when she turned to the sculptures. When these four pieces were done, she'd still only have eleven, but that might be enough for the show. Pete was right that staging had a lot to do with that. And speaking of Pete...

She'd begun watching for him, finding herself shifting from relieved to disappointed on days when he didn't show, and going from happy to confused on the days he did.

On Halloween night, she took time off for the Sober Halloween Party with her AA group. Although she and Pete hadn't come together, they arrived within a few minutes of one another, stayed together—talking, laughing, dancing—throughout the evening and left at the same time. Pete put her bike in the bed of his pickup and gave her a lift to the studio.

"How are the sculptures coming?" he asked as he waved to the guard at the kiosk and pulled through.

"Great! We're almost ready to pour the bronze. I worried we wouldn't get to this point, but if we can pour tomorrow—and Yusef thinks we can—I may still make it."

"Sounds great," he answered as he left. "I'll be waiting to hear."

"I'll let you know."

THE NEXT DAY things fell apart...literally. Skye arrived at the foundry to find two of her plaster molds on the floor in small, fragmented pieces. A small woman stood over the mess, sobbing and choking out, "I didn't mean to drop them! I didn't mean to!"

Yusef, purple faced, seemed to be struggling to control his temper, the big man holding his fisted hands at his sides while he berated the student, telling her how careless and irresponsible she'd been. Skye watched the scene in horror, feeling her knees begin to wobble.

Someone said, "She's here! Skye's here!"

Someone else came running to catch her before she sagged to the floor. Seconds later, Yusef was at her side, apologizing and promising they'd do their best to finish her work if possible.

Through the haze of shock, Skye realized it didn't matter. Nothing could be done to save those two pieces—at least, not in time for her to show them in St. Helena. She remembered what it was like to be a young student, so she chose to cut the kid some slack. She got her feet back under her and approached the sobbing student, whose straight, black hair hung in her face.

"Hey," Skye said, addressing her. "Please, look at me?"

The woman looked up, her face blotchy from crying.

Skye looked at her name tag. "Hey, Min-sun. It's going to be okay. Accidents happen."

"But you—" Min-sun's voice caught on another sob. "I'm so sorry!"

Skye touched the young student's shoulder, giving it a gentle squeeze. "It can't be helped now. Why don't you show me how the other molds came out?"

Min-sun nodded and took a deep, shuddering breath. "Come," she said. "They're here."

Skye approached the two unbroken molds…and got her second shock of the afternoon. "The pieces…" She carefully examined each of the molds again. "You didn't put all the pieces for each sculpture on the same mold. The pieces of the sculptures are all mixed up. Even if we successfully pour bronze with these two molds, we won't have everything we need to put the sculptures together." She looked over the second mold again. "I don't have all the parts for any of them. I won't have a single finished piece." She felt her knees weakening.

"Here," Yusef said from behind her. "I brought a chair."

Skye collapsed into it, her thoughts whirring as if she'd thrown them into a blender. She reached up, absentmindedly pushing her curls behind her ear. She'd have only the seven sculptured pieces she started with, and no time to create more. She'd been handed the greatest opportunity she could imagine, and she was blowing it. Suddenly she thought of the message in her painting *Missed Goal*. Then she began to laugh.

At first, it was a chuckle. Yusef, Min-sun, and the others in the room all looked at each other as if to ask, *What's funny?* Then the chuckles became laughter, and the laughter became giant belly laughs that mixed with tears and morphed into full hysteria.

That's when Pete arrived and Skye heard him come in. Perhaps later, when reality broke through, she'd be embarrassed that he'd found her like that, sitting in a chair next to a pile of broken plaster, hysterically laughing and crying while others in the room looked on, worried and helpless. She heard him say, "I'll take it from here, folks." He put his arm around her, and Skye leaned on him as he helped her to her feet. With his strong support, she made it to the door while others scurried to move objects out of their way.

"Hey, Skye," he murmured to her as they walked. "Come on, kiddo. You need to get hold of yourself." He walked her a little way down the hall and helped her to a bench. Then he sat beside her, rubbing her back and repeating "Shh, shh. It'll be all right."

Skye regained control with a gulp. "How can it…be…all right? I've failed, Pete. I can't make anything out of what's left, and I have only seven sculptured pieces."

"Then they'll be the seven most amazing sculptures anyone at the Jardin de la Vie has ever seen, and each will have plenty of space for its admirers to walk around it."

Skye shook her head. "You make it sound so easy. I've got to go tell Dr. Weems I can't make the deadline."

Pete helped her up. "I'm guessing you haven't eaten today?"

Skye tried to remember. "I guess I forgot."

"We'll get you some food. Then I can drive you to her office." He checked the time. "After that, I'll have to leave you there. I'm due at the Hot Shop this evening."

"Okay," she said. "Pete? Thanks."

"Isn't that what a Sherpa does?"

"Sherpa?"

"You know, the dude who comes along with you on your upward climb, handling the busy little details so you can make it to the top."

Skye smiled despite her sadness. "I get it—and Pete?"

"Yeah?"

"You make a pretty good Sherpa."

"Thanks." He looked pleased with himself. "Come on. Let's get you fed."

Chapter Ten

An hour later, Skye sat in the office across from Dr. Weems, explaining what had happened. "I can't make the deadline. I'm so sorry. I know you put your reputation on the line for me, and I've been working. Hard."

"I know you have." Vickie Weems's expression showed both her disappointment and sympathy. "I'll have to tell Filene you won't be able to fill the space she's reserved in the sculpture garden." She paused. "Unless you have a better idea?"

"No, I'm sorry, I..." Then Skye realized she *might* have a better idea. "How do you think she'd feel about filling the extra space with the work of an up-and-coming glass artist?"

A new expression lit the professor's face. "You're talking about Jamison Peters?"

"Yes, although you and I both know him as Pete."

Dr. Weems offered a knowing smile. "Yes, we do, and I think that's a wonderful idea. I'll get Filene on a video call right now." She reached for her computer mouse, and then looked at Skye again. "It might be wise...that is, it would be better if you weren't present for this conversation."

"Oh. Yeah. I get it." Skye stood and scurried to the door. "I'll wait in the hall."

"Thank you."

Skye found a bench a few yards from the professor's door, then she sat...and tried to think of something useful to do while she waited. She found herself thinking about taking drink or a hit, "just a little bit of something" to calm her nerves. It was the first time in a long time the craving had been this strong. But she'd always known stress could trigger that kind of response. She sat quietly repeating the Serenity Prayer as a kind of mantra.

When she first left rehab, Skye had used good chocolate as a substitute, eating a piece—or two, or three—when the cravings got bad. When she began gaining weight, she gave that up, too. *Then I became a chocoholic in recovery.* She chuckled at her own joke. She could resist the craving for drink or drugs, but she'd sure love some chocolate about now.

She reminded herself that even if the show in St. Helena was lost, she could still resist the temptation to relapse. No matter what happened, she was now the new and improved Skye and tougher than the cravings. Whatever the decision in Dr. Weems's office, Skye would come through just fine, and she wouldn't need booze or drugs to make it.

When she had waited for an interminable time, she began to think something had gone terribly wrong. Just then Dr. Weems looked out of her office and said, "Skye? Come on back." The professor gestured toward a chair.

Skye hurried into the office, closed the door, and sat. "Well?"

"Filene isn't happy." The professor looked weary, like she'd been through quite a battle. "She began by saying if you couldn't meet your obligations…"

"She cancelled," Skye said, cutting her off.

"She wanted to. Filene's a perfectionist. She doesn't like to deal with artists who are not."

"Okay then—" Skye started to stand.

"Don't worry." Dr. Weems motioned for her to stay seated. "I explained that, while you are a student here, you are not in control of the casting process. I told her it was an undergraduate student doing her apprentice hours in the forge who dropped and broke the molds just when the foreman was preparing to pour.

"I showed her your concept drawings for the women's series, and I showed her the photos I kept of your initial clay renderings. She loves them, Skye. She wants to be given the first chance to bid on the series when they're done."

"That's lovely, really, but—"

"The show is still on, and Filene wants to fill the empty spaces in her sculpture garden with Pete's glass work."

"Oh!" Skye jumped to her feet, unable to contain her relief. "I'm so glad. Thank you so much!" Emotion almost overwhelmed her. "You've saved me again. Can I hug you?"

Dr. Weems chuckled and held out her arms. "Come here." The two women shared a warm embrace.

Skye drew back. "Wait 'til I tell—"

"Oh, no you don't." The professor adopted a severe look. "I get to tell Pete. That's one stipulation on the deal."

Skye withdrew, nodding acknowledgment. "Of course. I'll wait for him to tell me."

"Good. I'll call him as soon as you're on your way down the hall."

Skye stood. "I recognize an exit cue when I hear it. I promise, I'll do my best to make you proud."

"I'm sure you will." Dr. Weems made the same shooing gesture Skye had seen from the foreman in the Hot Shop.

"I'm going," she said from the doorway. "Thanks again."

Dr. Weems nodded. "You're welcome. Now go, so I can make Pete's day."

"I'm gone." Skye sighed in relief as she eased down the hall.

PETE CLICKED HIS PHONE OFF, still stunned by the news. He'd need to get busy. He looked around at his small office near the Hot Shop. He had eleven pieces ready to go, but only three he'd display for the sophisticated buyers at the Jardin de la Vie. He repeated that in his mind: The Jardin de la Vie! Who'd have imagined…

He picked up his keys. What constituted an appropriate "thank you" gift for the artist who had given him this chance? Vickie had been careful to dodge the gratitude, telling him who made the initial suggestion. He knew a gift that might fit, but he couldn't afford to send Skye on an all-expenses paid tour of the finest art collections in Europe. He'd have to settle for what he could buy on the salary of a teacher's assistant who occasionally sold a nice piece of art glass. He'd never met a woman who didn't like chocolate.

Minutes later, he left the parking lot on his way to the best chocolatier he knew, a man named Ramon who fashioned his own elegant creations out of his shop on Pinell Street. Once inside the store, Pete carefully selected each item: sea salt caramel chocolates, dark semisweet covered rich vanilla nougat, honeycomb dipped in dark semisweet, chocolate covered sugared orange peel...

His choices filled a two-pound box with three pieces left over. "I'd buy more," he told the young woman behind the counter, "but this is all I can afford today." He flashed her a grin and handed over a debit card.

She rang it up. Then, with the kind of smile he often received from single women, she said, "Come back any time." She placed the three extra pieces into a small bag and handed it to him. Lowering her voice, she repeated, "Any time at all."

"Thanks." He nodded, keeping his expression pleasant, but not flirtatious, as he left the shop. He wondered what would happen if he started wearing a wedding ring. Would that fend off some of the unwanted female interest? He got the truck started. Then, thinking of similar come hither looks he'd received from obviously married women, he shook his head. A wedding ring wouldn't help much. Leaving that thought for another time, Pete smiled in anticipation as he drove toward the warehouse art studio and the artist whose good fortune had now become his.

SKYE WORKED STEADILY at her newest painting, the one she tentatively called *Crash and Burn*. Wild shapes in dark colors, accented with flames in red-orange and yellow, filled the four edges of the rectangular canvas. Darkest at the outside edges, they faded toward the middle. There, on a paler background, she'd paint the image of her broken sculpture pieces as she last saw them, piled in bits and shards like a heap of sun-bleached bones.

No one would know what it meant, but it would still feel like failure, and Skye painted emotions, taking what people felt and creating art. She repeated her success mantra as she worked: *I'm a great artist. I paint what people feel.* The more she said it, the more she believed.

She turned her brush into the paint she'd just mixed and dragged it through one upper corner of the canvas, leaving a trail of dark color that turned lighter as it moved toward the middle. Then she stepped back and studied the effect. *That worked well. I like it.* Studying the work again, she considered adding a similar streak on a lower corner but decided against it. She began working on the paler area near the center, where her broken sculptures would appear in acrylics.

Skye began mixing a soft salmon color for the central background. The back door opened with a bang and she looked up to see Pete striding toward her, wearing a triumphant smile. So Dr. Weems had told him. Good! Pete set down the box he was carrying, grabbed Skye in a bear hug and swung her before setting her on her feet. "Thank you!" he said and handed her the box.

"Um…you're welcome?"

"Ah, come on, Skye. You know what you did. I want you to know I was joking about hitching my wagon to your rising star, but I also appreciate the referral. I would never have gotten a Jardin de la Vie exhibit on my own. So…thank you, thank you, thank you!" On the final repetition, he placed both hands on her shoulders in a gentle grip, a kind of reminder hug.

"Don't be too gracious, Pete. It was a selfish gesture."

His features drew in as though he'd bitten into a lemon. "How do you figure that?"

"Filene had decided to drop me. I had to come up with a make-good option or my chance to do the show would vanish like spring rain, but if I picked another sculptor who works in bronze, her work would have competed with mine. What you do is so different that it doesn't occupy the same mental space for potential clients. If they leave with a glass piece and a bronze, they don't feel they've purchased two of the same, and they have no problem displaying them together."

He smirked. "And you figured all that out on the spot? I don't think so."

She allowed a secretive smile. "Okay, you caught me. I thought of your name on the fly when I got desperate, but I'm sure my subconscious mind had already thought it through."

"Yeah. Right." He was grinning again as he said, "I'm grateful either way." He picked up the box. "Here, open your gift."

"Okay." Skye pulled off the wrapping. "Oh! How did you know? I adore chocolate, and these are my very favorite. They're from Ramon's shop on Pinell Street, right?" He looked surprised but nodded. She went on. "When I first got out of rehab and felt *so* tempted to start using again, I substituted these." She held the box out. "Here, you can help me inaugurate this box."

He waved the box away. "No. I got them for you."

She moved the box close again. "Better take one now. This is the only time I'm going to offer, as I plan to cling greedily to everything else in the box."

"Then why not—"

"If you don't take one now…" She adopted a severe look. "I might think you're trying to poison me."

He laughed at that. "All right. You've won me over. My favorites are the sugared orange peel dipped in dark chocolate. I think those look like…" He chose a piece and lifted it, still in its little paper. "Like this," he finished.

"That sounds good. I think I'll try to find…ah, there!" She chose a piece that looked like his and lifted it into the air. "To Filene and the Jardin de la Vie. May we both knock her socks off."

"To Filene," he said, touching his chocolate to hers.

They bit into their candy. "You've done it now," she told Pete after her first swallow. "You know what happens to an addict who gets a little taste. As a devout chocoholic, I'm falling off the wagon even as we stand here."

"And loving it, I hope."

"Ummm." She licked her lips and took a second small nibble. "Loving every molecule. This stuff is chocolate perfection."

They were silent then as each savored the decadent flavors. Pete finished first, licking his fingers. "Looks like we both have work to do."

"Yes," Skye agreed, "but for me, the pressure is off. I won't be doing any sculpting before the show—thanks, in part, to you—and I have sixteen paintings ready or near ready, lacking only the touch up details. This one—" She indicated the canvas in front of her. "This is the seventeenth, and I expect to finish it in the next few days. I have ideas for at least three more and still have most of two weeks to paint. I think I'm going to be just fine. And you?"

"I have several pieces, but only three I'm willing to show to that crowd."

"Do you have pictures?"

"Yeah, I do." He pulled out his phone and quickly scrolled through. "Here's the one I like best." He showed her a familiar image.

"This is the piece you were working on that day I first came into the Hot Shop."

"I'm surprised you remember."

"That flame…that's definitely memorable."

"Well, this is what it looks like finished. I'm calling it *Agony of Pain*."

"That's what I see when I look at it." She'd seen how Pete formed emotion in glass, just the way she tried to paint emotion or style it in bronze.

"That's great." Pete narrowed his gaze, focusing intently. "Go on, please. Analyze it for me and tell me what you see."

"That dark shape standing up in the middle. It could just be a burning log, but some people might see a human figure, like someone being burned at the stake." She paused.

"Yes. Go on…"

"I don't see literal burning. I see you depicting a person who's done something that he or she regrets deeply, someone suffering the agony of a guilty conscience."

Pete's features widened in wonder. "You get it. I think you get me, where I'm coming from."

"We get each other," Skye said, taking his hand in a gesture of solidarity—two artists with a similar vision.

His hand gripped hers. "Yes," he said, beaming in wonder. "I think we do."

Chapter Eleven

The bond of that moment couldn't last, not when both artists had so much work to do before loading day in mid-November. Pete couldn't remember a time when he'd put so many hours in at the Hot Shop. He thought it lucky that his only class this term, other than completing his masters' exhibit, was in art studio methods. He could ace that just by being present in the Hot Shop. Now he needed to come up with five or six more pieces he'd be willing to display in front of the most discerning art collectors in the western states. That thought still amazed him, and he mumbled, "Thanks, Skye." He began mixing colors into the glass beads he planned to melt.

"Mr. Koury, can you help me with the glory hole? I'm having trouble holding the glass together when I reheat."

Pete turned to find a simpering coed—pretty enough, but she looked about sixteen. Definitely not his type. "Sure. Give me a second." He organized his own project and went to help Miss Sweet Sixteen, whom, he suspected, wanted his attention more than his assistance. He sighed. This was going to be a long afternoon.

WHATEVER THE PRESSURES, Pete always made time for his weekly racquetball game with Tim, a fraternity brother who graduated the same time he did. Tim, who managed to get the degree without the alcohol addiction, wore increasingly important job titles as he worked his way up the corporate ladder. For him, the game was a way of staying in shape. For Pete, who did plenty of heavy lifting in the Hot Shop, racquetball was his cardio workout and a necessary stress release.

"Honestly," Pete said, hitting the ball hard, "if I have to deal with one more fawning coed…"

"So, stop ducking!" Tim whacked the ball with a resounding crack. "As long as they're consenting adults, why not just take what they're offering and enjoy?"

"Most of them are hardly more than kids, and I don't like seeing myself as the dirty old man who takes advantage of little girls."

"Are they over eighteen?"

"I'm not sure about the one in the Hot Shop today. She looked like a baby, but yeah, for the most part, they're adults…legally, anyway."

"Then who's to say you're a dirty old man if all you take is what they're happily giving?"

Pete groaned and jumped for a high ball. "You make it sound like a straightforward business transaction."

"What's the big deal? You're a healthy male in his prime, they're—"

"Okay, stop. That's another point for me. You've got to focus more on your game." Besides, Pete didn't want to hear what Tim had to say about these girls. They might be legal adults, but most of them didn't have a clue what they'd be getting into when they came on to more experienced men. Pete didn't want to be the one to break it to them.

Tim whacked the ball again. "Honestly, you're starting to sound like some old guy."

"Maybe I'm getting tired of the party life."

"Oh? Have you met somebody? Thinking about settling down? You're young for that yet."

"Not too young." He put some spin on that hit. "But no, I haven't met anyone."

His conscience shouted, *Liar! You know you're thinking of Skye.*

He countered his own argument. *We've never even been on a date.*

He could almost hear his inner voice snickering as his mind filled with images of times he'd taken her to dinner or brought her meals, the way he'd swept her up in his arms when she'd fainted. He conceded that point to his inner voice just as the ball flew past him.

"Maybe it's time you paid attention to your game." Tim racked up another point.

"Yeah, yeah. Get ready to be trounced."

"You wish!" Tim said as he sent the ball flying.

FOR SKYE, the pressure was indeed off, and she found she could enjoy her hours in the studio. Molly, whose studio rent was covered by her grandfather—the one who wanted her to be an artist—often painted alongside her. Despite the rawness of her skill as an artist, Molly had a discerning eye and often advised Skye on her works in progress, pointing out small details Skye might have missed in her obsessive focus on the bigger picture.

"What's that little spot of blue?" Molly asked one afternoon in the first week of November.

"Blue?" Skye focused on the spot Molly indicated. A tiny dot in the middle of a leaf shape did indeed look blue; it almost looked like the paints she had mixed to get the blue-green hadn't fully combined. "I'm calling this one *Can't See the Forest.* Whoa! What if I turn that blue spot into an eye?" With a few quick, dark strokes and a little off-white, she added a human eye, peeking through the trees or tall grasses, the obstacles that had kept her imaginary artist's eye from seeing the bigger picture. "I like that! Thanks, Molly."

"No problem." Molly studied the painting. "I like that better, too. Nice work!"

"I owe it all to you, my friend." She set her brush down and stretched her hands above her head. "How's your painting coming?"

"Come see." Molly stepped back, turning her easel so Skye could better examine her work.

"Move over, Georgia O'Keeffe! Nice work, Molly."

"Thank you. I take that as quite a compliment coming from you."

Both women were silent as they looked from Molly's painting to Skye's and back again. "I still have a way to go to catch up with you," Molly said, "if that's even possible!" Then, in a sudden turn, she said, "I haven't seen Pete around here much lately. Are you two on the outs?"

"No, not at all." Skye explained how she brought Pete into the St. Helena show after her molds were broken. "He's under pressure to have enough pieces ready to fill the spaces in the sculpture garden. I don't expect to see him much between now and show time."

They were interrupted when Pete opened the back door and walked toward them. Molly raised an eyebrow. "You were saying?"

"I'm as surprised as you are." Skye turned to the guy in question. "What's up?"

"I have two new pieces done. I want you to come and see them. You can tell me whether you think they're up to the mark for the big show."

Checking the time, Skye saw she had a few minutes to spare, and Pete could use her affirmation and support. "Sure. Give me five minutes to clean up my work area."

"I'll do that for you," Molly said, stepping in. Then she turned and said, "Hi, Pete. Good to see you again." Back to Skye, "Go ahead and go. I know what to do with your things."

"Thanks. I appreciate that."

Molly grinned. "Happy to help. I owe you one or two."

Pete stayed close as they walked side by side down the hallway. She loved the way it felt to walk beside him even though Molly stared after them with a smug, told-you-so grin.

"THESE ARE GREAT, Pete. Honestly, you have a rare eye and the very rare skill to execute it well." She made a full circle around a piece done mostly in greens. "What are you calling this one?"

"I'll tell you, but first, tell me what you feel when you look at it."

Skye considered. "Honestly, I feel just a bit ill. I hope that doesn't hurt your feelings."

"Not at all. I'm calling it *Sea Legs.* I played racquetball with a buddy this week and he asked if I'd like to go out on his fishing boat on the delta this weekend. I told him I'm going to be too busy getting ready for this show, which is true, but it's also an excuse. The truth is—" he pointed to the green glass— "this is how I feel whenever I'm on the water."

"Me, too! I can get seasick standing on the dock, just watching the boats bob up and down." They shared a knowing smile. Then she asked, "Do you want to show me your second piece?"

"Yeah. It's over here." He led her to a different table in the Hot Shop and moved a large piece of fiberboard out of the way so she could see the work he'd positioned there. "What do you see in this one?"

"Hmmm." Skye stepped close, examining the piece from all angles. "First, this is obviously bigger. You're hoping it will command more attention."

"Yes, and…?"

"The emotion in it is brighter, happier. I don't know how to say it, but—"

"I'm calling it *Glass Half Full*."

"Ah, I see what you had in mind. It's about optimism, about looking forward with hope."

"Very much so, yes."

Skye admired the unique glass work, making comments that elicited Pete's beaming smile.

A few minutes later, Pete said, "Hey, it's almost eight. I'm betting you haven't had dinner."

"Not yet."

"Neither have I. How about we get something to eat?" Pete pulled his keys from his pocket. "It's time to lock up the Hot Shop, anyway. I chased most of the kids out an hour ago."

Skye still had more than enough to do, but she barely hesitated. "Great! Is your truck parked in the usual place?"

"Yeah, it is." He nodded, apparently impressed that she'd remembered.

"Race you there!" She jogged toward the door.

THE DAYS PASSED IN A HAZE. Skye kept up with class—barely, painted—steadily, and spent way too much time thinking about Pete. She relied on Molly to help her refine her vision for each painting, and she put the emphasis where it seemed to elicit the best emotional response. By the evening of November fourteenth, she had twenty-two paintings and eleven sculptures ready.

"I think these last three are among the best," she said to Molly as the two began preparing her work for transport.

"I especially like the one you call *Food Dreams*. Most people in your select audience are going to look at that and realize you're commenting on world hunger. The way you've done it is clear, but subtle enough that it won't be off-putting to anyone. It's an excellent piece of work."

"I've never been truly hungry," Skye said, "not like some of the people we see in the news, but when I lived with my mom in the commune—"

"The Children of Rah."

"Yeah. I'm surprised you remember."

"Stories like that are hard to forget."

"No matter how we try." Skye's tone became apologetic when she added, "Hope I haven't weirded you out by sharing some of that."

"No, but I'm glad you got out."

"Yeah. Me, too."

Molly laid a hand over Skye's. "Were you hungry there?"

"No, never hungry like the starving people you see on the news or the ads for aid campaigns. Never like the babies with the pencil thin arms and legs." She shuddered. "No, not like that, but when my sister and I finally got some medical care, the doctor declared us both malnourished. She said that if we hadn't received good care soon, the kind we were finally getting from our Aunt Olivia and Uncle Enrique, we'd have run serious risks of losing our teeth, or developing organ or skin problems."

"You were lucky to get out when you did."

"I say we were blessed. Our Aunt Olivia's concern saved us in more ways than I can count. She and Uncle Enrique became the parents we should have had."

Molly turned to another of Skye's paintings, one completed in the past six days. "That's what this painting is about, isn't it?"

Skye looked at *Blessed Rescue*. Although no one would find anything in it that looked realistically like the Rah cult, the emotions of desperation and relief almost jumped off the canvas. "It's one of my favorites, too," she answered, "and yes, when I painted this piece, I was thinking of the day Aunt Olivia drove us out of there. We'd gone with her before, on little outings, but we knew this time would be different. She told us to get whatever we owned because we wouldn't be coming back. I was only nine, but I already knew other people were living better lives outside our compound. I wanted out, and our aunt's rescue came when Sunny and I needed it most."

Molly sat back, gesturing around her at the other pieces, both painted and sculpted, that Skye had brought out for packing. "You're going to do great. You know that, don't you? You'll wow those art collectors. By the end of the month, your name will be on the tongue of every collector and curator in the state, maybe the whole American West."

"I appreciate your vote of confidence, but I don't think this show reaches that far."

"Oh, its reach is plenty big. Wait and see."

"Let's hope you're right." Skye sighed. "I expect to graduate in May. After that, I'll have to do well enough to create my own foundry or rent time at someone else's. Otherwise, I'll have to give up the bronze and stick strictly with paint."

"You won't have to give up anything." Molly looked toward the door when she asked, "Do you know how Pete is doing?"

"I'm assuming he's okay. I haven't seen him for three days. We've both been way too busy, but he tells me he has eight pieces ready to roll, and he seems fairly pleased with the last ones."

"I'm glad," Molly said. "I bet he's going to wow them too."

Skye smiled, eyes twinkling. "Pete wows everybody. He can't help it."

Molly nodded. "Point taken. The man is gorgeous, so let me rephrase. His *art* will wow everyone, and the fact that he's there to show it off will only help it sell."

Skye thought of the last pieces she'd seen in the Hot Shop. Pete's work was good, very good. "I believe you're right," she answered, knowing that if the collectors and curators were women, Pete could sell almost anything and do very well indeed.

In the Hot Shop, Pete prepared each of his eight chosen works for packing. Shipping glass art was an art in itself—that is, if he expected each piece to arrive in good condition. Angela, one of the other grad students who worked in the Hot Shop, came to help. She also seemed intent on flirting and ingratiating herself.

"This is *marvelous* work, Peter," she purred as she lovingly caressed *Sea Legs*. "I can almost feel the rhythm of the sea. You must be a true sailor."

"Not really," he said, choosing not to tell her what a mistake she was making if she wanted to impress. "Can you hand me the foam peanuts?"

"Sure." Angela managed to scoot two feet closer while moving the box near him. Her thigh brushed his as she put the packing foam into his arms.

He stepped away, pretending he needed the distance to manage the large art piece. "How about the packing tape?"

"Happy to help," she said, scooting near him again as she balanced the tape on his leg.

"Thanks," he said, and managed to stop short of rolling his eyes. Just as well Angela didn't know Pete couldn't remember her name when he asked Sam for helpers.

"This is my favorite piece," Angela said, delicately stroking *Glass Half Full*. "It's so very…sensual." She gave him a sultry, come hither look.

"Hand me a big box, please," he said, pointedly ignoring her come-on. Pete released a soul-deep sigh. He'd had a long afternoon. Now he was in for an even longer night.

Chapter Twelve

S kye stood inside the Jardin de la Vie near the entrance to the gallery where her paintings were hanging, each spotlighted with its title and price. Filene, in her role as curator, placed the *Sold* tag on *Random Thoughts*, but she also made three of Skye's larger paintings available for silent auction with the bidding started at Skye's suggested price. On this first evening of the week-long show, Filene already had multiple bids for each of the three with the prices slowly rising.

Meanwhile, Pete held down the fort in the sculpture garden, answering questions about his own work and referring interested parties to Skye when they asked about hers. This first evening, both Pete and Skye needed to be available at the artists' reception, but they'd leave early the next day in Pete's truck, going back to their school obligations until they were needed again in a week to pack up any works that didn't sell.

Skye hoped they'd sell out, so they would not need to return at all. She smiled broadly, greeting yet another patron who wanted to compliment her work. Whether the woman would buy posed a different question.

For this event, Skye had gone all-out, buying a new dress at a price she'd never consider under other circumstances. Although it was modest enough to wear in front of Uncle Enrique, it still showed off her willowy shape. Its brilliant scarlet red, finished in shimmering sequins, drew attention from everywhere in the room. She'd taken extra time with her hair. Her type 3A curls required effort to detangle without breaking while still fighting frizz and dryness. Using gentle shampoo and a hydrating conditioner, she'd allowed her hair to air dry. Then with the help of a lightweight conditioning spray, she'd eased the bulk of it into a classic topknot. The small curls that gathered at her hairline refused to be tamed or contained, so she exaggerated them, letting their spirals become part of her look. Clean, barely there eye make-up and glimmering scarlet lipstick completed the look. "You're absolutely darling!" Filene declared when she arrived, promising Skye she'd be an asset to help her work sell.

"How's it going?" Pete appeared at her elbow. He held a glass of sparkling water in one hand and a napkin in the other. "You've been busy in here. I thought maybe you could use some fortification." He set the goblet on the small table where Filene had placed a guest book. Collectors and art aficionados interested in receiving advance notice of Skye's upcoming displays had already filled one page with their contact information. Pete nodded toward the book. "Looks like you're gathering fans."

"One can always hope. How's it going out there?"

"Good. I'm surprised at the comments I've been getting, not just on *your* work, which I expected, but on mine too. Filene started a silent auction on two of my pieces and—"

"Let me guess: *Agony of Pain* and *Leading Edge*."

"Yeah. How'd you know?"

"Those are clearly your best. I mean, they're all good, but—"

"You don't have to explain. Those two are my favorites. I should have known you'd pick them, given your keen eye."

She shrugged. "I know great art when I see it."

He nodded, accepting the compliment. "Thanks. Coming from you—"

"Excuse me?" A richly dressed man approached them.

Skye said, "Yes? Can I help you?"

"Which one of you is the glass artist?"

Pete answered, "That would be me."

"May I ask a question about your piece called *Sea Legs?* If you follow me into the garden, I can show you what I'm asking about."

"Sure." Pete gestured to Skye—it looked much like a salute—and followed the guest outside.

"Excuse me, Miss. You're the artist who signs herself Skye?"

Skye turned to see a well-dressed, middle-aged woman. "Yes, I'm Skye."

"I'd like to talk with you about doing a commissioned piece."

"Of course. What did you have in mind?" Skye slipped easily into sales mode.

"A RESOUNDING SUCCESS. That's what Filene called it." Pete exulted in the praise as he drove them home the next morning.

Skye made her voice deep and nasal, mimicking Filene as she repeated, "Resounding, my dears. We must have you both back another time." She raised her hand and Pete responded, the two sharing a high-five. "She thinks we'll sell out before the week is over."

"She said four of my pieces already sold. That's half," Pete said.

"Six of my seven sculptures and at least half my paintings are spoken for." Skye practically hummed. "Maybe even better? I already have four commissions."

"I have two. That's never happened before. Honestly, Skye, I can't thank you enough for letting me be a part of this."

"I told you, it's all selfishness."

"Yeah. Right." He let his eyes tell her they both knew the truth.

For a short while, they let the truck's radio fill the silence. Then Pete said, "We need a celebration, don't you think?"

"Yeah." Skye agreed. "I think so. More chocolate?" She produced her best hopeful look.

He laughed. "Sure. I can provide chocolate, but I'm thinking we need something bigger."

"Like…?"

"One of the collectors gave me a hint. He liked the painting you call *Nightscape.*"

"The one with the shapes like a nebula and stars."

"Yeah, that one. I believe he's the guy who bought it."

"Great. But why did he talk with *you* about *my* work?"

Pete shrugged. "Who knows? But he's a big fan of yours. Anyway, he started looking at my *Sea Legs* piece and talking about your *Nightscape.* Seems he's a professor of astronomy at Berkeley. He's looking forward to a major meteor shower next weekend. What would you think about finding a place where we could lie on the grass and watch the falling stars?"

Skye couldn't help wondering what Pete had in mind. "Like...to celebrate?"

He shrugged. "If you like. Or just to unwind. Lie still and let the heavens do the work instead of pushing as hard as we've both been doing."

She chuckled. "That sounds like fun, but we'd need to get away from the light pollution."

"Yeah. I can't think of a good place—"

"I can." For her, that was a no-brainer. She could only hope Uncle Enrique would go for it. "I know exactly where to go. I'll have to make some phone calls and do a little planning. When would you like to do this stargazing?"

"Say, next Friday evening?"

She nodded. "I'm pretty sure I can make it happen. In the meantime, I need to get caught up on classwork."

"I have some catching up to do too." He paused. "When do you think you'll know—"

"I should be able to tell you by tomorrow."

"Great! I'll check back with you tomorrow."

"Sounds great." Skye began humming along with the music. Then she said, "Promise you'll bring chocolate?"

He grinned. "The best chocolate I can find."

"You're on. Now I *promise* I'll find a place."

"Note to self, Skye will do almost anything for chocolate." Pete said.

"Don't get ahead of yourself." She wagged a finger at him, smiling. "I'll find a place for *stargazing* in exchange for good chocolate. And it has to be *really good* chocolate even for that."

He chuckled. "Duly noted. I'll call you tomorrow."

THE FOLLOWING DAY, Skye called her Aunt Olivia. She wasn't home, but Enrique answered. He asked too many questions about "this young man you're bringing," but agreed to let them use the back lawn for stargazing. Then he quickly reversed himself, pointing out that her cousin Amber's place, where she lived with her new husband outside Destiny, would have even less light pollution. "When they turn off their lights out there, the only bright spots you can see are the ones in the sky."

Skye conceded the point. A week later, Skye and Pete lay side by side, not quite touching, on a large picnic quilt borrowed from her Aunt Olivia. Amber and Max shared a blanket of their own, positioned nearby, as did Amber's friend, Paris with her husband, Greg. Skye's sister, Sunny, had come from the valley along with her husband, Evan; their blanket lay on the other side of Paris and Greg's. Closest to Pete and Skye, almost closer than Skye was to Pete, lay Aunt Olivia's denim picnic quilt, with Olivia and Enrique close enough to touch.

"I'm sorry about this," Skye whispered to Pete as they watched the crowd move in around them. "This crowd scene is not what I planned."

He grinned. "I think it's cute. They're all being protective."

"They're all checking you out, making sure I'm safe with you."

He dropped his voice even lower. "You may have had times in the past when your family didn't feel that way about the people around you."

"You know it," she answered, "but that's a discussion for another time."

"Oh, look at that one!" Amber called.

Skye looked up in time to see a bright light streaking the sky. An idea jumped into mind for how she could use that in a painting. She sighed. Sometimes being an artist was a pain. Anything visual could always draw her into her work. She wanted to relax and enjoy the evening, but she couldn't turn it off. Like it or not, the artistic impulse was always with her.

PETE COULD NOT HAVE BEEN MORE amused. He knew Skye worried that he'd be offended by the crowd that gathered protectively around them, but he thought it was sweet. These people clearly cared about Skye, and that gave them gold stars in his books.

A bit after midnight, Enrique declared the star party should end. "We need to break this up and let everybody get some sleep." People began scrambling to their feet, picking up and shaking out blankets, and preparing to leave—all but Amber and Max, who lived there, and Pete, who'd spend the night on the couch in Max and Amber's living room.

"Sorry we can't offer you better," Skye whispered as she folded her quilt.

"No worries." Pete's glance shifted toward Sunny and Evan. "Will you stay here tomorrow and go home with them on Sunday? Or should I pick you up in the morning?"

Skye didn't have to think twice. "I'll go with you, if it's still okay."

"Sure. I'll come by about…when? Eight o'clock too early?"

"No. Eight's fine. See you then."

She noticed the way Enrique watched them, waiting to see if there'd be a goodnight kiss. She smiled at his confused expression when she walked away from Pete without so much a touch. Clearly, Tío Rico didn't understand their relationship. But now that she thought about it, she didn't understand it either. What were she and Pete to each other?

Aunt Olivia's mom antennae were good. The minute she had Skye alone, Olivia asked, "What's going on with you and Pete?"

Skye had been preparing for this question since her protective relatives had begun to gather. "Not much, really. We've never even been on a date, unless you can count tonight."

"Really? You two seem much closer than that, like you've been a couple for some time."

"Nope. We've worked together—on our art projects, you know—but that's it." She chose not to mention fainting on him or waking up in his arms or the way he brought her meals or took her out sometimes or bought her chocolates…

Olivia interrupted Skye's thoughts. "Well for sure, you've got your hands full with that one. He's as handsome and charming as the devil himself."

"Um, yeah. Believe me, I've noticed."

Olivia chuckled. "I'll bet you have! Keep your head together, *chiquita*. It would be easy to lose it over a man like that."

"Will do, Auntie. Thanks."

Late that evening, as she lay awake, Skye thought over the weeks she'd known Pete. They had started out with him thinking she was a stalker, and perhaps she was. Then she'd fainted on top of him and he became a sort of knight errant protector. Weird. After that, they were colleagues, working together toward the same make-or-break opportunity. Of course, they always had AA in common, along with their attempts to support each other in sobriety, That made Pete a friend. If it weren't for her crazy attraction to him, friendship might just be enough.

ALONE ON A COUCH in the home of strangers, Pete lay thinking much the same thing. He'd promised himself he'd help Skye out, keep her from destroying her health while she got ready for her grand opportunity. She had turned that show into so much more than it might have been, and, in the process, she'd made it a giant upward leap for him, too. He couldn't thank her enough. When he'd planned the stargazing for this evening, he'd hoped it might be a turning point for them with a warm blanket, a night full of stars, and some non-alcoholic bubbly. Maybe even a little romantic action, a move toward something more.

He had to grin, thinking of the way Skye's people had formed ranks around her, circling the wagons. He knew plenty of recovering addicts. Few had the kind of support Skye enjoyed. He sure didn't. His dad had written him off when he switched the engineering major he hated for the art he loved. His mom gave up on him after the second time he stole from her. Or was it the third? He only remembered trying to find ways to keep the bills paid even when he was a falling down drunk, no longer able to hold a steady job.

Then there was his brother. Michael still talked with Pete, but was always cautious, like he wasn't sure whether to trust, like he still thought Pete might be playing him. Well, Pete could hardly blame him, considering what he'd put Michael and the rest of the family through before he chose sobriety.

Following the process outlined in Step Nine, he'd gone to each of them, enumerating the ways and times he'd hurt them, and asking their forgiveness. His mother and Michael had both given him lip service, but they didn't want to be around him. His dad was a different story. Pete had disappointed him, but that was largely because his dad had selfish expectations. He'd never understood Pete at all and couldn't understand his work. His dad still imagined he was playing with a hobby, not becoming a serious artist with a following. Pete supposed his father might come around if he achieved great things— say, if he became another Dale Chihuly, celebrated around the world— but it was possible he wouldn't be happy even then.

No, Pete had nothing like the support system he had seen with Skye. But then again, who could blame them for sticking by her? She was a fantastic artist and amazing person.

He admired her work ethic and her dedication to sobriety. He respected the efforts she'd made to conquer the ghosts of a difficult past whether addictions or other problems. And he prized the relationships she had with her family so different from his own. Her artistic vision amazed him. She could paint things he could only feel and could not execute in glass.

On top of all that, she was lovely. He couldn't help smiling when he thought of the way little curls gathered around her face when she pulled her hair back. He loved her smooth, unblemished skin—a light reddish-brown like quality terra cotta—and the way her thick, dark lashes flickered unconsciously when she became angry or embarrassed. Even the tone of her voice pleased him. He could hear her across the room and start smiling, just knowing she was close.

He couldn't define what it was he had going with Skye, but he knew he wanted it to keep moving forward. He wanted to know her better and to have her come to know him, the real Pete that he hid from almost everyone. That decided, he rolled over and fell into a deep, dreamless sleep, the best night he'd had in ages.

Chapter Thirteen

Pete picked up Skye at the Reyes home the next morning, prepared for the discussion that might define what they were becoming to one another. It seemed Skye had come prepared for a different set of topics entirely.

"If it's all right with you," she began, even before she greeted him, "I'd like to make a stop on the way down the mountain. I want to show you something."

"Oh? What do you have in mind?"

"It's a place I want you to see. It kind of relates to what you said, about the talk we should have. Do you remember the health spa we passed on the way into town?"

"Not really. It was getting pretty dark by then. I think I remember the turnoff, though, and I noticed the signs."

"It's only about five or so miles down the road. Your turn will be on the right." When he seemed to hesitate, she added, "Don't worry. I won't keep you long."

"Okay." He paused. Then, with a smile in his voice, he said, "Interesting how our trip to see the meteor shower turned out."

She made a small, scoffing sound. "You mean the family circus?"

"They did make it something of a crowd scene."

"Nothing like a swarm of Reyes relatives to scare away the faint of heart."

He had to smile at that. "They don't know what to think of me, do they?"

"Don't worry about it. They haven't decided what to think of *me*."

"They love you, though. It's cute, the way they gathered around you. They're like a protective wall between you and the world."

"They don't know you've been my number one protector these past weeks."

That opened the topic Pete wanted to discuss. He started to speak.

Skye interrupted his thought. "There, just ahead on the right."

He took the turn at the sign reading, Destiny Health Spa.

"Pull up anywhere," she said.

He stopped the truck and reached for his door handle. "Are we going in?"

"No need. I thought you might like to see where I come from."

"Aren't you from Destiny?"

"Yes, but I was born here. Right here."

"Here? In a health spa?"

"The spa wasn't here then." She told him a story he found amazing about a sun worshipping, drug using cult that called themselves the Children of Rah and their self-styled guru who brought his followers to live in tumble-down shacks they built from whatever they could scrounge. She described how they squatted on land owned by an absentee landlord who allowed their presence only because he didn't know they were there; about free use of alcohol and drugs; about being delivered by a scared young mother whose fears were calmed with opiates and a would-be midwife who'd read two books about birthing before delivering her sister, Sunny.

"She'd delivered three babies by the time she got to me. I was the fourth." Skye looked carefully at Pete.

Pete saw the look Skye gave him, like she was wondering if he was weirded out by all this strangeness. He couldn't blame her for thinking he might be. Other people had probably responded badly in the past. "I'm sorry," he said, touching her hand. "I'm sorry you went through all that."

"That was just the beginning." She told him she didn't remember her first drink. "It happened when I was too young to remember. I've been drinking beer and wine since before I could speak. The grown-ups gave us whiskey in our baby bottles to 'help us sleep.' The older kids started experimenting with drugs by the time I was six or seven. They liked to try them out on those of us who were younger, just to see how silly we looked when we were blitzed out of our minds."

"Whoa." Pete had thought fraternity parties were crazy. At least those people were alleged adults. "I...don't know what to say. That's awful, Skye."

"When I...um, collapsed on you—rather unceremoniously, I'm afraid—that was as physically close as I'd been to anyone in some time—that is, anyone who wasn't family. It's like you got in under my radar without my even noticing."

Now he made the scoffing sound. "Not that you *could* notice. You were unconscious."

She nodded. "Yes, there's that." She took a deep breath, looked him straight in the eye, and laid her hand over his. "What I'm telling you is that I'd never intended to become involved with another recovering alcoholic or addict, ever again. I've had some negative experiences, guys who made promises and flaked, relapsing into their addictions when I relied on them the most—"

"Pretty typical." He realized instantly that he'd made a mistake. "Relapses happen."

Her voice grew icy. "Not to me. Not to the people around me. I don't tolerate it."

"I get that."

"Anyway, I told myself I'd had enough of that and made promises to myself about how I would not get involved in any way with another person in recovery. Then I went to that first meeting in the basement of the church and you walked in... I've gotta tell you, Pete. You made me want to rethink my decision. Then when you got up and walked out..." She patted his hand. "Tell me the truth. It felt like you were leaving because of me. Is that true?"

He hesitated before speaking. "Actually, yeah."

"What? Really?"

He took both her hands in his. "Skye, I left that meeting because I'd made the same vow you had—that I wasn't going to get involved with other people in recovery. I'd had some bad experiences of my own. Then I sat down near you and knew if I stayed, I'd be tempted to break that promise."

"You...what?"

"I left because I didn't want to be attracted to you."

She gave him an odd look, part incredulous disbelief and part hope. "Can you repeat that, please?"

"I didn't want to be attracted to you, but I was. Like crazy. It was electric, Skye, really crazy how powerful that feeling was. I knew if I stayed, I'd end up breaking my self-promise. You… what was that expression you used? You 'got in under my radar' almost immediately."

"Oh. Well." She sat back, her curly hair flattening against the car's head rest.

"I *am* attracted to you and I'm pretty certain you're attracted to me too. We're consenting adults, both past the promises we made to ourselves about not dating others in recovery. The next step seems quite logical."

Skye flashed him a look, part skepticism, part suspicion. "And that would be?"

"We go out. We date." He took her hand. "We spend time together, support each other in sobriety and in our art, and explore where this relationship can go."

"You make it sound so simple."

"It *is* simple, or at least, it should be."

"Yeah. I guess. It's just that…well, one day I woke up in your arms. I hadn't planned to be there, and it was kind of…disconcerting."

He tried not to smirk. "I had the impression you quite liked it."

"Oh, yeah! Definitely!"

"Good. Then we've got everything straight." He started the engine and headed the truck down the highway. But he hadn't quite covered everything, had he? He saw the pullout ahead and an idea jumped into his mind, an idea he hoped Skye would like.

Skye relaxed against the seat, settling in for the drive to the valley. She felt droopy and wondered if she could sleep.

That's when Pete slowed. He surprised her, saying, "Let's stop here for a second."

She gave him a questioning look but said nothing as he drove the truck into the wide space and brought it to a stop. "Look around," he said.

She looked. "Yeah?"

"No trees. No power lines. No lights. This—"

"It's what people call 'the pullout.' It allows drivers to make a U-turn if they realize they're on the wrong road. It's also the only place between the valley and Destiny where you can reliably get a cell signal."

"It looks like a great place to watch a meteor shower, don't you think? There are bathrooms and a water fountain… Maybe tomorrow night? Just you and me, no relatives invited. I'll throw a couple of sleeping bags in the back, maybe with some extra padding. We can lie back and watch the stars, or even get inside the bags—one bag each, of course—after the evening turns chill. If we fall asleep, we'll have only ourselves to answer to. I can bring snacks—"

"And I'll bring hot coffee and cocoa. Yeah. I'm in. Let's do it." Catching his vision, Skye got quickly on board. "It sounds great, Pete, just the kind of evening we planned in the beginning. I'm glad you said what you did about separate sleeping bags—"

"I might feel an electric buzz whenever I'm around you, but I can be a gentleman."

"I know you can. If you'd wanted to press your advantage, you've had plenty of opportunities." Skye hesitated to think of all the times Pete could have made moves on her. His hand lay on the seat between them. She laid hers over it. "Stars and a quiet evening." She sighed. "Yeah. I like the sound of that."

"We'll plan on it, then, and we'll call it a date." He put the truck in gear. "Day after tomorrow, do you need to be back early?"

"No, not particularly."

"Me, either. If we did go to sleep while stargazing—"

"No worries. We can just cruise back down the hill whenever we're ready—"

"And I won't have to worry about *Tío Rico* coming after me with a shotgun?"

She laughed. "No. You won't need to fear my uncle, especially since I don't intend to tell him we're here."

Pete smiled. He'd had almost exactly the same thought.

SKYE LAY ON A HEAVY PLATFORM, staring up at a starry night sky. Pete lay beside her, only something was different about him—off. "Ooh, look at that one," he said, pointing at a streak of light, and Skye watched the meteor fall. "Yep, a good one," Pete said and began to laugh. Only then did she realize what seemed so off about him. Pete was drunk.

"Pete, you've been drinking." She confronted him plainly, expecting a denial and prepared to throw evidence at him.

"Yep. Sure have." He giggled, apparently not the least bit bothered. He smelled like a brandy bottle with a tincture of sour sweat thrown in.

She struggled to keep her voice even. "I told you, sobriety is a requirement. Drunkenness? That's a total non-starter."

"And I told you relapses are common. Get used to it. It happens." Pete almost snarled his response. Then he leaned over her, held her down and began kissing her—slobbery, open-mouthed kisses that repulsed and terrified her.

She screamed and began wrestling, desperate to free herself.

Skye awoke soaked in sweat, panting for breath, tangled in her bedsheets. The normal appearance of her bedroom brought her around quickly. "It was a dream." She said it aloud. "Just a dream." Then she began to cry great tears of sorrow and relief.

More than an hour passed before she could relax enough to fall back into sleep. When she woke again in the morning, she'd had no other dreams—at least, none she could recall—but feelings of doubt and fear still hung about her.

She didn't need a psychologist to explain what that dream was all about, and she knew she could not judge Pete by the behavior of others or by what he did in a dream. She even recognized the dream's heavy platform when she remembered the flatbed truck that once delivered hay to the commune, feed for their dairy goats. Parts of her nightmare clearly came from a memory of what happened there on a sad day when she was seven or eight.

Bringing all that out of her subconscious mind helped her deal with the past but did little to chase the wisps of unease or the very real fear the midnight experience engendered. In fact, her negative feelings seemed to grow throughout the day. As she neared the evening hour when Pete planned to pick her up, her hands began to tremble.

Chapter Fourteen

I t took a flat fourteen seconds for Pete to realize something was wrong. Skye's smile when she met him at the door couldn't have been more plastic. She shrank away from him when he tried to touch her elbow as they walked. He made multiple attempts to start a conversation, but she answered in short, clipped monosyllables. And the harmonic vibrations coming off her rivaled those of the Sacramento Philharmonic playing a dirge or a requiem mass.

"What's going on?" he asked as they left the edge of the city and started up the highway.

"What are you talking—" She looked at his face, dropped the pretense, and sighed. Then she spoke, her voice so low, he had to listen carefully. "I didn't expect to be nervous about this."

"Why are you ner—" He also stopped mid-sentence. His face fell. "It doesn't matter why. If you don't want to do this, we'll turn around and I'll take you home." He signaled and prepared to pull off, ready to make a U-turn.

"No!"

Her strong response still had him pulling to the side. "Okay, talk. Do you want to do this or not? And can you tell me why?"

"It's silly. I…I had a nightmare." She laughed nervously. "See? Silly, like I said."

He turned off the engine. "Tell me about it."

"Well, okay, but it's embarrassing." She spoke haltingly, telling him about the last two men she'd invited to come to Destiny and how each had fallen off the sobriety wagon just in time to leave her humiliated and awkward in front of her family. Then she described how he'd appeared drunk in her dream.

"Ouch. No wonder you didn't want to date another recovering addict."

"I'm glad you underst—"

"But you should have realized I'm not going to fit into that category, that I won't do the same thing either of those guys did."

"I didn't think *they* would, either, but—"

"But you're not considering one big difference." He took both her hands and looked into her eyes. "You've already taken me to Destiny. I've met your family and I did that sober. And trust me, if I can get through that crowd scene sober, I can manage an evening of watching the stars."

She rewarded him with her first genuine smile of the evening. "You're right. I should have thought of that."

He looked at the road as a car whizzed by. "Can we still go to the pullout?"

She nodded. "Yeah, we can."

He drove back onto the roadway and resumed highway speed. "Tell me the details. I want to know all about this nightmare."

Skye laughed. "Not on your life!"

The chatter between them became easy again. Pete watched light and color come back into Skye's face. People she trusted had put her through rough experiences, things no one should have to go through. The betrayals of those two jerks must be small compared to some of what had happened, but he could see what made her wary. If he wanted to go forward with getting to know this amazing woman, he'd need to be prepared to take it slow and easy.

SKYE KNEW PETE WAS RIGHT. Her family had put him through a ringer last night—bless them all. If he could handle *that* sober, then he was not going to pull a Ryan or Doug scene on her. As for the rest, he'd seen her vulnerable several times already. He was not one to take advantage. The last threads of the nightmare vanished; Skye relaxed and enjoyed the drive.

The sky was fully dark by the time they parked at the pullout and rolled out their sleeping bags in the bed of the pickup. The moon had not yet made her appearance, so the sky was lit only by the shimmering stars and Pete's flashlight, which he used only as needed.

"I love the way it smells up here," he said as he straightened the sleeping bags. "I forget this clean, fresh, foresty scent when I'm in the city. I may have to do a glass piece that captures the feeling of coming back into the natural world."

"You do that, too? Always think of possible art pieces, I mean."

"Oh, yeah. I guess it comes with the territory, sort of an occupational hazard."

"Yeah. I guess so." Skye watched the way he kept the two bags close, but clearly separated. He was being careful, making sure she knew his intentions. After that weird dream, she needed that more than usual. She took a deep breath. What was this about, anyway? Some new brand of PTSD asserting itself after all these years? She'd been through this with the counselor in her rehab lockup. The counselor had warned her about the moments she called triggers. Sometimes Skye wondered if she'd ever clear them all.

For a while, they sat on their sleeping bags wrapped in warm coats and blankets—munching on snacks, enjoying the warm drinks Skye brought, chatting aimlessly. Then Skye saw a streak across the heavens, and they lay back to enjoy the show.

Lying there next to Pete, it seemed natural for him to take her hand —natural, comfortable, normal, as if they did this all the time. The conversation also flowed easily. There, in the privacy of the dark, it was painless to share confidences. After a while Skye asked, "I told you a little about how my addictions started. What about you?"

"I dunno. Usual story, I guess. I'm the firstborn son. My dad expected me to be his mini-me, wanting me to achieve everything he wasn't able to do with his own life."

She felt him move uneasily. "You don't have to tell me if you don't want to."

"It's okay. It's good to talk about it with someone I trust."

They paused to watch a pair of meteors streak through the sky, almost on parallel tracks. Pete continued. "I tried. Throughout my childhood, pleasing my father—winning his approval—ruled my world. My mom could see what was happening. She told me frequently how proud she was of my straight-A report card or my first place in the spelling bee or whatever, and she never failed to include Dad, to tell me he was proud of me, too."

Skye read between those lines easily. "But he never told you that."

"No. Not until I got into sports. That was the key to Dad's approval, being a top athlete." He sighed. "Turned out I was good at it. Success in sports made Dad proud, so I worked hard, and I got better."

She snuggled a little, drawing closer to his shoulder. "You were a high school athlete."

"High school and college."

"Oh? What sports?"

He gave her an impressive list. "But football was king. I suspected my dad wanted to be a pro football player and never got the chance. I mean, I know he played in school, but he never talked much about *playing*. I'm guessing he sat the bench a lot." He shifted, scooting closer. "Anyway, when I was moved up to varsity during my second year in high school, Dad crowed to everybody about his son, the football star, as if sitting the varsity bench made me 'star' anything. He and Mom came to every home game, and he traveled to every away game he could reach."

Skye squeezed his hand. "Go on."

"I got better. I made the starting line-up my junior year. Senior year, I made all-league."

"You made your dad proud."

"Yeah, finally, and it felt good. I played well enough that I got a scholarship. That got me into college where my dad expected me to follow in his footsteps—to become an engineer."

Skye wondered how this all related to addiction, but she let him take his time.

"Remember I said I did *everything* to excel?"

"Um-hm."

"That included hanging with the team. Partying. A lot."

"Meaning, getting smashed."

"Yeah. Getting wasted most weekends. By the time I left high school, I was already a serious drunk, although I still hid it fairly well and kept up my grades. But it got worse in college. Most of the guys on the team belonged to the same frat—one known for its parties. But drinking with my football buddies killed football for me. By senior year, I'd been drunk one too many times, showed up late and hung over to practice one too many times, played lousy one too many times, and they booted me off the team. I was also failing classes and hiding that from my parents too."

Skye thought of her former roommate, Lila, and all she'd hidden. "I've seen people do that. They couldn't hide it forever and the parents eventually found out." A wave of guilt smacked her as she realized she'd done it too—not to the extent Lila had, but she'd hidden plenty from Rico and Olivia.

"You're right on that one. The first time my dad came to a college game and I wasn't even dressing out, he went on alert. I made excuses about an injury, but it took him no time at all to figure out the coach had dumped me. We had a blowup that lasted for hours. In the midst of it, I screamed lots of things at him that I would never have said if I hadn't been half-blitzed at the time." He sighed. "I even said how much I hated engineering and how I wanted to major in art."

"I don't suppose that went over well."

He snorted. "He cut me off then and there. That was the last time I talked to my dad."

"The last time *ever*?"

He swallowed. "I've seen my mother since then, and my brother. But we have to meet outside the home. My dad said if I ever came to his house again, he'd get a court order to keep me away."

"I'm sorry. I can't imagine what that would be like. Even when I was in the worst throes of my addictions, my family always kept the door open."

"I know. That's the kind of thing your family does. I've seen how they rally around you." He paused. "Mom might have wanted to be that way too, but she wasn't about to cross Dad."

"I'm guessing few people are willing to cross him."

He chuckled low and dry. "For never having met my dad, you know him pretty well."

"I've known people like him, but I'm so sorry your dad is that way.

I'm surprised he hasn't come around, now that you're a successful artist."

"As far as my dad is concerned, I'm a failed engineer, a failed athlete, and a failed son. He considers art a trivial thing and nothing one could call a career."

"I'm so sorry. You're good, Pete, and you're beginning to draw the attention of the art community, including serious collectors who will support you in the future."

"Thanks to you." He lifted their joined hands, squeezing gently.

"You know I brought you into that show to save my own place after the mess-up at the forge. Besides, the only thing I did was give you the opening. Your work succeeds on its own merits." A large meteor shot across the sky and they both paused to watch it. As it faded, Skye asked, "What do you think it would take to bring your dad around?"

He snorted. "Is there such a thing as a personality transplant?"

"Not that I know of, but I'm sure that would be popular."

"The good news is, I've recognized that Dad's problems are his. I no longer feel the need for his approval."

"You wouldn't turn it down if he offered it."

"No. I'd be grateful. But I've learned to be happy with myself. If I'm doing what feels right for me, I don't need to be validated by others."

"That's a healthy place to be. I feel like I'm there much of the time. Other times, I still look for outside validation, even hunger for it."

"And you get it. Oh, look! That's a big one." They paused to watch another falling star.

Skye hesitated before asking, "What turned things around for you?"

"It was a combination of things. I changed my major to art and stayed in school. Renewed interest in my classes helped me do well enough to graduate, and I'd been taking art all along, so it didn't take too long to finish the degree. But it all went downhill after that. Dad was right about an art degree not leading to a job. I spiraled out of control, drinking more all the time, losing one minimum wage job after another, living in a trashy apartment…"

"The addiction took over."

"Yeah." He paused. "Then I caught a nasty virus that kept me flat in bed for almost a week. A couple of days in, I ran out of booze and was too sick to crawl out for more. By then, I'd burned enough bridges that I couldn't talk anybody into bringing me some."

"You must have been going through withdrawal at the same time as the flu. That had to have been…" She paused, looking for a word.

"Hellish," he said. "The worst time of my life."

"Going cold turkey like that? You could have died, Pete. Some people do die of withdrawal."

"I was lucky I didn't. But I got through it, and when I finally felt strong enough to leave the apartment, I was sober, craving a drink like mad, but sober for the first time in a long time. Taking a clear-eyed view of my life made me see what a wreck I was. I'd already had a couple of friends die drunk, and I knew it could easily happen to me. It might already have happened except for good luck or great timing. I could also see how I'd cut myself off from everyone who once cared about me."

Skye heard him sigh. She waited.

"By then, I was getting by on what I could scrape together from odd jobs…or what I could steal. I hate to even say that word out loud, but—"

"I get it, Pete. When addictions take over, it's the booze or the drugs that make the decisions, and you do whatever it takes to give them what they want."

"Yeah. I figured you'd get it."

"No judgment here. I'm still dealing with plenty of regrets myself."

"Anyway, I got dressed and left the apartment. I stood on the corner, trying to decide whether to go to the liquor store or to spend the few bucks I had on a healthy meal since I hadn't eaten in days. I must have stood there for most of an hour before I finally reasoned that I had nothing to live for, so I might as well drink myself to death. Smart, huh?"

"No, but I know what it's like when you're in that dark, dark place."

"Yeah. I guess you do." He paused. Then he gripped her fingers. "I started toward the liquor store. Then the strangest thing happened." He shifted. "A mom with a little girl, maybe four or five, came walking toward me. As they approached, the kid smiled at me, the biggest smile, so cute! And she said, 'It's a boo-tee-ful day, isn't it, Mister?' I looked around and realized she was right. Until then, I hadn't even noticed the weather. I said, 'Yeah, it is. It's beautiful.' As they passed me, the mother smiled, too. She said, 'I hope you have a wonderful day.' And it's weird, but that's when I knew I could."

"That you could have a great day?"

"That I *could*. I could stay sober and I could rebuild my life. I still had plenty of time and all the same smarts, talents, and abilities that got me into college in the first place. I could make a life for myself and maybe even make a living as an artist. Right then and there, on that street corner, I resolved that I'd had my last drink. I bought groceries, went home and made a salad. Then I started looking for AA meetings. I went to two a day that first week."

"In a way, your sobriety was forced on you too. You weren't in jail, but—"

"You're right. It took a nasty virus to give me the clear vision I needed to see my life in context and realize it's not what I wanted."

"And it took a cute little girl to help you see that your life was worth living."

"Yeah, that's it. I've learned to see both as my personal miracles, my AA miracles."

"I've had those, too." She paused. "When did you have your last drink?"

"Honestly, I don't remember, just that it was sometime before the flu came on. I can tell you about my D-day though, my decision day."

"The day you chose to be sober."

"Yeah, it was June nineteenth, four and a half years ago. I swore myself to sobriety a little past noon that day, and I celebrate that occasion every year."

"I'm impressed. Good for you for staying sober that long. You've done great."

"It didn't always feel great while I was doing it, especially in the beginning when the cravings were so bad."

"But you've never had a drink since?"

"Never. I remembered what one guy said at my first AA meeting: 'One drink is too many and a thousand is never enough.' I knew it would take just one drink to put the addiction back in control and I wanted to run my own life for a change."

She nodded. "I know what that's like."

"But you've come farther, faster."

"Not really. Like you, I had much of the degree work behind me—piecemeal, here and there—before my DUI arrest, and I had already begun to build a reputation as an artist. Being locked up put me out of that market for a while, and I wasn't sure how hard it would be to get back in. I'm grateful that collectors and gallery owners seemed pleased to see me when I returned. That's one of my personal miracles."

An easy silence settled between them while they watched the skies. Then Skye asked, "Pete? Why the name change? I mean, why are you Jamison Peters in your work?"

"My surname is Koury."

"Yeah? What about it?"

"It's Syrian. My grandfather came from Syria. Not exactly a white bread name, you know?"

Skye made a scoffing sound. "Do I look white bread to you?"

He drew his lips tightly together. "I guess we both know how that goes."

"Yeah. I guess so." Skye shivered.

"Just to clarify," he said, "I'm not ashamed of who I am or where I come from, but I wanted to reduce the risk of bias based on my name. Besides, using a different name distances me from my father. Given his attitude toward me, that seemed necessary."

"I'm sorry that has to be a factor." Skye shivered again, harder this time.

"Are you getting cold?" Pete asked.

"Yeah," she said, choosing not to mention that part of her shudder had little to do with the chill. "I think I'll crawl into the bag."

"I'm ready to warm up too."

Some awkward squirming and positioning brought them back to where they'd been, only warmer. Pete had arranged the two bags with their zippers side by side, so it didn't take long for their hands to find each other and their fingers to intertwine. It didn't surprise Skye to find that their hands were still linked when she awoke the next morning.

Chapter Fifteen

S kye returned to her studio filled with ideas for new paintings, concepts for her commissions, and plans to restart work on the broken pieces in her women's sculpture series. She found Molly there, the first time they'd both been awake in the same space since the show in St. Helena.

"Tell me," Molly said. "How did it go?"

Skye shivered with the flush of success. "All my pieces sold. Filene sent an itemized list showing each item with its buyer and price. I'll get a check later this week."

"A good check?" Molly looked as eager as if the success were her own.

"Better than I imagined. Filene ran silent auctions on a couple of the pieces and a pair of highly competitive collectors kept bidding each other up. I won't have to worry about rent money for a while."

"Great! I'm glad for you. And Pete? How did he do?"

"Quite well. He had one piece that didn't sell, but Filene agreed to keep it there so she can sell it when the right buyer comes in. She ran a silent auction on Pete's best pieces, too. I think she surprised him with how well those did."

"That's awesome." Molly drew closer, adopting a suggestive tone. "And the two of you? How are you doing? As a couple, I mean."

"You know we've never actually been a couple—"

Molly tittered. "Fool yourself if you think you can, but I've been watching, remember? He was here all the time—bringing you food, checking up on you, giving you rides to places. When he wasn't here, he was calling or texting or—"

"Okay. You're right about that, but it's not like we were *dating*. It was more like…" She paused, searching for a good way to describe their relationship.

Molly volunteered an answer. "Like you were married?"

"What?" Skye stared. "What are you *talking* about?"

"He's been acting like an attentive husband, the way he takes care of you."

"But…" Skye scrambled for an answer, a way to help Molly understand. "That was just for the show, to get us both ready for the *art* show. It wasn't like—"

Molly arched a brow. "It's been a few days since the show. Have you seen Pete?"

"Well, yeah, but—"

"Every day, I'm guessing."

"Well, not *every* day—"

"And on the days you didn't see each other, were there still phone calls and texts?"

"Yes, but that's because we were planning…" For the first time, Skye put it all together, seeing the bigger picture of the time she'd spent with Pete and how it surely looked to anyone watching from the outside— how it must have looked to her family, how she'd felt when she woke up beside him in the back of his truck, what he'd said about dating.

"Have you dated anyone else since you started hanging out with him?"

"No, but I wasn't seeing anyone before then, either."

"What have you done together since the show? Anything that has nothing to do with art?"

"Well, yes…" Reluctantly at first, Skye shared the story of the two stargazing adventures. She didn't mention how the second evening ended, but Molly read between the lines.

"You fell asleep out there, didn't you?"

"Well—"

"This just gets better and better! Did you spend the whole night?"

"Yes, but—"

Molly laughed. "So, he's spent weeks acting like an attentive husband, he's held you and carried you in his arms, he's met your family, and you've even spent the night together—"

"Not in *that* way—"

"Have you had the DTR talk?"

"The what?"

"The *define the relationship* talk. You know, the chat where you define what you are to each other and where you see it going."

"Well, we haven't exactly, but—" Or had they?

"But you think he's ready to?"

Skye gave an exasperated huff. "You keep putting words in my mouth!"

"And so far, they've been right on."

Skye sank into her one chair. "Oh my. This has all sort of…sneaked up on me." She thought about when she'd told Pete, that he got in under her radar. "I guess we did have that DTR talk. We decided we're going to date each other."

Molly's expressive face lit with a kind of triumph. "That's great! Oh that's great! I knew you too would be good together. You have your art in common, you look wonderful together, and you for sure aren't going to find anyone better looking than Pete."

Skye gave a thoughtful nod. "You're right about that."

Scooting back into her own space, Molly began cleaning her brushes. "I need to get to class, but I'm going to want more details when I see you again. Keep notes so you can tell me everything."

Skye threw up her hands. "What more is there to know?"

Molly left laughing, and Skye went back to work, but her life had taken on a whole new perspective.

BACK AT THE RACQUETBALL COURT, Pete had been listening to Tim's latest business success with half an ear while he focused on the game…and Skye. "One of the three middle managers is going to get that promotion," Tim said, "and it looks like it could be me."

"Good!" Pete answered, hoping the response would serve—and so would Tim.

"Hey, man." Tim held the ball. "Something's on your mind. Want to tell me about it? Or should I say, 'tell me about her'?"

Pete scratched at the neckline of his shirt. "You think you know me so well."

"I've known you for a while now, dude. You get a certain look when you're crushing on somebody new. Who is she?"

"*Dude*, get on with the game and serve."

"Don't want to talk about her, huh? Sounds like you're getting serious."

Tim was a bulldog when he bit into an idea, so Pete gave him something to chew on. "Okay. If you must know, there's a woman who interests me. We aren't exactly dating. Not yet anyway. We're sort of in the hanging out stage. Now will you please serve the ball?"

Tim held still. "Only if you promise you'll tell me all about it when *things* start happening." He gave his eyebrows an exaggerated wiggle.

"Nothing's happening for now, so serve or get off the court."

Tim laughed and served the ball.

SKYE DRESSED CAREFULLY in slim black slacks and a form-fitting peacock blue sweater. She loved that he was taking her out to dinner and that this time, he intended it as a date. Not a mercy meal to help her get ready for the show, or a celebration of their mutual success. He had asked her to dinner, no strings attached. Skye couldn't remember the last time she felt this excited about going out with a guy. High school, maybe? Probably not even then. Too many of Skye's dates, for far too long, had been covers for her various addictions. She'd get together with a guy to smoke with him or use, but never just to gaze at falling stars or have a nice evening out.

She'd done some dating since sobriety, since she'd begun to believe marriage and family life were possible. During the years of her addictions, she'd been too toxic to consider marriage, and motherhood was out of the question. Once sober, she'd dared to dream. Then the dream led her to Doug and Ryan and she'd again begun to doubt she could attract a decent guy. Dating Pete had rekindled the spark. If a good man like Pete wanted to date her, she might still have hope.

Her doorbell rang at seven. She answered it to find that Pete had also taken time with his appearance in neatly pressed black slacks, an open-collared black shirt, and black leather jacket. "You clean up well," she said, straightening his collar and putting some flirt into her smile.

"You look amazing," he said.

She resisted flipping her curls when she answered. "Thanks."

He drove them a few blocks to a trendy downtown restaurant she'd heard about, a place that offered a mac-and-cheese bar with eight different flavors of the comfort food favorite, including bacon-and-egg, lobster, and chicken chorizo. The chef had also created innovative ways of presenting entrees that included Asian street tacos, Korean fried He, and tuna poke nachos.

They found parking a few blocks away. As they walked to the restaurant, they moved closer together, shuffling in the autumn leaves and chatting about the weather. Skye breathed in and sighed. "Oh, I do hope that smell is coming from where we're going." Her mouth watered. "I can almost taste it!"

"Just wait 'til you do," he answered.

A few minutes later, they were seated at a cozy leather banquette, studying the menu. "This is a fun place." Skye ran through the food options. "I don't think I've ever eaten where they offer food on boards."

"Would you like to try one? The salami and cheese board looks good."

Skye looked at the price and immediately shied away. She imagined the day might come when spending almost twenty bucks on an appetizer wouldn't faze her, but she wasn't there yet, and she wouldn't let Pete spend that much to impress. She scrambled for another reason, one she could tell him. "I'm thinking of ordering one of the dinner salads, and I doubt I'll have room for it if I eat salami and cheese first. Thanks, though."

"Oh? Which salad?"

The small talk continued until they'd each placed their orders—Skye for a salad made of Thai-spiced skirt steak and noodles, Pete for a turkey, apple, and brie sandwich with garlic aioli and fig jam. "Sounds like we're in for a couple of interesting dinners," he said.

"I'll give you a taste of mine if you share a little of yours."

"Deal."

They sipped club soda while they waited for their food. At first, they seemed to be fishing for topics with a comment here or there about the meteor shower or the way her family had greeted Pete or the couple of messages she'd received from family since they'd been there, both asking when she'd bring Pete to Destiny again. They finally found a subject to stick with when Pete asked, "What got you started painting?"

Skye told Pete about her high school art class and how the teacher had encouraged her work, "but the real thing that kept me painting was the therapeutic side of it—the fact that I could get a lot of tough emotions out by putting them on canvas. I found that's what I wanted to do, to paint feelings. As I got better, I realized I could paint them in ways that other people could see them and find catharsis in my work as well."

"I feel the same way," he said simply. "Finding catharsis, I mean. I remember when you were working on your painting, *Blessed Rescue*. I didn't know where you were going with it while you were in the process, but when I saw it finished, it immediately brought back to me that morning on the street corner when I had just about decided to drink myself to death, and then a cute little girl and her mom came along and commented on the beautiful day. That was my moment of blessed rescue, and I could feel the emotions again when I studied your work: the initial sense of 'why bother?', then the turning point, and finally the hope." He paused, clearly embarrassed to be getting emotional.

"Remembering those moments and keeping them in the forefront of our minds and hearts is one of the things that can keep us in recovery."

"Yeah, I get that."

"How about you, Pete? How did you get started? I mean, glass-blowing isn't the kind of thing you find at the average high school."

"No, I didn't start that until I got into college, but I'd always been interested in art. Like with you, my art was an effort to get out ideas or emotions that I couldn't express in other ways. I'd been drawing—largely just doodling, I guess—since I was a little kid, and I got some positive attention for the work I did in my high school art classes. Even when I started college in the tightly structured engineering major with its demanding class schedule, I always took an art class to lighten my load. In my sophomore year, I discovered the Hot Shop. That was another day that changed my life. Over time, I realized that I want to do with glass what you do with paint—to help people feel. That's what drives me."

Skye thought of the struggles she sometimes had with her art—frustrations like what had happened when her molds were broken at the metal forge, but also many others when the paint wouldn't seem to go where she wanted it to, or the clay didn't take the shape she tried to impose on it. Doing what she did wasn't all raw talent. It required skill as well, and sometimes her skills failed her. "Do you ever regret it?"

Pete scrunched up his forehead and tilted his head to one side. "Regret my art?"

"Yeah. Do you have those tough moments when it isn't working, and you wonder if you've made a terrible mistake and you're in the wrong field?"

He chuckled. "I call those my I-should-have-been-a-plumber moments."

Skye laughed. "I always remember what my senior year keyboards instructor said, that I'd make a very efficient secretary."

Pete lifted his glass. "To plumbers and secretaries."

"I can toast to that." Skye clinked her glass against his and sipped her club soda. "I'm glad you didn't become a plumber, Pete. You're very talented."

"Thanks, I—"

"You sculpt in glass what I try to put into paint and metal."

He nodded. "I've always said I was trying to channel human emotions."

"You do a fine job of it."

Deep in their animated conversation, they barely noticed when the food arrived. Then the aromas wafted toward them as the delectable meals beckoned them to dig in. They leaned closer together when they shared their promised tastes, almost close enough to kiss.

Chapter Sixteen

It was still early when Pete drove Skye to her apartment. He didn't want their time together to end—not yet. He tried to think of a way to extend the evening that didn't sound like a come-on, but he kept getting stuck before he could speak. That's why he felt such relief when she said, "It's early yet. Would you like to come up?" He felt even more encouraged when she added, "Molly's out for the evening, so we'll have the place to ourselves." All his senses went on alert.

"Sure, I'd love that." From a different woman, he'd have considered that a loaded invitation. But he didn't know what to expect from Skye, not after that little talk about how he'd sneaked in under her radar.

"Have a seat," she said, indicating the couch. "I've got regular water and sparkling water. Either sound good?"

"I don't need anything now." He put his arm on the back of the couch and patted the space beside him. "Come sit with me."

She smiled but seemed to waver. Then she said, "I'm going to get a glass for myself and I'll bring one for you too, in case you change your mind. I also need a stop in the rest room. I'll be with you in a couple of minutes."

Pete reminded himself to let Skye lead the way in whatever did or did not happen between them. He sat back, eagerly waiting to see what would happen next.

ALONE IN THE BATHROOM, the door locked behind her, Skye took a deep breath and stared into the mirror. What had she been thinking, inviting him to her apartment? She'd even told him her roommate was out for the evening. She had to know how that would sound.

She calmed herself, rationalizing that she knew Pete. He wouldn't put on any pressure, would he? Or maybe she shouldn't count on that when she seemed to be following the script from a seduction scene in some cheesy movie. She took several deep breaths, steadying herself. With another long look in the mirror, she frowned at her reflection and finger combed her thick hair, pushing her spiral curls behind her ear. It was time to get control of the situation. She flushed the toilet to cover her delay and went back to face the situation she'd created.

WAITING FOR SKYE TO RETURN, Pete spotted a section from a recent newspaper focused on up-and-coming artists. He picked it up and began to read. He was impressed, but not surprised, when he realized Skye's work featured prominently. Most of the first article was about Skye and all the images were of her work. He studied the pieces the reporter had pictured.

"Ah, I see you found the vanity piece." Skye reentered the room.

He looked up. "That's a nice article about you."

"I hang on to that section to pick me up on my should-have-been-a-secretary days."

Pete shook his head. "Don't even think about it. You're amazingly talented. These folks aren't the only ones who've noticed." Again, he patted the sofa.

Skye sat, closer than Pete expected. She had other magazines and newspaper sections she'd collected, each a window into the art world. Together, they flipped through the images as they continued the discussion of her work, his, other art they both appreciated, the direction they thought art might be headed. It pleased him that she never scooted away, that when he put his arm around her, she snuggled into the crook of his shoulder.

SKYE SNUGGLED CLOSER, delighted with the direction their evening had taken. When had she ever enjoyed this kind of closeness? They were bonding over the natural high that came from sharing their art and enjoying these affectionate moments while stone-cold sober.

"You're right," she said in response to a comment he'd just made. "That's exactly what I thought when I painted that picture."

Pete pointed to another of the featured paintings. "And this one? With the bright background? I'm guessing you did this work around the time you embraced life-long sobriety. All that light is hope, optimism for a brighter future. Am I close?"

Skye swallowed hard, astonished by how he could read her. She leaned toward him. "Yes. Exactly. How did— how could you—"

He reached for her hand and she wound her fingers with his.

He sighed. "I recognize that bright moment. I've been there too."

"Yeah. I guess you have." She snuggled against him. When he leaned closer, so did she, their faces barely inches apart.

"Skye," he murmured, "I really want to kiss you."

Her lips almost touched his when she murmured, "Please do."

The kiss began gently, little more than a touch of his lips on hers. Then, as it warmed and deepened, Skye melted into it, wanting… wanting way too much. She pulled back, her hands against his chest. "Whoa. Let me catch my breath."

Pete pulled back, panting. "I thought you liked—"

"Oh yeah. I definitely liked. That's the problem."

"I don't under—"

"Please, Pete. The dinner, the whole evening, it's all been great. Lovely. But it's time for us to call it a night."

"If I've done something—"

"No, you've been good, great." Skye eased away, hoping she could explain her thoughts clearly. "I'm just not ready to hurry into any… anything more."

"Okay," he said, but the look on his face spoke more of bewilderment than understanding.

"Maybe there's something I should tell you," she said, wondering if this was the right time, then deciding to forge ahead. "Remember I told you about the older kids in the cult and how they liked to experiment on the younger ones?"

"How they tried out the drugs on you kids just to see what you'd do."

"Yeah. That."

"Sure, I remember. That must have been rough." He stroked her hand.

She pulled away. "Well… those weren't the only kinds of experiments."

"Okay, but I don't see—" And then his face changed, his expression becoming sympathetic. "Oh. Maybe I do."

Skye went on. "The adults in the group were, um, pretty free with their various…" She paused. "The first counselor Sunny and I saw, the one Enrique and Olivia sent us to when we were kids? She called it 'indiscriminate coupling.'"

Pete interpreted. "They did a lot of random hooking up."

"Yeah." Skye offered a grateful half-smile. "And they weren't cautious about hiding it from us. We saw things little kids should never see. Then the older kids…" She took a deep breath and let it out slowly. "Pete, do you understand what I'm saying?"

He nodded, leaning away from her. "Yes. Sadly, I think I do. You said you don't want to hurry anything. I get that now." He touched her shoulder—gently, a gesture Skye found both supportive and endearing. "You know I'm not trying to rush you."

She nodded, too emotional to trust words.

Pete drew his brows together in a look of concentration. "Just so I know what we're talking about, what is it you're looking… uh, waiting for?"

Skye dug deep. "I'll need to know the guy is serious, that he's in it for the long term. I'll need someone who's committed."

"By committed, you mean…?"

"Completely committed—one hundred percent."

"To…?" He gestured, waiting.

"To sobriety, of course—"

"Of course."

"And to his work, whatever his passion is." She waited, hoping he'd fill in the rest.

"And…?" Still he waited.

She breathed out a sigh. "And to me. He will be completely committed to me."

"Committed as in…"

"As in a long-term, stable relationship, probably marriage."

Pete drew away, his expression incredulous. "You don't want any… anything before *marriage*?" The way his voice rose at the end suggested total disbelief.

She heard his doubt and understood it, since she felt at least part of that herself. "I think that's the way I'm headed. I've watched my sister marry and then my cousin. Some others too, friends of ours. If a guy stands up in front of family and the community and makes a legal commitment, I'll know he's serious about me, not just about what I might do for him today or how I might make him feel in the moment. He isn't thinking of me as a starter relationship he can easily escape if things don't work right away."

"That makes sense, I guess, but—"

"Please try to see where I'm coming from. When I was little, people did things with me and to me that I was powerless to stop. I got away from the worst, but there was enough…" She paused. "I had enough bad experiences, both as a child and later when I was drunk or high, that I have to feel deeply trusting before I can let anyone get close. It's a mark of trust that I allowed you to get this close tonight, that I kissed you, that I'm telling you any of this."

"Okay," he said. He seemed calmer. "Now you need to understand where I'm coming from. All I know of marriage is misery. My parents have stayed together, but I've always known that dad stays because he doesn't want a divorce to mess up his business relationships with his big-money clients. Mom only stays because she likes the money and she has no training to make her employable. They live under the same roof, but they don't really live together. They haven't for years. You're talking about marriage, and I don't know what that is. Not the kind of marriage you're talking about. Bottom line? I don't plan to risk it. Ever. At all."

"Never?" The concept seemed foreign to Skye. "What about children?"

He shook his head. "I've never wanted kids. All I know of

parenting is my parents' impossible expectations and their constant disappointment. And considering the way they've disappointed me, well... I see no point in repeating that cycle."

"I know things haven't been good between you and your dad—"

"I'd call that a serious understatement." His sardonic smirk said much.

Skye thought of her aunt and uncle who had raised her and Sunny in a warm and loving home. Of course, not everything had gone right with them either. They were ordinary folks who made mistakes, and heaven only knew she'd made more than her share, yet her family had been there when she needed them. Had she not known Enrique and Olivia, had she only known the parenting she'd seen in the cult, she'd probably feel as Pete did. But couldn't he see there were better examples? "That isn't all there can be to marriage and family," she began.

"It's all I've ever seen." He stepped away. "Listen, Skye. I'm a mess. I've been clean for more than four years, but my life is only now getting onto an even keel so I feel like I know where I'm headed. I can barely take care of myself. I don't know if I—" He looked toward the wall, then turned back, his expression blank. "I don't think we're headed the same direction, and I...I'd better go."

"Okay," Skye said. "But I think we should still discuss this. I know I haven't been explaining myself well... Will you call me tomorrow? Then we can talk more."

He said, "I don't know," but he shook his head as he said it. "You're looking forward to marriage and I never want to marry. I don't think that leaves us much to talk about."

"So that's it?"

"Unless you want to consider rethinking your plans. I can't see changing mine, and that means we're headed too far apart." He scrubbed his hands through his hair and blew out a breath. "We've spent a lot of time together, worked well together, but we're looking for different things, planning different futures, different kinds of relationships." He moved toward the door. "I wish you well, Skye. I hope you find what you want."

Had she swallowed a large chunk of ice? Or did it just feel that way? Skye put her hand to her chest to stop the ache, like something under her breastbone had just frozen solid. She tried to keep her voice even. "Thanks, Pete. I wish you the same."

"I guess I'll see you around." He nodded a goodbye and went out the door, closing it behind him. She heard his footsteps on the outside stairs and her hopes sank with him.

She ran to the door and opened it. "Pete?"

"Yeah?" He looked up from the bottom step.

"Don't worry about changing AA meetings. I'll find a different one."

He hesitated. Then his voice rang clearly. "That won't be necessary. We're both working in art, so we'll see each other. There's no reason we can't still go to the same meetings; that is, if it won't bother you."

Bother her? Skye feared it would wound her all over again every time she saw him, but she didn't have to make things worse. "Okay then. I'll probably see you Thursday."

"Fine." He started for his truck but looked back. "Skye?"

"Yeah?"

"No regrets. I care about you, and I hope you have a great career and a good life. I'll keep watching for your work."

"Thanks. And I'll watch for yours."

"Good. That's good." He smiled and nodded to her again. Then he got in his truck and left.

Skye stepped back into her apartment and resumed her place on the couch. It smelled like him. The couch smelled of whatever gingery scent he was wearing, and of the Hot Shop, and of Pete. Until that moment, she hadn't realized how many hopes she'd begun to pin on him. Then she did something she had sworn she'd never do again, certainly not over a man. She curled into herself and had a good, long cry.

PETE SLAMMED the ball against the wall of the racquetball court again and again, working off frustration while he waited for Tim to show.

"Hey, dude. You look like you're trying to murder that thing. Pretty lady turn you down or what?"

"*Dude*, shut up and play."

"I'm guessing you don't feel like talking."

"Not much. No."

"Okay then. Let's play." Tim got into position and served.

The game went on almost wordlessly. Pete used the time—what free mental space he had around his game strategy—to ruminate on Skye, what had happened, how something that had seemed so right had gone so wrong. He wondered if she'd ever find the guy she wanted. Huh, surely not at an AA meeting.

But hadn't she told him that? She'd said that, just like him, she'd sworn not to date anyone she met at AA or NA. This wasn't the reason he'd sworn off dating recovering addicts, but it certainly added to the argument for why he'd never let it happen again. Who'd have guessed that a recovering addict wanted the whole white-picket-fence gig with the ring and ceremony, the whole works? He snapped at Tim. "You gonna serve that thing or what?"

"Don't worry, man. You're about to suffer a vicious beatdown." Tim served.

"You wish!" Pete shouted as he played, though he thought it likely he'd endure an embarrassing defeat. His head was most definitely not in the game.

Skye sat through class the following day, barely keeping her eyes open. If asked to repeat the brief lecture or the discussion that followed, she'd have drawn a complete blank. Having fallen asleep in one of Dr. Randolph's classes, she knew she couldn't afford to do that again, yet her errant, half-dreaming thoughts wandered elsewhere.

An image began to take shape in her head, a painting she tentatively titled, *Loss*. Her fingers began to move in the shapes she'd use as she covered the canvas—first in dark colors filled with the gloom she'd felt since Pete walked out of her apartment and her life. Somewhere near the middle, but slightly off center, she'd leave room for a bright spot. Or maybe the bright spot should go in first. Then the dark despondency could crowd in around the hope.

She was trying to decide on a color for that bright spot—bright white? Maybe bright yellow? Perhaps something pinkish to signal love and romance? The darker colors could be deep wine tones fading toward black. That's when Dr. Randolph said, "Do you agree, Ms. Ray?"

Skye looked up. "Me?"

"You *are* Ms. Ray." Professor Randolph made his disapproval clear.

"Please, one moment to collect my thoughts." Skye felt her face warm. Knowing she'd been caught, she struggled to remember…

The professor had been speaking on the importance of an art piece's placement within an exhibit. That had been a few minutes ago, but maybe she could still pull this off.

"Ms. Ray? You can simply admit you weren't with us if you choose—"

"No, sir. I don't think that will be necessary. I admit my mind wandered. I just got an idea for a new painting and I'm rather excited about it, but—" She looked at the faces around her, some smirking, others seemingly interested in the art she mentioned, and a few rooting her on. "You were speaking of the way a particular piece is displayed within an exhibit. I remember a display of French impressionist paintings I saw several years ago. Many artists were represented, but the anchor piece was one of the large paintings from Monet's *Water Lilies*, there on temporary loan.

"The exhibit was set up as a labyrinth with the aisles doubling back on one another and leading the viewer through. Within each aisle was a break between the walls so *Water Lilies* was clearly visible. Every few feet, as the viewer got closer to the big attraction, she or he got a glimpse of it from a different distance and angle, all with changing emphasis in the lighting."

She stopped, hoping she hadn't just made a huge mistake.

Dr. Randolph nodded. His attitude had changed, and his interest piqued. "Yes, that was the point. Exactly. So…tell us your reaction to seeing *Water Lilies* from different angles and in different light."

"It was amazing!" Now aware that she had guessed correctly, Skye felt free to ramble on, extolling the virtues of all the other French impressionists she saw that day, and then adding, "It was as if someone had been moving along in high gear and suddenly discovered a higher one. Everything paled in comparison to Monet's masterpiece. That painting was *perfect*, absolute perfection! From every angle, in every light, no matter how far away the glimpse of it or how up close and personal." She shook her head. "I'll never forget it. That exhibit showed me some excellent art with truly rare, exceptional talent at its center. I felt privileged to be there in that gallery, in front of that painting, like I was standing on sacred ground."

By the time she finished, people were giving her admiring looks. Though she suspected some were admiring only how she'd gotten away with woolgathering in class, she knew others were picturing the exhibit and wishing they'd seen Monet's *Water Lilies* too. The most important expression was her professor's. "Thank you, Ms. Ray. That's an excellent example."

She nodded and reminded herself to keep her head in the game. She'd been lucky this time, but she couldn't expect that to happen again. As she turned her attention to Dr. Randolph and exhibit placement, she allowed one final thought. If that new painting was all she got out of the breakup with Pete, would it be worth it? Knowing the answer already didn't help. She sighed and gave her attention to the class.

THE STUDENT COMING on to Pete today seemed more insistent than most. During the last hour in the Hot Shop, she'd complimented his work, his attitude, the "artistry of his hands," and the way his polo shirt stretched tight across his back. She'd found every opportunity possible to touch him, first brushing her hand against his when she handed him a tool, and eventually standing close enough that when she turned, her breast rubbed against his arm. As the crowd in the shop thinned, she made her offer more obvious.

The moment came when she looked around the shop, saw they were alone, and asked him to follow her into a dark corner, behind some equipment. "Please? There's something I want to show you." Pete saw that she'd pushed a bench into that dark, protected spot. Just as he was wondering how she'd make her pitch, she sat astride the bench, unbuttoned her blouse, and said, "I've always wondered what it would be like to do it in the Hot Shop."

Pete stood there, stuck for the right response. He could hear Tim's voice echoing in his head: *As long as they're consenting adults, why not relax and enjoy?* But as he watched the girl—Leanne, was it? Launa, maybe—and saw her positioning herself on the bench, he found that "relax and enjoy" did not rank among his initial responses. He found himself vaguely disgusted and wondering why she didn't have more self-respect. Knowing he needed to say or do something, he asked, "You want to go…right here? Where anyone could walk in on us?"

"Yeah. Sure. 'Hot Shop' sounds hot, right? And the idea that someone could walk in and see us just makes it more interesting." She'd removed her shirt; she reached for the hooks of her bra.

"Stop. Put your shirt back on."

"What?"

Pete scrambled for something to say. "You must realize I can't take you up on…what you're offering here."

She frowned. "What are you talking about?"

"Technically, I'm your teacher. If there is any chance we'd be caught—"

The girl sighed deeply, rolling her eyes. "Oh, I get it. You're gay. I should have realized."

Pete opened his mouth to deny it but realized that wouldn't help. "Let's just say this is a bad idea for lots of reasons."

Babbling more curses than he'd heard since he played team sports, the girl put her shirt back on and flounced from the room. Her parting line was a promise never to get near him again.

He bit his lip and stopped short of yelling, "Thank you! I'll count on that!" She slammed the door behind her, and he heard every step as she stomped away. To his surprise, he began to chuckle. Then the chuckles turned into full-blown laughter. His bigger surprise came in realizing the girl's offer hadn't tempted him. Not at all. In fact, he felt relieved that she'd gone, and he was embarrassed by her total lack of dignity.

Pete knew he wasn't ready to think about marriage, or even long-term commitment. Not yet. Maybe never. And that meant there'd be nothing more between him and Skye, but he also knew that casual hookups weren't for him. He plopped down on his workbench, uncertain whether to be angry or grateful.

Chapter Seventeen

Winter

December arrived almost before Skye noticed and with it came her Uncle Enrique's birthday. Skye went alone to celebrate two days with the family enjoying turkey tamales and traditional Mexican dishes, along with a huge birthday cake. When people asked what had happened to Pete—and almost everyone did—she said he was a friend and coworker, but they weren't dating.

In the kitchen on Sunday afternoon, alone with Aunt Olivia, she said something about her newest painting only to have her aunt come back with a mention of Pete. "I always thought that one was way too handsome for his own good."

"I remember you said he was as handsome and charming as the devil himself. I found that rather odd, since images of the devil are usually about as ugly as they can get."

"Hmmm." Olivia considered that. "I know that's how Satan is always pictured, but scripture tells us how he leads us away through flattery. If there really is a devil, and if he's really that ugly, can you imagine anyone following him, or being flattered by his attention?"

Skye raised her eyebrows. "You have a point. No, I don't think anyone would be flattered by an ugly red creature with horns on his head and a forked tail."

"A true devil would have to be breathtakingly handsome and so slickly charming he could lead people along without them realizing it." Olivia finished with a nod.

"And that's how Pete struck you?"

"Oh yeah! If I were just a bit younger—and of course, assuming I didn't have your *Tio* Rico—that man could lead me almost anywhere."

Skye laughed. "It's funny to hear you say that."

"It's true. Your Pete is about as pretty as a man can get and still look like a man—and that one is *very much* a man."

"Yes." Skye nodded. "He certainly is."

"So tell me, what really happened? Because you say you were never dating, but I saw the way you looked at each other. You weren't just coworkers, were you?"

Skye sighed. Because this was Aunt Olivia, and because Skye knew what they said in the kitchen wouldn't go further, Skye gave her a quick outline of how things had developed, completely eliminating any reference to falling asleep in the back of his truck and sleeping side by side through the night.

"And that's why he broke up with you? The old male excuse that you 'wouldn't put out'?" Olivia spit the words like poison.

"No, no. It wasn't like that," Skye said. "We just have different goals in a relationship. I'm dating to find a companion, aiming toward marriage and children, the whole happy family sitcom scenario. Pete isn't looking for that."

"Then what is he looking for? A quick hook-up?" Olivia looked ready to spit nails. "Because if that's what he's about, then I've half a mind to go tell that man what I think of him, leading you along. I knew he looked like the devil himself."

Skye chuckled. "Slow down, auntie. I don't think Pete fits into the devilish category you're imagining. I think he wants something lasting, just not necessarily… legal, and he doesn't want children. At all."

"And *you*, my dear, are cutting him way too much slack. If he cared for you, he'd realize that being with you and around you is the reward for his efforts. He wouldn't feel wounded that he can't have more than that until he's ready to invest in a more serious relationship."

"Aunt Olivia—"

Olivia held up one hand. "No, don't defend him any further. You deserve a better man than that, someone who isn't that…that superficial."

Skye laughed. "He isn't superficial, and you are entirely missing the point, but it's clear I'll never need a guard dog with you around. It's a good thing Pete isn't here. I suspect you'd bite him on the ankle and hold on until he shouted for Uncle Enrique to come and pull you off."

Olivia narrowed her eyes. "Maybe I would. Yes, I definitely would." She pursed her lips and added, "It's a good thing you didn't bring him. I don't need another dental bill."

Skye laughed freely, feeling easier about the breakup with Pete than she had since it happened. An hour later she said her goodbyes, citing the need to return to complete her final projects before the term ended. As she approached her apartment, she realized it was the first time in days that she hadn't looked for Pete's truck. She hummed to herself as she skipped up the stairs, pretending happiness more than feeling it, but knowing it would be real, given time.

PETE WALKED along the American River at the parkway in Sacramento. For the past couple of Thursdays, he'd found reasonable excuses to avoid the AA meeting where he expected to find Skye. That told him quite a bit. If Skye meant nothing to him, he wouldn't mind running into her. He looked at his watch. AA would be starting in less than an hour. He'd told her she didn't have to find another meeting. Maybe it was time for him to prove it.

Grudgingly, he acknowledged that he needed to get himself to that meeting and he needed to play it off gently if and when he saw Skye again. As he walked, he noticed the bright yellow in the valley oak trees along the river. It was the same color as the yellow in Skye's painting about sobriety and hope. Hearing his own thoughts stopped him short. He couldn't get Skye out of his head. How had she gotten under his skin so quickly?

But he couldn't get serious either. He wasn't ready for that and might never be. He was still putting his own life together. He couldn't consider marriage or any kind of stable, long-term relationship other than the one he was developing with glass. Anything else would get in the way of the art he'd worked so hard to develop, the life he planned. He thought fleetingly of the coed who'd offered herself so freely in the Hot Shop. The image almost made his skin crawl.

He tried to imagine what that would have been like, tried to picture himself with her. All he could manage to feel was the same disgust he'd felt at the time, the urge to tell her to have more self-respect. An image of Skye came to mind. There was a woman who had learned to respect herself, and he had to respect her for it. His disgust turned on him because he couldn't be what Skye wanted. As he passed a bright yellow cottonwood, he kicked his foot against a rock in the path and winced when it left his toe bruised and aching.

Limping back to his truck, he drove toward the old church to meet with fellow alcoholics.

THE USUAL SUSPECTS were gathering at the church when Skye arrived. Less apprehensive than she'd been in weeks, she entered the room, exchanging pleasantries with others she'd come to know. Despite his claims to the contrary, Pete hadn't attended since their split, so she felt no worries about running into him now. Then, just as the meeting came to order and people took their seats, he arrived, looking every bit as handsome and charming as the devil himself.

Skye gasped when she saw him. Bernie, the older man sitting beside her, asked, "You okay? Did something happen?" He looked toward the door, saw Pete, and hovered protectively.

"No, Bernie. I…I, uh, just remembered something. Don't worry. I'm fine." She quickly looked away from Pete, desperately hoping he sat nowhere near her.

As if he'd heard her, he took a seat across the circle. Unfortunately, that put him right in her line of sight every time she looked up. To avoid staring, she made a point of focusing anywhere else each time she peeked up from her AA manual. Then, realizing that always looking away was also a clue, she determined to glance at him, give him a vague smile, and turn away again.

She followed through, lifting her head, the vague smile already glued in place. But then she saw him. He looked at her with such bald emotion, such intense yearning, that she gasped again, ducked her head, and fought tears. She reminded herself that they hadn't really dated, hadn't come to mean that much to each other. She was most definitely *not* in love with him.

Bernie, sitting beside her, caught her hand and asked again, "You okay?" He punctuated the question with an icy stare across the circle in Pete's direction.

"Yeah." Skye nodded. "Yeah, Bernie. I'm fine."

But Bernie wasn't the only one who noticed. As the meeting went on, following the usual order and the usual rules, people all around the circle were looking from Skye to Pete and back again, expressions seeming to signal their attitudes. Skye imagined various folks wearing "Team Pete" or "Team Skye" t-shirts. This couldn't go on. One or the other of them had to leave the group. She determined she'd speak to Pete right after the meeting. Then, just as they were moving into the sharing portion of the meeting, Pete took an exaggerated look at his cell phone and said, "Excuse me. Business calls." He practically ran from the room.

Skye blinked back unexpected tears as she answered Bernie's worried look with a brave smile. Before the meeting could conclude, she too used the excuse of pending deadlines to leave early so she wouldn't find herself answering difficult questions or fending off pitying looks.

Once she was well away from the meeting, she sent a text:

We need to talk. When can we meet?

The response came back quickly:

No need to talk. I'll find a different meeting.

Skye's emotions tanked as she read Pete's text. Until that instant, she hadn't realized how much she looked forward to seeing him again. That's when the craving set in. A drink? A quick hit? Something, almost anything to take the edge off, and chocolate wouldn't do. She'd left the meeting early, so she had a little time. The closest liquor store wasn't three blocks away, and she knew of a dealer who frequently hung out near there. It would be easy, so easy.

Skye knew better. Opening that door, even a little, would be like opening the floodgates. She'd learned the lessons well. Once the chemical pathways in the brain have been rewritten so the drug takes precedence, it will take over any time it can. Skye knew that; she recited all

141

those facts over and over again as she returned to her lonely apartment.

Noticing the light on in the living room, she took a deep breath. Molly was home and Skye was grateful. Left alone with cravings this large, she might be tempted to cave. Skye pointedly stopped herself. *Don't allow that thought!* She popped into the apartment with a smile on her face to greet Molly, glad she wouldn't have to face her demons alone, or meet again with the man as handsome and charming as the devil himself. Not tonight, anyway.

PETE PRACTICALLY KICKED himself as he found his way back to the Hot Shop. The forge had shut down for the evening, and he knew it was too late to work, but he needed someplace private to think and he had the keys to let himself in.

From the moment he entered, he knew it was a mistake. He couldn't work with the forge closed down. No, he should probably be at the gym trying to murder another racquetball. He smiled, thinking of the way Tim had described his recent efforts to work out his frustrations. He found a drawing pad and charcoal, thinking he might turn his emotion into a design he could sculpt in glass later, but he found himself unable to focus enough to create.

He couldn't let this go on. His art had been in freeze-frame since his last talk with Skye. Though he hadn't shared any of his current dilemma with Tim, the guy could read him only too well. His advice during their last game hung in the back of Pete's mind: "Dude, if the girl you want won't scratch that itch for you, find one who will." He shuddered and thought, *Tim, you're a scuzzbag.* He glanced toward the work bench in the corner, the place where his student had made it all seem so cheap. Instantly he wished he hadn't had that thought. He felt dirty, like he'd touched something unclean and needed to scrub.

He started cleaning up in preparation to leave. Then he heard the door open.

"What's going on in— Oh, it's you, Pete." Sam came through the door. "I was getting ready to leave for the night and I saw the light on. Everything okay?"

"Sure, Sam. I thought maybe I could get some work done, but it isn't happening." He grabbed his jacket. "I'll lock up." He moved toward the door.

Sam moved toward him, concern written on his features. "You okay, son?"

Pete hesitated, but if there was anyone he could talk to, Sam was. Before he knew it, he'd dumped out the whole story including a summary of his own sketchy upbringing, his reasons for not wanting marriage or children, and how the woman he'd been seeing wanted nothing less. "I can't give her what she needs, Sam. I'm not that guy. But I can't stop thinking about her either."

"Hmm." Sam rocked back and forth, sucking his lip and nodding. "Seems to me you're cutting yourself short. You don't strike me as the casual hook-up kind of guy."

"Well, no, but I'm no priest and I'm no saint. I've matured since my fraternity days, and I want a relationship, but I've always imagined living with a woman I care for, someone committed to her own career. A two-career household where we both have other interests, both know the score. No need for legalities. No talk of kids."

"Um-hm." Sam paused. "Is that what you still want? 'Cause I've watched you invest a lot of yourself in this woman, and I think you like her more than you're admitting."

"Well, yeah. I like Skye. I like her a lot. But I'm not ready to change my whole worldview, my whole life plan."

Sam seemed to take that in. Then he stood, yawned, and stretched. "Pete, it's late. Let's shut this place down and get some rest. We can pick this up again later if you like."

"Sounds good. You go ahead. I'll get the door."

"See ya." Sam nodded his goodnight and Pete returned the nod. He followed Sam out, locked the Hot Shop and drove home—no longer quite so agitated but still short of answers.

THE CLOCK TICKED down December and the school term drew toward an end. Skye completed the last of her exams and turned in her final projects. Looking forward to a couple of weeks of down time with family and friends in beautiful Destiny, and hoping they'd have a white Christmas in the foothills, she packed a small bag. Molly had plans to be away for the holidays as well, so Skye was in the process of locking windows and getting ready to be away for a while when she saw she had a voice message from Dr. Weems.

She looked to see if there had been other messages. No. The only one was the message: "If possible, I need to meet with you before you leave town for the holiday. Can you come to my office at eleven this morning? Send me a text to say yes or no. I'll wait to hear."

Skye checked her watch: 10:36. She had time for a meeting if it didn't take long. She sent the text:

See you at 11.

Then she got her bike out of the storage locker where she'd already stowed it for the holiday, locked her front door, and made her way to the other side of campus to meet with Dr. Weems.

She expected to find her professor there, and maybe even Dr. Randolph or one of her other professors, especially if there was a problem involving her work. What she had not expected, and what she saw the moment Dr. Weems opened her office door, was Pete—a.k.a. Jamison Peters—looking very much like the charming devil himself.

Chapter Eighteen

"What are you doing here?" Skye heard the accusation in her tone and looked toward her professor, preparing to apologize.

Dr. Weems spoke first. "I invited him here, just as I invited you." She looked from one to the other, her eyes narrowing. "Are we going to have a problem?"

"No. Not at all." Skye worked to get her voice and expression under control. "I'm just…surprised, that's all."

"Let's get moving then. Have a seat, please. I don't want to keep either of you long."

Skye sat. Professor Weems began by commenting on both Skye and Pete's participation in the shows at the Soho Gallery and in St. Helena, complimenting the pieces from Pete's impending master's exhibit, and asking about Skye's current projects. When both answered that all was on track, she congratulated them. Then she began to sketch out an offer she'd received from "a very wealthy, influential, and highly eccentric art collector." She explained that a man named Arthur Vincent, a financier in the Bay Area, had attended the show in St. Helena. He had purchased both Skye's painting, *Can't See the Forest*, and Pete's sculpture, *SightScape*.

"He thought the two of you had produced excellent depictions of the same theme, just in different media. He has made an interesting offer to have you do that again."

Skye watched the professor and tried to focus on what she had to say instead of watching Pete, who kept glancing at her just as she glanced at him. She listened carefully, but what she heard still made little sense. As Dr. Weems concluded her explanation, Skye wondered if she'd understood the words at all. "Any questions?" Dr. Weems asked.

Unable to come up with anything short of asking her to start over—a request she didn't expect would go over well—Skye looked to Pete, who appeared as discomfited as she.

"He wants us to do paired art?" Pete sounded equally disbelieving.

"Yes, essentially." Dr. Weems nodded approvingly, beaming at Pete to let him know he understood. "He has listed eight of what he calls 'themes,' mostly emotions like love and hate, but also ideas like seeking deep perception. He would like the two of you to work together on each of those themes with Skye producing a painting and Pete creating a glass piece. The two would communicate the same ideas in different media but would work together. He is offering a very large sum of money—even more if the two of you attend a party he's giving in early April to discuss your themed and paired art pieces."

Hearing it all for the second time, Skye felt she was beginning to understand, though she still had a hard time accepting it. She decided to restate it in her own words. "He wants us to work together, with each of us creating a piece related to each of the eight themes he's provided. Then he wants those pieces to be finished and ready to show at some big party in the Bay Area where we make a personal appearance. And he wants that all done in…how long?"

Dr. Weems picked up a calendar. "The date when you'd have to be ready to ship is about eleven to twelve weeks away, if you start the day after New Year's."

Skye looked at her professor, then at Pete. "I don't know about Peter, but I'm still very much involved in finishing the commissions from the St. Helena show, especially the sculpture series on women that I promised Filene. We got the brass poured last week. Now it's just a matter of putting the pieces together, finishing and staining—"

"I'll put in a good word with Filene, if that's what it takes. I've told you what Mr. Vincent is asking. Let me show you what he's offering." She held up her notes, with the central figure, a dollar amount in multiple thousands, written large in black permanent marker.

Skye gasped when she saw it, jumping to her feet. "That much? For the two of us to—"

"That much for *each* of you."

Skye gulped and dropped into her seat. "Oh my." She looked at Pete, who appeared just as stunned as she was.

"I've never worked with this man, this Arthur Vincent before," Weems went on, "but I spoke with Filene about him. She says he buys a great deal of art and is 'very particular.' Coming from Filene, that means something!"

"Definitely," Skye murmured.

Dr. Weems went on. "She also says he has money to burn and if you please him with this weird nineteen-sixties-style art 'happening', he could keep you in rich commissions for years." She paused and looked from Pete to Skye and back. "This isn't something you should have to decide immediately, but you have little time: Mr. Vincent wants a yes or no by tomorrow and will have written contracts here when the department office opens in January if you accept."

Dr. Weems stood and picked up her keys. "I'm going to the mailroom. I'll check my box, maybe have a chat with my husband while I'm there. You two talk. If you want to do this, I'll do my best to run interference for you. If you don't want it, I'll understand, but I warn you." She paused, emphasizing each word, "I've never seen an offer like this to any student or art faculty member during my entire tenure. I don't expect to see another like it. If you can possibly make it work, I encourage you to go for it."

She picked up her purse. "That said, I'm out of here. See you in a while."

She nodded to each of them as she left them alone in her office.

PETE HEARD all the words but found it hard to wrap his head around what Vickie Weems was saying. The number on her notepad blinded him to almost anything else, even the bleak, almost frightened expression on the beautiful young woman who sat across from him, looking as stunned as he felt. He'd just realized this was the "big break" every artist talked about, but few ever saw. He'd wondered how he'd move forward after completing his Master of Fine Arts in the spring. With that kind of cash, he could buy his own forge, build his own hot shop, and become a serious, working glass artist. With that entrée to big buyers, he'd have a built-in market for his work.

He looked at Skye. "What are you thinking?"

"I'm thinking it sounds impossible. Then I look at that amount of money and realize I could buy a metals forge. I could set up my own studio for both bronze sculpting and paint. I could be a real, working artist, just as I've always dreamed."

"Just as every art student dreams." Hearing his own thoughts spoken aloud brought Pete up short. "I've been thinking that, given the awkwardness between us, we probably couldn't work together." He gave her a half-hopeful look, as if seeking reassurance. When she said nothing, he went on. "But we agreed that we're good together when we're working on our art, and with that kind of money on the table, we ought to at least give it a try. It could be our big break."

He watched her turn to stare at the window. She started to speak, stopped, and licked her lips. She had never looked more beautiful, or more desirable, and Pete felt himself stir uneasily. Then she looked straight at him. "Pete, we've had personal differences, but we've always understood one another as artists. This weird offer means too much for us to let it go without trying. What do you think? Can we work together? Let other things go and focus on our work?"

Pete realized he'd begun nodding even before he knew what he'd say. "Yeah, let's do it. It's like you said. When we work as artists, we always click well."

"Yes," she said. "We do."

For a moment, Pete entertained the thought that anyone passing in the hall might see a pair of bobble head dolls nodding in rhythm. The ridiculousness of that image paled next to the numbers of zeroes in the rich guy's offer. Pete picked up the notes on Vickie Weems's desk. "Can we look at his themes? Maybe we can both ponder them over the holidays. We can—"

He stopped in mid-sentence when Skye took the seat beside him and leaned in, looking at the notes in his hands, all business. "Let's see. The first theme is love, but not romantic love. What does that note say?" She pointed.

"Vickie's writing isn't clear. I think it says, 'platonic or familial' love."

"Hmmm. In some ways, that will be easier to work with than romantic love." She closed her eyes, and Pete wondered if she was seeing a canvas in her mind. "With romantic love, everything that pops into mind is a cliché—hearts and flowers, Rodin's *The Kiss*, all of it done and done. With platonic or family love, we can come up with something different, even though that theme has been used before too. I think it'll be better to work with. What's the second one?"

They went on like that, discussing each of the eight themes. Some, like "antagonism," were challenging because they seemed obvious, and others proved more esoteric. Skye looked positively regal when she said, "American class consciousness. I think we can ace that."

When Dr. Weems returned some twenty minutes later, Pete had seen Skye transform from a scared student into a confident, talented artist, brimming with eager energy, ready to take on the contract the eccentric Mr. Vincent offered, no questions asked. *She's spectacular*, he thought as he watched her. He might not be the guy for her, and he knew he couldn't be what she wanted, but someday, some guy would hit the jackpot when he married Skye Ray.

Pete also discovered that Skye's enthusiasm was contagious. When Vickie asked if they wanted to go for the contract, he spoke as confidently as Skye did, assuring the professor that they were ready to give Mr. Arthur Vincent the pieces he hoped for, presented with all the frills and flourishes. He spoke with greater confidence than he felt when he said, "We've begun talking about the themes. We'll have no trouble doing paired works."

Dr. Weems looked from one to the other, nodding approval. "All right. I'll call Vincent's office and tell them to have the contracts drawn up. When these offices open again at the first of the year, both of you can scoot in here and sign on the dotted line. That will be a couple of weeks before classes start again, but don't wait for classes. We'll want to get everything official as soon as possible. After that, I'll be available if you need me as a sounding board. Otherwise, it looks like you're on your way. And incidentally, if either of you had concerns about what to do for your final projects this spring, I believe we've just answered that question."

Skye raised an eyebrow. "We can get paid and get class credit, too?"

"Why not? In an ideal world, we'd be preparing all our students to make it as professional, well-paid artists. Reality doesn't allow for that very often. Let's enjoy it when it happens."

Pete grinned. "I like the way you think."

Dr. Weems stood. "Okay, you two. Get out of my office so I can go on vacation. And you do the same. You need a break before you dive into this all-consuming project."

"Yes, ma'am." The spirited gleam in Skye's gaze mocked her meek reply.

"Will do," Pete replied. He'd been planning to stay away from Skye, but now he'd have good reason to spend time with her without the pressures of their differences. The idea pleased him, making him cheerier than he'd felt in some time, probably since that night in her apartment.

Pete's truck and Skye's bike were parked in the same lot. The two left the faculty offices, walking side by side. Any lingering awkwardness already seemed to be dissipating as they discussed the eight themes and possible ways of portraying them.

They were deep into a discussion as to how they might portray "American materialism" when Skye laughed and mentioned her planned visit to Destiny for Christmas, the most material American holiday of them all. "It's too bad we can't spend some of that time working. We could do a lot of planning over the next ten days, especially surrounded by all that inspiration." Then she gave him a totally guileless look and asked, "Where will you be for the holidays?"

He hesitated. "Here, I guess."

She blanched. "Oh. I forgot. I'm sorry, Pete. I didn't mean to rub it in."

"It's okay," he said, although it didn't *feel* okay. "I didn't think you were trying to rub it in that you still have family who want you and I don't." He smiled, trying to play it off as a joke, but her stricken look told him how flat that attempt had fallen.

"You wait here. I need to make a phone call, but I'll be right back."

"No. Skye, don't do that. Really!" He kept talking as she strode away from him and around the corner of the building. She was going to call her people in Destiny to wangle an invitation for him, and he couldn't allow her to do that. Given the awkwardness between them, he knew he couldn't face her relatives, especially when they were always so kind.

He glanced at his truck, less than twenty-five yards away. He could just lope over there and take off before she got back. One way or another, he couldn't go with her to Destiny. He was still musing, pondering how to deal with a polite refusal, when Skye popped back around the building. "Come up to Destiny with me. There'll be plenty of food for the holidays, and Aunt Olivia says Greg and Paris are planning to spend the week with his family here in the valley, so you can stay at their house."

"Your friends are going to leave their home open? To me? They don't even know me!"

"Well, they do, sort of. I mean they met you when we—"

"That was *one evening*. We weren't together for more than four hours. At most!"

Skye shrugged. "It's Destiny. People see no reason not to trust you, so they do."

"I can't... Skye, I can't possibly—"

She caught his arm in a pleading gesture. "Just say you will, Pete. It's easier than arguing." Her smile penetrated his resolve. He'd made up his mind not to be the stray Skye dragged to her family holiday, but he didn't want to spend another Christmas alone either. And they really could use the time to work.

"You know, we can still work together with me here and you there. Email, text, phone calls, photos back and forth. I can sketch out an idea, shoot a pic, send it to you—"

"Pete, why are you arguing? Just come with me. We can share this time together as coworkers and...and friends." He saw how she hesitated with that word. But they had been friends, hadn't they? Before he tried to change things?

He made up his mind. "Throw your bike in the back. I'll drive you to your place. Give me an hour to pack a bag, and I'll pick you up then. We can talk about art themes on the way."

"And for the next ten or eleven days," she said, giving him that triumphant smile that said she knew she'd persuade him. "It's a win-win."

As Pete watched her walk her bike toward his truck, he turned his thoughts inward, hoping he could enjoy his Christmas in Destiny and not feel too much like the interloper he was.

Chapter Nineteen

hey started their road trip discussing the themes they were intending to portray and quickly realized they didn't always share the same ideas of how those themes should be shown. The differences first surfaced in their discussion of calumny.

"The key is in the emotion, so how would I have to feel to behave that way?" Skye asked. "I mean, to go after someone with deliberately false and degrading statements meant to destroy their reputation. That's pretty vicious."

Pete shrugged. "Happens all the time, especially in politics. In academic and art circles, it's typically more subtle, more planting comments intended to undermine. It can get nasty, though."

Skye nodded. "I guess it can. I try to stay away from politics, any kind, including at the university and in art. But staying away can be tough, especially when people try to pull you in."

"Which also happens too often." Pete slowed as he approached the winding road that would take them up the mountain. "I keep wondering how I can show that in glass."

"More of your flames of a guilty conscience?"

He shrugged. "I've kinda done that, y'know?"

"I know. I try not to repeat myself, either. I've been thinking I might start my painting with a white wing, like a goose wing, near the middle. Then show disembodied goose heads, with their beaks all pulling feathers from the white wing. As the feathers leave the wing, they begin to turn black and fly away in the breeze. I might want to call it *Feathers on the Wind*."

"That could work. It's sort of like the old idea of gossip, how rumors spread like feathers and can't be regathered."

She sighed. "You're right. It's trite. I'll need to think of something better."

"No, it might still work depending on how you do it. I can't imagine anything in glass to pair with that, though."

"Why not try—"

"Huh-uh. You don't want me creating your ideas, do you?"

"Ooh. I hadn't thought of it that way."

Before long, a simple idea occurred to them both. Whatever symbols one of them chose to represent a theme, the other would try to use the same or similar, and where that didn't work, they could choose to work with similar colors. That way the two pieces could appear paired even if they took different approaches to their topics. "It's an obvious answer," Pete said. "Why didn't we think of it sooner?"

Skye took the question seriously. "Maybe because we're still kind of tiptoeing around each other, more worried about what the other may think than about getting the job done."

Pete had to agree. "I think you're right. We're pros, though, aren't we? We can do this."

Skye smiled. "Yep. We can do this." She held up her hand.

He gave her a high five. Then he became more thoughtful. "Skye? About the reputation thing? Am I going to have problems with your relatives because...well, because we're not dating but I'm coming to celebrate the holidays with your family?"

Skye chose not to mention her chat with Aunt Olivia. "I wondered about that. When I went home for Rico's birthday, everyone who met you at the star party wondered where you were and why you hadn't come with me. I just said we were friends and we worked together on art projects, but we weren't dating. That calmed things down."

"I guess it would, but what will they think—"

"Maybe I should warn you that when I called to ask bringing you for Christmas, I made you sound like the poor, lost orphan child, the male equivalent of the little match girl." She tried to play it off lightly.

"Oh? How'd that go?"

"I just said we were working on a big art project, something really exciting that I'll tell them all about when we get there. Then I said that I wanted to bring you along, partly because we could be working on ideas in our down time, and partly because I didn't want you to be alone on Christmas."

"Whew." Pete looked uneasy. "So I'm the sad little stray, huh?"

"My Aunt Olivia has been taking in strays most of her life. Sunny and I are the obvious examples. You don't think of things like that when you're a kid, but later I realized what a great responsibility she assumed when she picked us up at the Children of Rah compound that day and took us back to her house. From that point on, she and Tio Rico were raising four kids instead of just their two. It had to be expensive in time and energy as well as money, but they did it. They saw the situation we were facing and stepped in to save us."

"And now your Aunt Olivia is taking in another stray, this one for Christmas?"

Skye smiled shyly. "Yeah. Something like that, but you won't be the first. Rico and Olivia have often had Christmas guests they've never met before. Hope you don't mind the way I presented you."

Pete shrugged. "It doesn't matter, does it? I mean, it's true. We *are* working on a project, we *can* make good use of our down time this holiday, and I really *did* have nowhere else to go." He raised a brow. "No calumny there."

"Sorry, sport. That old 'use it three times and it's yours'? You really need to use it better than that if it's going to count."

"Hey! I thought that was pretty good!"

The banter continued as they made their way up the hill. For Skye, it was confirmation that they could, indeed, work together again, putting the awkwardness of the past behind them. When they pulled in at the Reyes home, any leftover stiffness had disappeared and they were back to the way they'd related before that one disastrous kiss and its aftermath. This may not be the relationship she'd hoped for, but it was so much better than trying to avoid him.

"Here, let me get that suitcase for you." Pete helped Skye with the things she wanted to carry in at her family home.

"And the box?"

"The box, too. I'll come back for it." Pete smiled at the beautiful woman beside him. Yes, he could respect her as an artist, and if that was the only option for being around her, he was certainly less miserable now than he'd been when they were avoiding each other. He couldn't help yearning to be closer to her, but that couldn't happen. Not if she needed a commitment and he couldn't make one. Unfortunately, that thought dumped him right back into the gray-brown world of glum. He followed behind Skye as she walked up to the front door, opened it, and tapped three times before calling, "Hello! Anyone home?"

She was answered by a cacophony of children's voices yelling, "Skye's here!" mixed with a dog's eager barking. Moments later, two red-haired dynamos and a half-grown beagle careened around the corner. The children threw themselves at Skye; the dog, unable to stop, slid out the door and against Pete's legs. Pete reached down to take the dog's collar. "I don't know who you are or where you belong, pooch, but I'm pretty sure you're not allowed out near the street."

The pup looked up at him with a floppy-eared smile. Pete couldn't help grinning back. A flurry of greetings kept Skye involved for a minute or two. When things quieted, she turned to Pete. "These little disasters are Will and Kate," she said, holding them with clear affection. "And that little guy you're protecting from himself is called Scooter. He's about a year old now but still thinks he's a puppy. Kids, this is my friend, Pete."

"Hi, Pete," the two chorused in unison.

"Hi." He stood there, the suitcase in one hand and the beagle tugging at the other.

"Well, come on, everybody. Let's get inside." The children backed farther into the room and Skye stepped out of the doorway, holding the door open for Pete. As he passed, she said, "Aunt Olivia is keeping an eye on the twins while their parents do some Christmas shopping."

"I see," Pete answered. "And this fellow, too? Did he need a babysitter?" He pulled the dog inside, closing the door behind him.

"He didn't wanta be all 'lone," Will answered. "It's almost Christmas."

Pete nodded, still serious. "I see. We don't leave our friends all alone at Christmas, do we?" He kept a mostly straight face but added a hint of a wink in Skye's direction.

She rolled her eyes and turned toward the back of the house, asking, "Is your Gramma Olivia in the kitchen?"

"Yeah," Kate said. "She says that since you're here now, we can dedicate the tree tonight." She looked at Pete. "Are you gonna help us dedicate the tree?"

"Dedicate...?" Pete tried to make sense of the question. Then suddenly, it snapped into clarity. "Oh! Decorate! Is that what you mean?"

Kate frowned in disgust. "We're gonna put on lights and ornaments and stuff. We're gonna dedicate it."

Skye's amusement showed as she gave Pete a meaningful look that invited him to play along. "Yes, love. Pete will help us with the tree this evening. Won't you, Pete?"

Pete agreed. "I will be happy to help with your tree."

"There you are." Olivia came from the kitchen, wiping her hands on a towel. "Sorry I didn't get out here sooner. I'm in the middle of a batch of Christmas cookies and I didn't want the ones in the oven to burn." She gathered Skye into a full embrace. "So glad you could come!"

For a moment the two women reveled in the greeting. Then Olivia's gaze fell on Pete. In that look, he saw her assessment of him, her suspicions, and her hesitancy, backed by her determination to be a good hostess. She didn't touch him, didn't even offer a handshake, but she did say, "Welcome, Pete. We're glad you could join us for the holiday." She crossed quickly to a bowl on one end table and picked up something. "Paris and Greg took off for the valley this morning, but they left the keys to their place. Greg said to use whatever you need."

Pete took care not to touch Olivia when he took the keys. "This is amazing. I'm astonished they'd leave their home in the hands of a stranger."

"After the evening spent watching meteorites, they feel like they know you." She gave him a meaningful look that said, *Don't mess this up.* Her voice had an edge when she added, "Greg also mentioned that Skye knows how to find you, should anything go wrong."

Pete, taking it as a joke, chuckled drily. Turning to Skye, he said,

"I'll take my stuff to their house, but I'll be back to help decora...uh, dedicate the tree. What's a good time?"

"Come for dinner," Olivia said. "We'll eat about six, so get here around five-thirty."

"Will do," he said. He asked Skye, "Is your sister coming?"

"She and Evan will be along later."

"Great. I'll expect to see them then." He nodded to both women as he went to the door.

He was closing it behind him when he heard Olivia say, "What's that about dedicating the tree?" Skye started to answer as he shut the door behind him. Clearly, Olivia wasn't buying Skye's argument that she and Pete had never dated. The lady was sharp. Pete knew he'd have to keep his wits about him when he was around Olivia.

Somehow, the thought didn't disturb him as much as it once had.

"Are we ready for the ribbon?" Skye picked up an unopened package.

Olivia said, "Yes, I think so. We have the lights and ornaments all in place. Let's start wrapping from the top down." A few years ago, Olivia had seen a tree wrapped in gold wire ribbon. From that moment, she'd given up tinsel and finished each tree with ribbon instead.

Pete participated in the decorating, but mostly he observed. Even when his family was together and more or less functioning, he'd never known this kind of familial togetherness. He watched, curious to see how they'd work with the ribbon.

Max, father of the twins, climbed a ladder. "Hand me a straight pin, will you, honey?"

"Sure thing." Amber went into the ornament box. She pulled out a pin and lifted it to her husband.

"Thanks." Max took it and fastened the ribbon around the top of the tree, just below the place where the star would rest. "Okay, we're there. Let me hand it to you..." He reached for Amber, but the room was high, the tree tall, and Amber couldn't stretch to the place where the ribbon needed to go.

"Let me help." Pete stepped in. He took the roll of ribbon from Max and, using Amber's direction, wound it toward the front. Pausing every couple of feet to use a straight pin, he continued wrapping until he reached a height more comfortable for the women. Amber took over first and then Skye. Kate and Will each took a turn as the ribbon reached the lowest branches.

Olivia finished it off with another straight pin in the back. "There we go. All done." She turned to her husband. "What do you think, Enrique? Are we there?"

Enrique polled the group. "Well, *familia*. What do you think?" He looked first to his wife, then to their daughter, Amber, her husband, Max, and the twins. Finally, his gaze took in Skye and lastly, Pete. "Well, people, is this tree ready for the Christmas star?"

"And the dedication," Kate said.

Someone had clearly spoken to Kate because she added, "We *decorated* it. Now we need to *dedicate* it."

Someone had spoken to Enrique, too. As family patriarch, he took his place at the top of the ladder. "We all agree? We're ready?" He was answered by an eager chorus. "All right then." He took the star in hand and fastened it to the top of the tree. As he did so, he said, "I hereby dedicate this tree for this Christmas holiday. May it shine into the New Year."

Everyone clapped and cheered. Skye leaned close to Pete and murmured. "Amber asked *Tío* Rico to do a dedication. I think she even fed him the words."

"I noticed Kate got the words right this time."

"She's very proud of that. I expect dedicating the Christmas tree will become a family tradition now—thanks to Kate."

"It's a nice tradition."

"Hang around, my friend. You're going to see lots of traditions over the next few days."

Pete smiled. "Family, friends, traditions. Isn't that what Christmas is all about?"

"That and the reason for the season," Olivia added. He heard that edge to her voice again.

Skye said, "We're a religious family. You're going to see lots of Nativity scenes and other mementos of the Holy Family and the birth in a stable."

"We didn't have that when I was growing up." Pete hadn't realized he missed it until now. "It's good to see a family celebrate that part of Christmas, too."

"Yes," Olivia said. "It is good."

Pete thought he heard the edge leave her voice. That was good too.

Chapter Twenty

When Skye awoke the next morning, her first thought was of Pete. Then she realized what she'd just done and warned herself to change her train of thought. By now she knew better than to get involved with him personally. They were only on the same page when they worked together, and when they supported one another in their sobriety. She needed to let that be enough.

Although the air outside registered below-freezing temperatures, Skye decided she could use a walk in the cool air if only to shake some of the cobwebs loose. She bundled up for the temperatures outside, yet the chill in the air proved more than she felt ready to manage. When it dawned on her that she'd started in the direction of Greg Frantz's home, the place where Pete had stayed the night, she was both too chilled and too embarrassed to continue. She turned back to the home of her aunt and uncle.

She entered the front door to the scents of cinnamon, vanilla, apples, oranges, and chocolate, reminding her of all that was good and homey about Christmas here. Aunt Olivia had one of her potpourri mixes simmering on the back burner, and she was baking for Christmas. The mixed aromas added up to the scent of Christmas, of home. Serene, peaceful feelings came with that awareness. Skye thought of Pete, essentially banned from his family, even at Christmas time. She'd been blessed with a loving, forgiving family who kept letting her try again until, with their help, she'd been able to conquer her demons.

Filled with gratitude, she said good morning to her auntie, then hurried through her shower so she could help in the kitchen. A half hour later, she emerged from her old room down the hall and entered the kitchen with her hair left in a towel turban to dry. The sight of Pete, lifting a tray of cookies from the oven, brought her up short. "Pete! I hadn't expected you this early. I might have done something with my hair—" She saw Olivia watching her carefully.

"Your aunt invited me to help with the baking. I'm not much of a cook, but I follow directions fairly well."

"Yes, he does," Olivia added, and Skye heard the approval in her voice.

"I'll put this towel away and join you." Skye hurried down the hall, reminding herself that she'd worry about her appearance in front of a date, but not before a colleague and friend. Since she had assured her family that Pete fit into the friend-colleague category, she needed to appear unconcerned that he'd caught her with her hair wild. She used a spray-in detangler, hurriedly worked in some product, did a quick finger combing to create a few spiral curls near her face, and rejoined the pair in the kitchen.

As she entered the room, she heard Pete say, "I'm glad Amber and Max will be here for the holiday. I'm guessing it's a different kind of celebration when you have kids around."

"I agree," Olivia answered. "It would be fun if we had Ty's family here, too. Tyler is our son. He's older than Amber, but his kids fit right in with Max's twins." She paused. "They're celebrating with Ashley, that's Tyler's wife, and her family, but they plan to come up later."

Skye joined in. "How about Sunny and Evan? Last I heard, they planned to be here."

"They still do," Olivia answered. "But they're both working right up until the holiday. They should arrive late tomorrow afternoon, in time for dinner and Christmas Eve at church."

"Does that mean we go caroling tonight?"

Olivia nodded. "That's the way we do it. But because we have the twins with us this year, we'll go earlier in the afternoon, the way we used to when you kids were little. We'll have a big pot of soup and some fresh rolls waiting for when we get home."

"Sounds good." Skye looked at Pete who nodded to acknowledge he'd heard.

For a time, they worked together in the kitchen, helping Olivia through two more kinds of cookies. Skye began to wonder if she'd missed breakfast. She was on the verge of asking when Olivia said, "Okay. We'll let those cool. Time for some brunch, don't you think?"

"Oh good! I thought maybe I missed it." Skye tightened her apron.

Pete asked, "How can I help?" and Olivia put him to work cracking and beating eggs. Before long, the smell of cooking bacon brought Enrique from the garage. A companionable foursome sat down to eat. Skye told herself not to get used to this scenario, but it sure felt comfortable.

PETE STARTED to reach for the bowl of scrambled eggs, but Skye gave him a look, barely shaking her head. He frowned in confusion, but nodded understanding when Enrique bowed his head to offer a blessing. He had never lived with people who said a prayer before eating. He wondered how his life would be different if he'd had this kind of upbringing. Might a background in religion have offered protection when he began to tumble into alcohol abuse? Religion hadn't saved Skye from addiction, but her belief and occasional attendance may have helped her return to sobriety. The twelve steps of AA always emphasized relying on God for healing.

He tried to focus on the words and quickly realized Enrique's prayer was mostly expressions of gratitude. That was different too. His parents hadn't prayed since... He couldn't remember the last time, maybe when his mother's mother was still living.

And gratitude? He'd always heard his parents complaining about what they wanted and didn't have. This family clearly didn't have as much material wealth, but they had something he'd never had. Pete told himself that if he ever did have children, he'd want them to have this sense of belonging, of unity. The realization startled him. Just knowing he was thinking about marriage and kids seemed startling enough. When had that thought entered his head? Then he looked at Skye, who smiled brightly from across the table, and answered his own question.

Everyone chatted easily over breakfast. Skye told her aunt and uncle about the fantastic offer made to her and Pete, if they could figure out how to do companion pieces on the eight themes their eccentric host wanted them to portray.

"Will you be able to do that?" Olivia asked.

"We're working on it," Skye answered. "We've come up with a few ideas. Nothing's set in stone, but we have a sense of the direction we need to go, at least for a few of the themes."

"What kind of themes?" Enrique asked.

Olivia said, "Yes. Tell us about them."

Skye looked to Pete, who read the list from the email in his phone and listened carefully to the observations Skye's aunt and uncle shared. When they began to talk about the theme of "abundance," he knew what he wanted to sculpt. He didn't yet know how he'd show it, but he wanted to depict the emotions he'd felt a few minutes ago, when Enrique offered the blessing with such rich expressions of thanks. This family knew a kind of abundance he had never known, a kind he wanted to keep and hold onto, a kind he might want to know better.

POST BREAKFAST CLEANUP went quickly with all four adults pitching in. Enrique went to the garage and fetched a stack of inexpensive but festive looking plastic trays. Olivia explained she'd found them at a discount store in the valley. She added, "I hope I have enough."

Pete asked, "Uh, enough for what?"

Olivia laughed. Skye answered, "We're caroling tonight. That's what the cookies are for. We'll spend the next few minutes making up mixed trays of holiday treats to deliver wherever we sing. We have these six kinds of treats, some of which you helped to bake, and Aunt Olivia has a couple of others ready."

Olivia added further explanation. "When we have the trays prepared, we cover them in red or green plastic wrap and tie each with a ribbon. They're our gifts for friends and neighbors."

Pete looked in apparent awe at the table covered in Christmas treats. "I've never seen anybody do this kind of thing for friends, and certainly not for neighbors. Where I come from, we barely know who our neighbors are."

Olivia brushed off the comment. "It's a tradition here in Destiny. By tomorrow evening, we may have the table filled again, this time with the treats others have shared with us."

"I don't know what to say. This is a different kind of Christmas than any I've ever seen."

Enrique said, "I'm glad you could join us."

Skye watched the exchange in silence. She knew how strange this must look to Pete. She remembered how foreign it had seemed to her when she first came to live with her aunt and uncle. Christmas had barely rated a mention in the Children of Rah compound, although it did give the group occasion for a feast, when they could afford it. They didn't give gifts, and certainly didn't recognize anyone outside their own membership. Any relationship the cultists had with their neighbors was generally fraught with tension and suspicion—not good grounds for gift exchanges, or even pleasant greetings.

"Here, Pete," she said, stepping in to include him. "You take charge of these three kinds of cookies. Stack three or four of each, depending on the size and space you have, on this end of the tray." She set the oatmeal scotchies, jam thumbprints, and fudge brownies within his reach. "Tio Rico is starting each tray with the gingerbread people and frosted sugar cookies. Aunt Olivia will add the fudge and caramel. I've got the Russian teacakes, lemon bars, and snowballs. Your three will finish off each tray."

"This table is full. Where should I put the trays when I finish them?"

Enrique answered. "Look behind you. I've set up a folding table against the wall."

Pete grimaced. "I should have noticed. Okay. Let's do this!"

As they worked, the talk turned back to the art themes the collector expected Pete and Skye to show in their paired works. Skye wondered how she could capture the emotion around this table, this bonding of familial love that came from working together to benefit others. If she could capture this feeling, it would be the hit of their show.

She looked at Pete, caught his gaze, and swore he must be thinking the same thing. When he said, "I've been thinking about that theme of familial love," she knew he had. She couldn't help wondering why a guy who seemed so right for her should end up being so wrong. She sighed, then covered the sound with a pretend cough into her elbow and a quick, "Excuse me."

"Just don't cough on the cookies." Olivia took a step away long enough to count the finished trays and the ones in process. "We still have a way to go, I think."

Skye watched Pete pitch in as if he could think of nothing he'd rather do on a crisp December morning. Again, she reminded herself that this man, no matter how nearly perfect he might seem, was not headed in the same direction as she, and wishing would not make it so. She needed to guard her heart. That would make it easier to split from Pete when the time came.

But even as she thought it, she wondered if it were true. At least for the coming weeks, she'd need to work closely with him and to be around him regularly. Protecting her heart might be more difficult than she'd imagined.

JUST AFTER FOUR O'CLOCK, Max and Amber pulled into the driveway. The car had barely come to a stop when the twins tumbled out of the two back doors. This time, Scooter did not accompany them. "Mom made pumpkin bread!" Will barely seemed able to contain the news.

"We don't have room on the trays—" Olivia began.

Amber interrupted. "I wrapped each loaf separately. We can give one tray and one loaf wherever we sing."

"You may not have enough to go around—"

"We'll hand out as many as we have. If we run out, we run out." Amber shrugged.

"That sounds doable. Do you have room in the back of the wagon for all our trays?"

"Depends. Are they stackable?"

"Yes, I believe we can stack if we're careful."

Pete spoke up. "If they don't all fit in the station wagon, I can follow you in my truck. I know they'll all fit there."

"That's an idea." Max looked at the half-filled back of the family's new wagon. "We don't have a lot of room here, especially if we put up the third seat."

"The truck then." Enrique made the decision.

Just like that, everyone went to work, loading the trays into the back of Pete's truck. As they prepared to leave, Enrique and Olivia joined Max and Amber in their wagon, telling Pete and Skye to follow. Skye said to Olivia, "Each time we make a stop, you'll need to tell us where we're going next. That way, we won't ever lose you."

"Sounds good." Olivia loaded in behind Will and Kate in the third seat. Enrique squeezed into the small extra seat that remained.

"You can come with us, Tio Rico," Skye said. She looked to Pete, who nodded. "We have a bench seat with extra room."

"No, thanks. I like to be with my lady when we go caroling."

"Good enough." Skye watched as he settled next to Olivia.

Three hours and eighteen families later, they all returned to the Reyes home, the goodies distributed, the singers ready for hot soup and rolls. "That went well!" Amber declared.

"Better than well," Skye said. "We made the day for some folks. Did you see Mrs. Kamphouvong dabbing at her eyes?"

"Old Mr. Mackey just kept saying, 'thank you, thank you,'" Max said. "I never thought about how lonely he must get."

The group gathered around the table and Olivia brought out the food. Enrique asked Max to say grace. For Pete, the whole experience was almost surreal.

Over the years, he'd thought very little about the possibility of marriage. Then, once he was in recovery, he'd definitely ruled it out. He supposed he'd go through his adult life the way he had his young adult years, moving from one girlfriend to another when things got difficult in a relationship. He'd pictured himself married to his art. When it came to children, he'd always wondered what the point was if he'd just end up estranged from them the way he was now separated from his own parents. What he saw here, in the company of this loving, multi-generational family, had given him a reason to rethink those conclusions.

He paused, aware of the direction his thoughts were taking. He knew better than to change his mind on a whim, but he also knew he had begun to consider the possibilities of having a real, committed, and lasting marriage, something like what he saw with Olivia and Enrique. Here before him were a couple who'd taken in two little girls who needed them, raising Skye and Sunny as their own. And here was their daughter, Amber, who had taken on Max's children, loving them, making them hers. This visit had shown him examples of familial love he'd never considered before.

Skye interrupted Pete's thoughts. Quietly, she murmured, "You're lost deep in some thought-forest. What are you thinking?"

"You'd be surprised," he told her. "It even surprises me."

"Well…?"

"I'm not ready to talk about it yet."

"Maybe someday?"

"Yeah, maybe. We'll see. It has to do with that theme of familial love."

"Sounds good," she said.

He laughed along with the rest of the family when Will tried to put a roll in his coat pocket, planning to take it home to Scooter. "That isn't going to work, buddy," Amber said, clearing the pocket. "Let's ask Gramma Olivia if we can have a zip bag for that roll."

Pete watched the whole tableau with a kind of glow, basking in a type of family warmth he'd never known. He could learn to like this kind of family.

Chapter Twenty-One

For Skye, the family caroling had been a moment of rich nostalgia, and a peek into a possible future. All those years as an addict, she knew she'd never have children. Why perpetuate the cycle into another generation? Then, once she got clean, she had wondered if she'd be able to have healthy children, even if she decided she wanted them. Had she done irreparable damage to her body that would extend to the next generation?

She'd talked with doctors, run tests, been told her chances of bearing healthy babies were as good as anyone's. But then she'd seen how difficult it was for a recovering addict to build a lasting relationship and realized she might never marry. Today as she watched the family celebrating together, she ached to think of all she'd be missing if that were true.

She helped the family carry in the goodies given them by neighbors, and she waved as Amber, Max, Kate, and Will left. Watching the twins tonight, remembering what it was like to be a child in this family, she'd realized how much she wanted that. What if she did find someone, the right someone, to marry? What if they could create a stable home and she was able to conceive healthy babies? Wouldn't she want that? The emotion that welled in her answered the question.

She turned her smile inward. Now, how did she capture that deep longing in her art?

CHRISTMAS EVE DAY DAWNED BRIGHT, cold, and cloudless. "What are the odds of a white Christmas this year?" Skye asked as she entered the kitchen.

"Not bad," Olivia answered.

"Really? It doesn't look that way now."

Enrique spoke from the folding table where he organized the treats from the night before. "We should start seeing clouds by midafternoon. The snow could start as early as midnight."

"Now *that* sounds like the Destiny Christmases I remember." She peeked into the pan where Olivia stirred tortilla wedges. *"Chilaquiles?"*

"Yes, ma'am. Would you like to cook the eggs?"

"Happy to help. How many are we expecting?"

"It's just the three of us this morning. Amber has plans with her family until midday or so, though they'll be here before Ty and his family arrive."

"Great. We will still have a crowd for our humble dinner this evening." And she didn't expect Pete for a few hours yet. She swallowed an unwelcome sense of disappointment. She got out the eggs but took a quick look into the saucepan Olivia stirred. "Green sauce today?"

"I thought about making both red and green. For Christmas, y'know? Then I realized how much leftover sauce I'd have. I settled on green. I have *cotija* cheese and sweet onions, too."

"The perfect combination." Skye set to work, trying to recapture the emotions she'd felt with the children the night before, wishing Pete didn't flash into her mind any time she thought about the future. He'd made it clear that the only future they were likely to have together was in their art. She'd be wise to quit daydreaming about anything else.

"Is everything okay?" Olivia looked as concerned as she sounded.

"Oh. Yeah. I was just thinking about the art projects I'm supposed to be working on."

"Anything I can help with?"

"I don't think so. Maybe you could help if I didn't have to coordinate with Pete—"

"How is that going?" Olivia dropped her voice and turned away from Enrique. "How is it working with him after…you know."

"It was awkward at first." Skye moderated her volume to match that of her aunt. "But we're good when we keep the focus on art. Now that we've recognized we don't have any future beyond that—"

"I wonder."

"You wonder what?"

"I saw the way he looked at you when we sang together last night. I suspect he's reconsidering his position."

"I don't underst—"

"That man wants you, Skye. Not just for the moment and not only as a fellow artist. I see the way he watches you and I suspect he's beginning to weigh what it would cost him to have you back in his life."

"I don't know…" Skye tried to keep her tone doubtful, though her heart had begun a happy dance.

"I do." Olivia patted her arm. "Keep an eye on that one. He may surprise you."

Skye's amusement came out in little huff. "You've sure changed your tune. What brought you around?"

Olivia pursed her lips. "Remember I said he's as charming as the devil himself?"

"Um-hm."

"Well he is, and I hope I'm not just falling for that, but… well, he's deeper than he first appeared, and I'm quite beginning to like him." She nodded at Skye's answering grin. "I suspect he's full of surprises."

PETE SURPRISED THEM ALMOST IMMEDIATELY. The doorbell rang while Skye was still cracking eggs. Looking out the front window and seeing Pete's truck, Olivia said, "You'd better answer that. It's for you."

As she wiped her hands, Skye asked, "Do we have enough for an extra person?"

Olivia nodded. "We will if you prepare more eggs."

"Will do." Skye hurried to the door and flung it open. "Hey, stranger. We weren't expecting you for a while."

He hesitated. "I hope it's okay for me to show up like this."

"It's good," Olivia called from the kitchen.

"Thanks, Olivia." Pete looked more confident when he stepped inside. "I saw Gale's Produce Stand had a sale going on holiday fruit trays. I thought that might help with breakfast."

Enrique entered. *"Chilaquiles* and fresh fruit? We'll think we're in Mexico, for sure."

Skye said, "Come right in. We'll set the table for four." She told herself that her heart hadn't really raced when she heard the doorbell and knew Pete had come. She went back to the kitchen and cracked two more eggs.

WHEN THE FAMILY bowed their heads for grace, Pete saw that Enrique, Olivia, and Skye all held hands. He'd been too flabbergasted to notice before, but now it seemed quite natural. On his left, he reached to clasp Olivia's fingers. On his right, he intertwined his fingers with Skye's.

She looked up, startled.

He smiled and bowed his head. It touched him to hear Olivia's prayer include him, thanking God for letting him spend the holiday with their family. A few years back—possibly even a few months ago —he'd have wondered if these people were for real or if they were trying to sell him on some agenda.

But there was nothing forced or artificial about the Reyes family. Seeing how their neighbors responded to their caroling and gifts, they must have been caring people all the years they'd lived here. There was something wholesome and real and *good* about all of this. He thought about Max and Amber and the happy connections he'd seen in their family. He wondered if the little town of Destiny attracted this kind of people, or if it shaped people to become this open and caring.

He was a city boy, born and bred. Until that moment, it had never occurred to him to consider small town living. Maybe he needed to open to that possibility.

"What do you call this?" he asked as he dug into his meal.

"Chilaquiles," Enrique said. "A standard Mexican breakfast."

Pete lifted a bite on his fork. "Well, *chila*...whatever. Where have you been all my life? This stuff is fantastic!"

Olivia glowed beside him.

"Chil-a-kee-lays." Skye pronounced it slowly. "It's worth remembering, if you ever want to order it sometime."

Pete, his mouth full of deliciousness, nodded. He swallowed and said, "Good to know. Maybe I can get you to write it down for me later?"

"Happy to," Skye answered.

Then Pete laughed. "It just occurred to me: If we can make art pieces that capture the sensation of eating *chila*... um, this, we'll have our entry for 'contentment.'"

Skye chuckled, too. "Now we just need to figure out how we'll make that happen."

As before, Pete helped with cleanup. Then he asked if Skye had immediate plans.

Skye looked to Olivia, who shook her head. "No, nothing I can think of."

"I wonder if I might borrow you for a little while."

"Sure. I want to be back before Ty and his family get here. Can we do...whatever you're planning and get back by four or so?"

"That's lots of time. Sure."

"Then let's go." He grabbed his jacket and hers as they went out the front door. Commenting on the chill in the air, he pulled on his coat.

"Rico says we may have snow by the morning."

"How about that! A white Christmas." That was something else he'd never known.

"So...what's the big secret? What do you need me to help you do?"

"Christmas shopping." He gave her a *help-me* look. "You know I wasn't planning to spend Christmas with anyone—"

"And no one expects you to go out of your way."

"But you've all gone out of your way for me." When Skye started to protest, he held up his hand in a *stop* gesture. "I want to leave a gift for Paris and Greg, something nice for letting me take over their house. And I want to have something, even if it's something small, under the tree for each member of your family."

"Pete, that isn't—"

"Please don't argue. I have a glass piece titled *Home*. It doesn't fit into anything we're doing in this new project, unless we really put a twist on the idea of familial love." He looked at her expression. "No. I didn't think so, either, but it will be the perfect gift for Greg and Paris."

"You don't have glass for everyone, and certainly not for the kids—"

"No, I don't, and that's why I need you. If you're game, I want to make a quick run down to the valley. You can help me pick appropriate items and maybe help me wrap them." He tried for a charming smile. "I seem to work better with glass than with wrapping paper."

"For the record, I protest. No one expects you to do this."

He thought of the unsolicited gifts taken to friends and neighbors the night before. "Aren't unexpected gifts the best kind?"

"You have a point. Okay then. Off to the valley."

They took their places in Pete's truck and fastened their seat belts. As he started the engine, he said, "I should mention that I may have a glass piece for Max and Amber, too, and maybe another that's appropriate for your aunt and uncle. You can tell me when you see them."

"Okay. Shall we start at the Hot Shop?"

"No, I took all my finished work home before the holiday. Do you mind stopping by my apartment?"

"No, of course not." She said the words, but he noticed a sudden tightness in her. As he turned his truck down the hill, he promised himself he would be the consummate gentleman.

AT PETE'S APARTMENT, Skye helped him choose, package, and wrap the glass sculptures he wanted as gifts for her family. She could easily see how *Home* would work for Greg and Paris. When Pete asked, "What about your cousin, Tyler? What's his home-and-family situation?"

Skye gave him her best answer. "I'd like to tell you, but the truth is, I don't really know. When I got buried in addiction, he wanted to keep his family far from bad influences like me, which means I haven't seen Tyler in a while—or his wife, Ashley, either. I know his kids are close to the ages of Will and Kate. If I remember correctly, his oldest is about eight, a girl. His boys are younger, maybe six and five."

"And the twins are—"

"Seven, so they really should fit well together. That is, assuming they get along."

174

"I'm guessing they will. The twins seem able to get along with just about anyone."

Skye chuckled wryly. "You should have seen them when Max and Amber first started dating, but that's a tale for another time."

"Maybe you'll find a moment to share it with me later."

"Yes. Maybe."

He liked the twinkle in her eyes when she said it. It suggested there would be other, more personal, times. With Skye's help, he chose another glass piece for Tyler and Ashley, and still another for Sunny and Evan. When the glass gifts were ready, he drove them to a big box store where he hoped to find last-minute items for the kids. Looking at the human zoo in front of her, Skye said, "I'm sure glad I finished my shopping early."

"Yeah, well, I would have if—"

"No excuses necessary. Let's see what we can accomplish."

After a whirlwind trip through the store, they left with Pete's shopping list completed and all his gifts packaged and appropriately wrapped. As they drove back to Destiny, Pete asked what Skye knew about Ashley.

"Not much. I met her once or twice when she and Tyler first married. One thing we don't discuss much outside the family is Ava, their oldest. She was an infant when Ashley and Tyler met. Tyler adopted her as soon as he married her mom. Ava knows she's adopted, but she's always thought of Ty as her dad and it's easier for her if everyone treats her like she's Ty's biological daughter. She was still little when Tyler realized some of the stuff I was getting into, became the protective daddy, and cut me off. Beyond that, you know as much as I do."

"There's some tension for you around this visit?"

"Maybe, but it's mostly just the unknown. Tyler's a great guy, and he's always been kind. I know he'll warm up, as soon as he realizes I'm no threat to his family."

"I hope that works. Remember the piece I chose for them? I called it *Yin and Yang*. It has two opposing colors crashing together in the center like waves, mixing into a third shade. It could just as easily be called *Blended Family*. Maybe it's exactly the right gift for Tyler and Ashley."

"Yes, maybe," Skye answered.

They arrived at the Reyes home and unloaded the gifts, placing them around the tree. Skye brought out her box and placed her gifts around the tree as well. Max and Amber arrived just as they finished.

"Do we get to open them now?" Will asked.

Max answered. "Come on, son. You know better than that. We told you we're opening gifts tomorrow, on Christmas morning."

"But it wouldn't hurt to open just one now, would it?" Will had found a gift with his name on it. He stared at it wistfully.

This time, it was Amber who answered. "Tomorrow, Will. Just as we planned. We will open gifts at our house first. Then we'll come here and open gifts with Nana and Papa Rico."

Max added, "It's only a few more hours. You've waited this long already. Surely a few more hours won't hurt?"

They were interrupted by the quick toot-toot of a car horn. Enrique looked out the front window. "Looks like Tyler and Ashley are here."

Pete felt the wave of anticipation flow around him, filling the room.

Chapter Twenty-Two

S kye hummed as she worked in the kitchen. Without being asked or invited, Ty's wife had jumped in to help and had slipped right into the rhythm. She couldn't do better if she'd grown up here. Their children were fitting in just as easily.

"Are you ready for the carrots?" Ashley asked Olivia.

"Oh, you have the carrots ready! Yes, put them right in the pot."

Skye watched as Ashley stepped over to stir. Ashley said, "I like this tradition, the simple supper. You've been doing this as long as I've been in the family. How long has your family been celebrating Christmas Eve this way?"

"As long as I can remember," Skye answered. "Aunt Olivia, how long have you and Rico been having your humble Christmas Eve dinner?"

"Since the first year we married." Olivia brought over a clean spoon to have a taste. "Umm. The rolls are ready to bake. Looks like the soup will be ready about the same time."

Skye liked the tradition, too. On Christmas Eve, the family always ate an early dinner of meatless soup—usually Olivia's favorite lentil recipe—and rolls, a humble meal to commemorate the humble birth in a stable, the cradle in a manger. Their tummies warm and filled, they went to Christmas Eve service at church. When they returned, they enjoyed a few rich treats, but only a few. They saved the feast for Christmas Day. Skye loved it that they had both the simple supper to honor the humble circumstances and the feast to celebrate the birth.

Minutes later, Olivia declared the food ready and sent Skye to round up the troops. She'd last seen the children—Will and Kate, Ava, Andrew, and Liam—all surrounding the Christmas tree, looking for gift tags with their names. She found them now in the room that had once been Amber's. Ava had discovered the stash of old children's toys left there for young visitors and had organized both children and toys into a game, almost a puppet show. The baby doll she voiced seemed to be in charge, giving the orders to Will's soldier action figure, Kate's teddy bear, Andrew's plastic dinosaur, and Liam's superhero. Each followed her instructions, speaking the lines she gave them and moving their toys according to her script.

The scene reminded Skye of times she and Sunny had played with Amber's toys when they came with their mother for brief visits during the years before Olivia's rescue. The older girls' toys always ran the show, but Skye managed to get a win here and there. This pretend play struck Skye as the beginning of art, of imagining a world beyond what they could all see.

"Come on, kids. Dinner time."

"Then church?" Will asked, some small level of distaste showing in the way he said it.

"Then church," Skye answered, keeping her voice bright. "And after that, treats and sleep, so Christmas morning can come."

Ava stood and held out her hand. "Come on, Will. Let's go. The soup smells fabulous!"

The way she spoke that last word told Skye it was a new addition to her vocabulary, one the eight-year-old felt proud to show off. Skye tried to mimic Ava's exact tone when she said, "It *does* smell fabulous, doesn't it? Come on, everyone. Your moms and your grandma have made some wonderful food."

She watched the scramble as all five children rushed to the kitchen. She'd always envied the level of energy little children brought to their play. If she could bring that to her art, who knew what she could accomplish? It occurred to her that childhood was an energy storm no one appreciated while they had it. Could she do something with that idea for the *alternative energy* theme their contract required? She followed the child-storm to join Pete and her family in the dining area.

PETE SAT beside Skye in the chapel, the two of them at the end of the pew with the Reyes family beside them. Olivia and Enrique sat on Skye's other side with Amber and Max next. Then came Will and Kate sitting with Ava, Andrew, and Liam. The other set of parents, Tyler and Ashley, took the opposite end. Pete watched them all, filled with admiration.

Olivia and Enrique had taken on so much when they brought their nieces to live with them. Now he knew that both Amber and Tyler had married people who already had children. Olivia and Rico raised two girls who weren't their legal responsibility. Now their children were each raising children to whom they had no obligation except what they chose, and both had adopted.

That thought brought another. Here he'd been wondering whether he wanted to be bothered with raising even one child, one born to him. He remembered someone saying that people who didn't want to raise children most certainly shouldn't have any, and he quite agreed. But was he really one of those people? He found he quite enjoyed being around these charming little folks. Maybe he'd just never seen how happy families could work.

He listened to the reading of the Christmas story in the second chapter of Luke and thought seriously for the first time about the "reason for the season," as Olivia put it. Sure, he'd always celebrated Christmas, but to him, it had meant Santa Claus and presents and a list of obligatory+ gifts to buy, greetings to send, and parties to attend—whether he wanted to or not. He'd never thought much about the religious tradition.

Of course, as a devotee of twelve step programs, he'd spent several years now giving his addictions "to God as we understand him." He'd always been happy to think of God as the amorphous power of the universe. He'd never attended church, never seen the need for religion, yet as he sat in the congregation, listening to a group of believers sing, "O, Come All Ye Faithful," he wondered. What if there was a personal God? What if he'd been missing something important and didn't even realize it?

Suddenly, it all seemed too much. Could he allow one holiday to change his worldview this completely?

He turned toward Skye, watching her as she sang—her face alight with the joy she found in the people and place and the religious celebration; her black hair gleaming, spiral curls framing her face; her lovely complexion warmed by the joy in the room and her own inner glow—and he wondered if he'd ever seen a more beautiful, more nearly perfect woman, or if he'd ever find anyone this nearly perfect for him. He picked up a hymnal and began to sing.

SKYE AWOKE Christmas morning to see that her uncle's prediction had been fulfilled. Their Christmas was white indeed, snow four to five inches deep blanketing everything. Destiny was lovely in any climate, but when it was white like this, with the trees all lacy, she found it hard to imagine anything lovelier. She felt privileged to call it home.

She hurried to shower and dress but took some care. After dessert the night before, and before they all parted for the evening, Olivia had made a point of inviting Pete for Christmas breakfast. She and Pete might only be colleagues, but she wanted to look her best…

Ah, who was she kidding? She stared at her reflection, remembering Step Ten and the need for constant self-examination, regularly taking a moral inventory. A lie to herself was still a lie. She should just admit it—she wanted to impress him, wanted him to want her enough to consider dating her again, to consider the possibility that they could be serious about each other.

Wonderful aromas wafted down the hallway from the kitchen—caramel rolls fresh from the oven, cinnamon-rich Mexican hot chocolate, spiced cider, scrambled eggs with chorizo. Her aunt and uncle always made Christmas breakfast a treat. They had always been wonderful to Skye, even when she'd treated them badly and disappointed them terribly.

When the doorbell rang, she was already on her way. "I'll get that!" she called.

Olivia responded. "Good! We're busy in here. Besides, it's for you, anyway."

Was Pete for her? She buzzed with excitement as she opened the door.

~

Half-buried in happy children and mounds of wrapping paper, Pete watched the buzz around him, amazed at the family's warmth and kindness. He'd grown up thinking families like this only existed in TV sit-coms. Those he knew were all much like his own—everyone concerned about keeping up with their neighbors, preferably outdoing them, one-upping each other. No one here seemed to care about that. In fact, they didn't seem to care much about *things* at all.

This family had taken him in as if he were one of them and no one knew he was coming until just before he got here. Still they'd had gifts under the tree for him—thoughtful gifts he could use like the super-warm wool gloves from Olivia and the super-tough leather gloves from Skye, perfect for the Hot Shop. They'd all been gracious about his gifts to them as well.

At that moment, Ashley tapped into his thoughts. "I still can't get over how beautiful this glass art is and so perfect for our family. It should fit well on our fireplace mantle. The kids are less likely to destroy it there."

"I love ours too," Amber said. "You're such a talented artist, Pete."

That led to a round of compliments and thanks as each couple commented first on Pete's glass work and then on the bronze pieces Skye had made. Tyler wanted to learn more about their paired art project, which gave everyone something to discuss as they cleaned up. When the room was orderly and the children were in Amber's old room playing, Max said, "While it's just the grownups here, we have something to tell you."

Everyone looked expectantly at Amber, who said, "Actually, we have several things to tell you. First, there's our Christmas gift to Will and Kate. I don't want them to have a stepmother. I want them to have a mom. We've been working on it for a while now—"

Olivia gasped. "Really? The adoption went through?"

Max nodded. "Finalized this week."

"Wonderful!" Ashley and Olivia spoke simultaneously.

Amber said, "The kids are officially ours, *both* of ours." She took her husband's hand.

"My former in-laws gave us all kinds of grief," Max said, "but Amber assured them that, as long as they're respectful of our decisions, they can still see their grandchildren."

"I didn't want to deprive the kids of all the family they can have," Amber added. "Why not three sets of grandparents?"

"Why not?" Tyler said. Lowering his voice and glancing toward the hall where they could hear the children, he said, "Pressure from Ashley's in-laws was part of the reason we married quickly, and also why I wanted to adopt Ava as fast as I could."

"Really? Your story is more like ours than I knew." Amber wrapped her arm around Ty.

Tyler and Amber, brother and sister, sat side by side, talking about their experiences with adoption while Pete watched, fascinated. He could do worse than becoming a part of this fam— Whoa! Where had that come from? Shocked by his own thoughts, he said, "Will you excuse me?" and stood.

Amber said, "Wait a moment, Pete. We want you to hear this next announcement." She looked at Max. "You tell them, honey."

"You're probably already guessing it, and you're right! Our kids will have a new brother or sister at the end of May."

"Congratulations," Pete said, but it came out sounding flat, even to his own ears. No one else seemed to notice as the room exploded in joyful excitement. As soon as he could do so without seeming rude, he excused himself for the bathroom. He didn't really need it, but it gave him a plausible excuse for leaving.

Alone and locked inside, he looked in the mirror. *What are you doing, man? You need time.* He began calming himself, using skills he'd learned in AA for overcoming addiction triggers. Eight minutes later, he returned to the conversation in time to hear Amber say, "I had a call from Paris last night. She and Greg are in Reno."

"Reno! Why?" Olivia's response came quickly.

"Her Aunt Jessica is getting married!"

Max looked at the group. "We didn't know Jess was seeing anyone.

Were any of you aware?" His question was met with head shakes and blank stares. "That's what I thought."

"Apparently she's been seeing him off and on for a while," Amber explained. "His name is Jacob Winston and he's also a math teacher. They met at conferences but could never figure out a way to be together. When Jess heard that Mr. Singh at the junior high planned to take early retirement at the semester, she told her guy. He starts here at the new year."

"That's wonderful." Olivia seemed genuinely pleased.

"One more thing," Amber added. "Her new husband has two sons, ages eleven and thirteen. Jess is going to be a mom now, too."

This news brought another round of excited comments.

Enrique said, "Everyone seems to have good news."

Skye answered, "That's what we look for at Christmas time."

Pete barely heard it all. When there was a lull in the conversation, he touched Skye's shoulder. "Can we talk alone for a minute? Maybe outside?"

"Sure." Skye excused herself, opened the door, and stepped onto the front porch.

Pete followed, closing the door behind him. He took a deep breath and tried to look composed. "Just want to talk about our return to the valley. We have a lot of work to do."

"We certainly do. I'd like to stay through tonight if that works for you. We can have dinner with the family. That's planned for midafternoon. Then in the evening, when people start getting hungry again, we usually bring out leftovers and top it off with Christmas treats. By tomorrow morning, the slump will be setting in. That's a good time to leave."

"Yeah. Okay. About how early—"

"I'd like to help Aunt Olivia with breakfast. Of course, you're welcome to join us. Then we can stop back by Paris and Greg's house to change sheets and so forth—"

"I can do that before I come here in the morning. I'll be the perfect guest and wash my used sheets and towels."

"Great. I guess we can be on our way by ten o'clock or so." She paused. "I didn't realize you were in that big a rush to get back."

He took a deep breath and reminded himself not to show her the roller coaster he'd been riding. "Just eager to get working."

She shrugged. "We do have a lot to do. Okay, sure. I'll be ready to go by midmorning."

"Great," he said, and opened the front door. He had more work to do than Skye could imagine.

Chapter Twenty-Three

For Skye, the rest of that day seemed almost magical. The cousins played beautifully together. Of course, they wanted to use the sleds Pete had given them. Since the snow held so well and given the nice hill down to the playing field at the high school, they had the opportunity. Skye watched Pete start one slide down the hill and then another, making sure everyone got an even number of turns. He kept the kids going until they began to talk about having seconds of Nana's pumpkin bread.

Skye couldn't help wondering how Pete was taking this family holiday. She suspected it was quite different from any Christmas he'd known. Though he seemed to be having a good time, he spoke little. Skye couldn't help noticing there were times his expression floated between blank and confused. She wished he'd share what was happening in his head. At other moments, she wasn't sure she wanted to know.

She touched the lovely bracelet Pete had given her as a Christmas gift. She'd come up with something uber-practical in those leather gloves she'd given him, gloves she picked up at the big box store when they were shopping.

His gift to her was anything but practical—and he hadn't bought it at the big box store. The bracelet had tiny charms, each handmade of colored glass, each associated in some way with her: a paint brush, a palette, a pickup truck, a shooting star, a canvas on an easel, and even one that looked like her favorite sandwich. It seemed he had put a great deal of thought into each of the charms as he made them. The bracelet was delicate, of course, and she'd have to be careful whenever she wore it, but it touched her that he'd obviously put so much time and care into it. When had he done this? Obviously not in the time after she invited him, so he must have been working on it before. What did that say about him, about them?

She looked at Pete, watched him pick up little Liam under both arms and swing the boy in a circle while Liam giggled. She sighed and rejoined the group.

THE REYES FAMILY Christmas dinner was unlike any Pete had ever seen. It included a variety of spicy Mexican dishes mixed with traditional English/American fare in a feast with something for everyone. He took small portions, hoping to taste every item, and found that, despite a healthy appetite, he didn't have room enough for everything. Skye gave him a knowing look. "Don't worry. The leftovers will warm up nicely later. You'll get a shot at all of it."

"Good to know." He set his fork down and let his meal settle.

If the meal left him perplexed, the family's after-dinner traditions baffled him. "You play cards?" he asked, his tone disbelieving.

"That confuses you?" Skye seemed as amazed by his bewilderment as he was by the games.

"Well, okay then." He intertwined his fingers and bent them backward, cracking his knuckles. "Let's break out a deck. My favorite is your basic five card stud."

Skye burst into laughter. "Not *that* kind of cards."

"What other kind is there?"

He was about to discover Uno, Go Fish, and Racko. When the children left to play with new toys, he learned about One-High Rook, a game that involved bidding, suits, and trump cards but resulted only in winners' bragging rights. He couldn't remember ever playing a card game where no money changed hands.

He leaned close to whisper, "I'm not sure I understand this game."

"Hang in there," Skye said. "You'll catch on as we go." Over the next couple of hours, Pete learned a great deal, mostly through the process of losing. Since the group had divided into teams, men versus women, the other guys were getting uneasy with him until the men finally won a round. Pete, who had seen meaningful looks pass among the women, suspected they'd given their men a mercy win.

Despite any confusion or unease, Pete realized he'd enjoyed the games—even the silly ones with the kids—and the warm camaraderie of the family.

The rest of the day and evening went well. As Skye had promised, the leftovers warmed nicely, and Pete got his opportunity to try everything, finding each new dish as delicious as the last. As he listened to the family talk, he realized every recipe had been lovingly prepared by one or more members of the clan. These people knew how to enjoy great food as much as they enjoyed each other. This was so different from the awkward holiday dinners in his family home, with most dishes made at the local deli.

After the Christmas meal encore, the family—from Enrique to young Liam—all enjoyed more treats and sang carols around the tree. By the time he left to go to the Frantz home for his last night in Destiny, Pete had a lengthy list of questions to consider. Maybe he could raise some of them with Skye on the drive home tomorrow. He thought of beautiful, amazing Skye and immediately felt tongue-tied and inadequate even to bring the questions to the fore. Somehow he doubted he'd get much rest that evening. It surprised him when he woke before the alarm the next day, feeling remarkably rested.

SKYE HAD her bags packed and ready before Pete rang the doorbell. Following another great breakfast, they said their goodbyes to her family and turned the pickup down the mountain.

"What did you think of your first Destiny Christmas?" Skye asked as they passed the turnoff to the health spa, housed on the former grounds of the Children of Rah.

"That was really something," Pete answered. "Is it like that every year?"

"Like what?"

"All that food. So many people. Caroling, card games, sledding—"

"Yes. And no. We always have plenty of food, usually a good mix of the traditional Mexican dishes my Reyes grandparents enjoys, and family recipes handed down through my Aunt Olivia. We always go caroling, and the family does lots of baking and candy making as small gifts for the neighbors. And now I've forgotten what else you listed."

"Does the family always gather? Do you always go sledding and play cards?"

"Yes, some portion of the family always gathers, although the mix can differ from one year to the next."

"Like your sister, Sunny, and her husband. What's his name again? Ethan?"

"Evan. You're right. Sunny and Evan weren't with us for Christmas morning because they went to be with his family. They'll be back for a day or two before the New Year. Maybe they'll be here for Christmas morning next year, but Tyler and Ashley will be with her folks, so the mix varies."

"Is there a time when everyone gathers together?"

"That's one of the things we've been talking about. We've realized that if we don't plan for it, we may not all predictably be together. Olivia and Enrique are trying to be more intentional with their organizing so we can all be in the same place at the same time. It's even possible the first annual Reyes family reunion will occur this coming summer."

"That's great." He nodded his approval. "It's good to see families that care enough to want to spend time together."

"Our family has had its rebels—namely, me—but for the most part, we've done well with hanging together. How about your family?"

He simply shook his head.

She offered a sympathetic look. "As for the rest, we don't sled if we don't have snow, so that's not an annual event. The card games are, though. That started a few years ago, when we were all adults. Then we limited it to a Rook tournament. We started adding in the kid games when the next generation got old enough to want to join us."

"It's touching that the adults are willing to play Go Fish just to spend time with the children."

"It's surprisingly more fun to play with the kids. Their excitement is contagious."

"I noticed, especially when they win."

They continued chatting about family and food and Christmas, which led to the topic of gifts. "Pete?" Skye said his name in a way that let him know she had something serious in mind.

"Yeah?"

"This beautiful bracelet you made..." She fingered it gently. "You didn't just throw this together after I invited you to join us for Christmas. When did you work on this?"

Pete hesitated before answering. "The idea came some time ago. I saw women wearing charm bracelets and realized they were becoming popular again, which got me thinking about whether I could make glass charms. One day in the Hot Shop, I had little bits of colored glass that didn't fit in with my design. After I had my art piece finished and placed in the cooler, I went back and started fiddling with the leftover bits, trying to see if I could produce miniatures that could become charms.

"Last week, when the term was winding down and the students were all taking their work home from the Hot Shop, I realized I had eighteen miniatures that had turned out fairly well, so I took them home to see if I could make a bracelet." He glanced at her. "I was thinking of a second income stream, you know?"

She nodded. "Go on."

"I took my miniatures home. I designed them with a tiny hole in the top for attaching to a bracelet. I'd already bought a chain. My plan was to put it together during the break."

She wondered if that was the entire story. "That's how *my* bracelet came to be?"

"Well, yeah." He cleared his throat. "When you invited me, I wanted to bring gifts and that's when I realized several of the charms —the ones I made when we worked together on the St. Helena show— were well-suited to you."

"You had others that weren't?"

"Yeah. Some of them didn't turn out at all." He gave her a sheepish grin. "I tried my hand at making a giraffe, but it ended up looking like a long-legged, spotted table lamp."

She smiled at his humor.

"Many of them turned out well, though, some of which seemed to fit you so …I decided I could make a nice bracelet for you. I already had the chain, the connectors. It took no time to put the finished piece together."

"It's beautiful." Her voice was soft as she reverently touched each tiny glass sculpture. Pete had created a uniquely beautiful bracelet, one that indeed reflected so many aspects of her personality and life. She didn't want to probe further, but she found his gift deeply meaningful. Surely it said something about what she meant to him. The question was what.

Chapter Twenty-Four

They started work the next day, meeting at Skye's apartment. Molly was still with her family, and neither the Hot Shop nor Skye's studio gave them the same room for sketching and chatting. Since their proposed contract required close cooperation, significant planning seemed necessary before they began their hands-on creative work.

They sat together at Skye's small dining table with their sketch pads in front of them. "Let's look again at 'calumny,'" Skye said, flipping to the preliminary sketch she'd already done. "If I stick with *Feathers in the Wind,* can you come up with a paired piece?"

"I've been thinking about that." Pete began sketching, explaining his work as he went. In just a few minutes, he'd shown her his concept: a table-top-sized piece in charcoal glass, variegated from nearly clear to almost black, ending in a kind of wing shape. "I'll place a bit of opaque white glass here, near the center." He completed the sketch, he tentatively called *Windy Words.*

"I'm not sure." Skye realized she was frowning and adjusted her expression. The pieces were too much alike, but she didn't want to change her own design—unless she decided it was too cliché and scrapped that whole concept. Maybe working with another artist always meant accepting compromise. Did this Vincent guy know what a difficult thing he was asking? Or maybe that was why the money looked so impressive.

For four hours, they worked almost without a break until Pete said, "I know you can go on like this for days, but we both need to eat." He took her to lunch at the same place where they'd eaten together on the day she passed out. That day set a pattern they continued throughout the week. They got together by midmorning each day and worked until late afternoon, sometimes with an encore session in the evening.

Pete took responsibility for assuring meal breaks. By the time their holiday week ended, they had roughed out ideas for four themes and detailed plans for two more. When the metals forge reopened after the holiday, Skye needed to finish the women's series of sculptures for Filene and then get to work on a couple of commissions she'd promised for January. When Pete had help in the Hot Shop again, he had commissions of his own to complete. They needed to do all they could on the Vincent contract while they had time.

The day of New Year's Eve, they met to review the work they'd completed and to agree to disagree about the final two themes since they still needed to straighten out exactly how their finished art would tie together.

"I think this is about as far as we can take this during the break," Pete said as they looked through their sketches and designs. "It's New Year's Eve. We should celebrate." He told her about the place where he'd made reservations, a trendy restaurant that planned to close to the public at nine. After that, those over twenty-one could stay, pay a cover charge, and enjoy drinks, snacks, and live music. "We'll want to stick with soft drinks, of course, but they have two good bands booked and their food is excellent. I'm hoping you'll come with me."

"Of course. Sounds fun." She didn't add that, on an earlier trip home from Destiny, she'd brought all her bridesmaid dresses. After Pete left, she pulled out the deep purple gown she wore for Sunny's wedding, steamed and fluffed it. When she finished, she liked what she saw.

She liked it even better when Pete saw her in the dress that evening. The way his eyes widened made the extra effort well worthwhile.

"You look terrific," he said.

"Thank you," Skye replied with a flirty turn. She couldn't help herself. She greeted him with a quick hug. "You're looking quite dashing yourself," she told him. Pete wore black dress pants with an open-collared white shirt and black leather jacket. His dark hair gleamed, and his close-cut beard and mustache made him look even more devilishly handsome than usual. "Just let me grab my purse and my jacket. I'll be right back." Skye hurried to get her things. For

tonight, pretending they were just coworkers could be even more difficult than trying to coordinate their artistic visions. But it sure sounded
like fun.

SHE'S FANTASTIC! Pete knew he'd have to stop staring, but he couldn't
seem to help himself, and he wasn't the only one. Men all around them
stole furtive glances as he escorted Skye to their table. Throughout
their dinner, which he found both creative and delicious, he had to
keep reminding himself to admire the food and the atmosphere, and
not just his companion.

When had a woman ever captivated him the way Skye did? He
could look at her all day, and it wasn't just her appearance, either. He
could listen to her, too. She was clever and interesting, talented, and
kind as well as beautiful.

For a moment, he thought of his buddy, Tim. What would Tim say
if he could hear Pete's thoughts now? He suspected he knew, and it
didn't bear saying aloud. Tim would probably leapfrog from one
"chick" to another until he was too old to know what to do with them.
Pete almost snickered until he realized that was the future he'd been
expecting for himself.

"Something funny?" Skye raised an eyebrow.

"Just thinking of a frat brother who needs to get more of a life.
What do you think of the guinea hen?"

Skye gave him a quick review of her dinner, agreeing with his own
thoughts, but her expression called him out, making it obvious that
she'd caught him daydreaming and changing the subject. He didn't
mind in the least and continued to marvel at how amazing she was as
the last hours of the year ticked away.

WHAT WERE they going to do at midnight? For the past few hours, they
and the others around them had been entertained by food, drink, and
music. Now the impending moment became real. As Skye looked

around the room, she saw dozens of other couples celebrating the advent of the New Year, all of whom would be embracing each other with a new year's kiss. What would happen with Pete? What did she want to have happen?

She gazed at the man who had occupied so much of her mind and heart from the first moment he'd walked into that first AA meeting. She knew what she wanted—more than she chose to admit—but if they opened that door, could they ever close it again? And what about the great differences in their lives and their plans for the future? That wouldn't be overcome with a kiss at midnight—or not even with months of working together. Maybe a kiss on the cheek? That seemed one way to go, but she didn't know whether she'd get the chance.

As the clock ticked down to midnight, people around them stood to toast the departure of the old year. She and Pete joined them, raising their glasses of club soda. Then, watching the clock on the wall, the crowd counted down the final ten seconds. "Happy New Year!"

Pete placed his hands gently on her shoulders, drew her close, and said, "Happy New Year, Skye." He placed a quick, chaste kiss on her cheek.

Skye repeated, "Happy New Year, Pete." She hated the stab of disappointment that told her she'd hoped for more. Sighing, she cheered the New Year with the rest of the crowd.

THE DEPARTMENT OFFICE opened and Skye met Pete in Dr. Weems's office to sign the contracts that had come from Arthur Vincent as scheduled. All three carefully read over them before signing, checking to make sure everything was as agreed.

Skye had already been to the academic advisor's office, double-checking that she'd met the requirements for graduation. All that remained were the two classes she'd enrolled in this term and her solo exhibition, the final checkmark for each student graduating with a Bachelor of Fine Arts degree. She and her advisor had agreed that her exhibition would come early in the term so she could show the paint-ings she planned for Mr. Vincent, together with the sculpture series on women that she'd promised to Filene. Together they would constitute her final show as a student.

Skye thanked her advisor profusely. As she and Pete left the office, she asked, "How about you? What classes and school projects do you have that might get in our way?"

"Not much. I have my final exhibition to finish, but the work I'm doing for Vincent, together with the pieces I've already submitted, should complete that. I still have to work with students in the Hot Shop a couple of days a week, and I'm student assistant in the senior seminar. Other than that, I'm cleared to graduate this spring."

"Then we know what we need to do. Now we just have to *do* it."

He nodded. "Let's get going."

As they moved into January, they established a new pattern—they chose a theme, decided what they'd each produce and how they'd coordinate their work, then they separated to work on their specific projects and checked in with one another along the way. They saw each other almost daily and often several times a day. They also continued attending AA together. Skye gave Molly a heads-up that Pete would be around more often. His usual spot to plunk down was the dining table. Skye began to expect Pete, even at odd moments when they hadn't made plans.

One evening, the second week into the New Year, Pete showed up with a take-out dinner for Skye. Molly waited until he left before commenting, "Just like an attentive husband." Skye responded by rolling her eyes, but the observation thrilled her. She realized she'd begun to think of Pete as a fixture in her life, even when she didn't wish to.

With some degree of sadness, she admitted she'd fallen in love. What did it say about her that she'd chosen a man who didn't believe in commitment? She sighed and squared her shoulders. She'd overcome other addictions. She could beat her addiction to Pete Koury as well, and she'd need to if she didn't want her heart to be irreparably broken.

~

DESPITE THE HARD WORK, Pete still did his best to keep up his racquetball games with Tim, but after he'd missed two in a row, Tim asked, "So who's the chick?"

"Dude, what're you talking about?"

"The chick you're so involved with that you're ditching your old frat buddy."

Pete patiently reminded Tim of the contract he'd signed, and the marvelous opportunity involved in this show for Arthur Vincent.

"And the chick?" Tim asked.

Rolling his eyes, Pete carefully explained that the only woman was another artist, a painter whose works had to be coordinated with his own. Then Tim asked the critical question: "Bro, since you started hanging out with this other artist, have you dated anybody else? Picked up on any other girls?"

Pete had to think about it. "No, I haven't."

"For how long now?"

Again, Pete had to calculate. What was that first day Skye had come hunting for him in the Hot Shop and fainted? "I guess it's at least four months now. Maybe a little longer."

"Four months? Dude! When in your whole life, since puberty anyway, have you gone four months without trolling for women?"

"That's you, dude. Not me."

Tim laughed. "Don't you see what's happening? You're in love with her, even if you haven't figured it out yet."

"Shut up and play racquetball," Pete growled.

He'd parked some distance away that day, and as he walked back to his truck, he thought about what Tim had said. Was Tim right? Was this love? He'd had crushes before, but had he ever felt this combination of admiration, respect, caring, this wish to make everything right for her if not for himself?

Deep in thought, he barely noticed the father-daughter pair walking toward him on the sidewalk. The little girl, maybe four or five, held her father's hand and skipped along, humming a tune he vaguely remembered from his own childhood. As they neared Pete, the child looked up and grinned, her face aglow. The father said, "Nice day," and Pete responded in kind, although his mind boomeranged to that day when he'd walked by another little girl and her mother, the little girl who had helped him see the beauty of the life around him. That was his D-day, the day he had chosen to live, to get clean and to become what he wanted to be.

And then it hit him—here was another D-day. Maybe he was ready for a new step in life with a new dream of becoming more. He had come this far. Now he could dream of becoming a fully developed adult, the whole picture, complete with a wife and little girls or boys of his own. He turned to watch the man and child as they walked away. It was easy to picture a little girl who looked like Skye holding his hand, calling him Daddy.

Skye's face came clearly to mind—so open, so beautiful, so achingly dear. He had admired her, wanted her, enjoyed being around her, but until this moment, he'd never been sure he loved her. Now he knew. He loved her completely with all the deep, tender emotions he had never expected to feel. He'd thought himself too hardened, too scarred, too damaged ever to feel this way, but Skye knew all about this kind of hardness. She had scars of her own, and still she ventured forward, hoping to have it all. Maybe he could too.

After what he'd told her about never wanting marriage, he'd have an effort persuading her that he might be worth her trouble. Yet that persuasion suddenly seemed a goal well worth pursuing. He had changed his life; surely he could change her mind. Grinning to himself, he hurried along the sidewalk, vaguely humming the little girl's nursery school tune.

Chapter Twenty-Five

By mid-January, Skye and Pete were pleased with their projects for the themes of "calumny" and "class consciousness." Dr. Weems had delivered the news that Filene wasn't happy about putting off delivery of the women's series sculptures or having them displayed in an exhibition before she got them, but she still wanted them enough to accept what she called "unfortunate timing." Knowing what she did of Filene, Skye considered that a win.

Pete met with Skye at her apartment so they could choose the next theme to develop. Skye wanted to work on familial love, but Pete hesitated, an odd behavior for him that Skye found annoying. "You have something special you want to do for this theme. Why can't you do it now? Our time is limited."

"Yeah. I know, but the timing has to be right. Why don't we work on 'antagonism'?"

Skye had to take a deep breath to steady herself, but she said, "Okay, we can try that. In fact, I roughed out something I'd like you to see." She paged through her sketchbook and laid out a sketch she'd done in colored pencil.

"Whoa!" Pete stepped back in surprise when he saw it.

Skye had drawn a human face, but, typical of her work, it was more abstract than real. The shape was distorted, much wider than a normal human's, and it was painted in vertical stripes. The stripe at the far left was a pale Anglo flesh color. Next to it was a darker color, like the olive skin typical of Mediterranean people. To the right of that came another hue, a pale terra cotta like Skye's own complexion. The stripes grew darker until the farthest right shone in a deep brown-black shade, like the darkest people of Africa.

The face wasn't just contorted in shape, but also in expression. The eyes were wide open, showing whites all around the irises—one pale blue, one nearly black. The mouth opened partially in an angry snarl and sharp teeth bit into the bottom lip, biting so hard that it bled. The overall effect was stunning, even in a small sketch.

"Whew!" Pete took a couple of deep breaths. "That's amazing, Skye. It's like the whole human race all in one person. We're one soul, but we're at war with ourselves."

"Yes. That's what I wanted you to see."

He held out his arms in a wordless offer of support. She stepped forward and he wrapped her in a gentle hug. "You are an amazingly talented artist."

Skye felt a warmth expand inside her from her heart outward at the feel of Pete's arms around her. It was all she could do not to burrow into his chest.

"Are you thinking of a large canvas?" Pete asked, clearing his throat.

Was Pete as affected by the embrace as she was? Or was he merely being supportive? She wanted to ask him, but not when she was feeling so emotional. Instead, she pulled away and busied herself with her sketchbook. "Maybe two-and-a-half feet high and four or five feet wide."

"It will be perfect." His expression changed. "I have no idea what to pair with that."

She took pencil in hand. "Let's consider that." They sat down together and began thinking of what might work, designing a paired sculpture to show the same emotion in glass.

CLASSES STARTED in the third week of January, but Skye took time away during that week and the next to complete the women's series, ready now for the show. Working in the shop at the metals forge, she dusted and polished each piece and placed them in the way she wanted to see them displayed. By the last day of the month, the series was complete and the four pieces made a strong statement. She'd done good work and she knew Filene would be pleased. Skye could now finish her paintings for the Vincent contract and she'd have her final student exhibition done.

She nodded to the shop foreman. "They're ready, Yusef. You can have your students pack them up for transfer now. The show is still a few weeks away, so is it okay if I store these here for a while?"

"No problem." The usually gruff foreman offered a supportive smile. "You're one of our favorites, Skye. Ever since you saved the day for Min-sun over the broken molds, everybody has been ready to donate blood if you need it. Min-sun will happily give you a kidney."

She laughed. "Thank them for me, but I won't be needing blood. Or a kidney either. At least, I hope not."

"Well then, whatever you do need, it's yours." Yusef nodded, turned away, and immediately began organizing students to pack and store Skye's work.

Skye thought of Pete, imagining how pleased he'd be when he saw her projects progressing. Again she wondered, as she often did lately, what might happen between them when they completed the Vincent contract. He had warned her that he was not a family man, so thinking of a future with him was only setting herself up for disappointment.

She caught a glimpse of her reflection in a piece of polished steel. She even looked like a woman in love. Images and swirls of color began coalescing in her mind. *Stop it!* she told herself. *You can paint* Hopeless Love *some other day. Focus on what you need to do now.* Unfortunately for her, the next thing on her agenda was another meeting with Pete followed by at least three more in the week to come. She cleaned up her space at the metals forge and prepared to go meet the man who had put her world into+ such delightful turmoil.

PETE TOOK a deep breath and bounded up the stairs to Skye's apartment. It was February seventh with Valentine's Day a week away, and the perfect time for what he planned. There was no reason to be nervous… But he couldn't help it. He had too much riding on the outcome of the next few minutes.

He rang the bell and Skye answered. "Hi Pete. Come on in and… What's this?"

"Flowers. For you."

"They're lovely, but…I don't understand."

He grinned. "How about we put these in water. Then we'll sit down together, and I'll tell you what I have in mind. It's about our plan for familial love."

The confusion cleared from her face. "Oh. Good. I don't know what that has to do with flowers, but I'm glad we're moving on that front. I have some ideas, too—"

"Okay, but I get to tell mine first."

"Deal." She set the newly filled vase on the kitchen counter and sat beside him on the couch. "Now tell me. What are you thinking for family love?"

He pulled a sketch from his pocket and handed it to her. Then he put his arm behind her on the couch. Almost trembling with anticipation, he waited.

Skye unfolded the sketch. It depicted two stick figures holding hands. He'd filled out the face of the taller one with a full beard and mustache. The smaller figure had thick, black hair that wound in spiral curls. "I'm thinking of us."

The confusion returned. "I don't understand…"

He took no time to close the small gap between them, pulling her toward him gently. "May I kiss you?" he asked

"I don't understand," she said, but she moved toward him in an action he took as an answer. He drew her into a gentle but insistent kiss. She responded, eagerly kissing him back, and he relaxed, knowing this was going well. When he finally let her go, he repeated, "When I think of family love, I'm thinking of us, Skye, of you and me. I love you."

He didn't know how to describe her expression. He'd hoped for joy or excitement. What he saw looked more like…shock, maybe? What she said was, "You do?"

He laughed and kissed her again. "I do. I'm in love with you, Skye." Then he added, "I hope I'm not too late, and I'm daring to hope that you love me, too."

Her eyes filled with tears. "You know I haven't changed my mind about...about—"

"I know," he answered. "You want the whole enchilada, or maybe it's chilaquiles. The white wedding, the mortgage, the kids, the works, and I'm in. For all of it." He straightened. "I realized the other day that I haven't wanted anyone else since I first met you." An image of the student offering herself so casually in the Hot Shop popped into his mind. He suppressed a shudder.

"I want to take you out next week for Valentine's Day—not as my work partner or my friend, but as my girlfriend. I want us to start dating and planning for a future together. I want to start thinking of ourselves as a possible future family."

"You're thinking long-term commitment—"

"Yep. Assuming things go well for us, I'd like us to start thinking toward a wedding."

Her eyes widened. "You're serious?" She touched his hair. "You haven't been hit on the head, have you? You weren't accidentally drugged?"

He threw back his head and laughed "You're wonderful, Skye. A lot of things have been changing for me since I met you. I didn't know what a family could be until I went to Destiny and spent time with your family over Christmas. I never thought I'd want children, but lately I've been noticing families with kids and I know now that I do. Want kids, I mean. I know we aren't ready to plan a wedding yet, or even to call ourselves engaged, but I'd like to see us dating each other exclusively and moving in that direction." He waited. When Skye said nothing, his nervousness returned. Then he said, "It's your turn to talk now."

"I...I don't know what to say." She made an odd sound. It could have been the start of a sob, an interrupted sigh, even a giggle. "Can I just say yes, I'd like that, too?"

This time his laugh was all relief as he hugged her closer and kissed her again. When he finally let her go, he said, "I'm ready to work now, if you are."

She grinned. "I suspect that could become an issue for us in the future."

He wrinkled his brow. "What could?"

"Deciding when to play and when to work."

He grinned back. "I suspect you're right."

With that, they began to work on their *other* plans for showcasing familial love.

For Valentine's Day, Pete presented Skye with a lovely necklace that depicted two entwined hearts, each containing a small central diamond. She gave him a "gentleman's grooming kit" (or so said the sophisticated looking label) that promised to help him keep his facial hair neatly trimmed and fashionable.

The following week, realizing they were ahead of schedule for their contract, they spent the weekend in Destiny, where their new status as a couple was met with joy and congratulations from Skye's family and friends and an intense interrogation in Enrique's office for Pete. "Never doubt that your uncle is fiercely protective of you," he whispered to Skye when he finally came out. The rest of the weekend was filled with family closeness and excellent food.

Skye couldn't remember ever being happier. She'd found a man who understood her completely—one who could empathize with the battle she'd fought to overcome her addictions and understood when she struggled to get through a difficult time, tempted to use again, but fighting that demon and winning. An artist like her, whose work would never compete with her own, yet who had the same sensibility and a similar way of understanding the world. Someone as handsome and charming as the devil himself who wanted only her. She'd never imagined she could be so lucky, or so blessed.

Their plans coalesced quickly. Both would complete their degrees by late spring and graduate in summer. By then, Skye's sale to Filene, their various other commissions, and their contract with Arthur Vincent would all be complete. When they graduated, they'd have the means to buy their own separate spaces and build their own artist studios, or to put a nice down payment on a home and establish a studio and hot shop together. Artist's agents had begun approaching them, and they'd agreed to consent only when they found someone who could represent them both. Each morning, Skye looked at herself in the mirror and thought, *How did I get so lucky?*

As they worked their way through the winter, Skye saw her life moving forward as it never had before. Mid-March came and, with her eight paintings for Vincent completed, Skye worked with Dr. Weems's staging class to set up her final student exhibit. The Vincent paintings, the women's sculpture series, and the additional paired paintings —*Hopeless Love* and *Dreams Come True*—made a nice exhibition. Best of all, Pete was there, encouraging her every step of the way.

She looked at the finished exhibition, ready to open the next evening, and sighed in contentment. For Skye, this moment was worth all the work of getting sober, all the struggle she'd gone through to hone her art, all the effort to study and develop her skill, everything she'd had to do to get here.

Even though spring was just around the corner, Skye knew she'd never again have a winter like this one. She and Pete were on top of the world with everything lifting and supporting their dreams, their success. Or so it seemed.

Chapter Twenty-Six

By the third week of March, both Pete and Skye had completed their final shows as students and their advisors had signed their paperwork for graduation. With the help of Dr. Weems's staging class, Skye's sculptures in the women's series were carefully prepared and shipped to Filene in St. Helena. Then each paired set of paintings and glass art was packaged and sent to Arthur Vincent to be set up for display according to the contract.

Skye had received two more commissions, both of which promised to pay well. Between her work to complete those paintings and her efforts to finish the final report for her degree, she still had plenty to do, although the schedule seemed absolutely lazy compared to the way she'd been pushing for...how long now? It seemed forever. Ever since she'd been sober, anyway.

She was in the metals forge, helping Yusef clean out the last of her personal tools, when she took a call from Dr. Weems. "Skye, can you meet me for dinner this evening? Tom is out of town and Pete will be covering the Hot Shop on the late shift. Meet me at Arjun's at six?"

Skye had never had that sort of invitation. A girls' night out? With a faculty member? But she liked Dr. Weems and she loved Indian food. "Sure. I'd love that." She confirmed the time and clicked off. Then, because she still had four hours before dinner, she went back to work.

Just before six, she walked into Arjun's, freshly showered and wearing black slacks and a white wraparound blouse. Reminded of what Pete had said about the day when Dr. Weems asked him to call her Vickie, she felt she'd received another reward, the opportunity to meet with her former advisor as a peer. A host greeted her and escorted her to a table where Vickie Weems was already seated.

Skye took the seat opposite. Dr. Weems lifted a bottle of red. "Wine?"

Skye waved it off. "Just water for me, thanks." She reminded herself that she'd never told Dr. Weems she was a "friend of Bill's," the AA phrase to describe a recovering alcoholic.

Dr. Weems nodded, her expression sober. "Let me know if you change your mind. I'm afraid I have bad news."

"Okay." The news couldn't be too bad, could it? Otherwise, why would her mentor have picked such a public place for delivering it? Skye sipped her water and waited.

"Filene called this morning. She is shipping your women's sculptures back."

Skye felt her heart begin to race. "Why? What's wrong?"

"She said she was never happy about having you delay delivery. She had a show at the end of February, all pieces by rising women artists. She wanted your sculptures for that. When your work didn't arrive until after that show ended, Filene didn't see how she could use your pieces, so she's sending them back."

"But she agreed—" +++

"Not really. She accepted the delay, but she never wanted it."

Skye felt weak. "We had a deal—"

"Yes, but you never had a contract. I'm sorry, but she can return the work as long as she hasn't paid for it, and she hasn't."

Skye steadied herself. It was a setback, but not a career killer. She and Pete were close to signing with an agent. She'd find someone to buy the women's sculptures. She nodded, "Okay."

Vickie Weems reached toward her. "I'm sorry, Skye, but that's not the worst."

Skye swallowed and folded her hands in her lap. "Go on."

"Arthur Vincent has decided to keep Pete's glass pieces, but he's sending back your paintings."

Skye almost came out of her chair. "What? He can't do that! We have a contract—"

"Yes, you do, and that contract includes a clause... Well, here, I brought a copy with me." She handed Skye a sheet of printer paper. Skye recognized the second page, or maybe the third, of the contract she'd signed. In bright yellow, Dr. Weems had highlighted the phrase, "to be paid when the work is delivered in good condition and approved by the buyer."

"I don't understand. Did something happen in shipping?"

"Not that I know of. He just says he doesn't like the paintings. I'm afraid this phrase gets him out of having to pay. He still wants Pete's glass art and he still wants Pete to come and talk with his guests at the big party, but he's cancelling every part of the contract that has to do with you and your paintings."

Skye could feel her heart pounding in her throat. "And he can do that? It's legal?"

Dr. Weems took a deep breath. "I suppose you could sue, but that word *approved* is like a hinge. Everything turns on it. I'm afraid you'd spend a lot on an attorney and end up losing."

"So I'm out? Just like that?" She took a quiet moment to absorb the blows. "Does Pete know?"

"He was in the office when I got the fax from Vincent. He wanted to be the one to tell you, but he was due at the Hot Shop—and I didn't want him to do it anyway. I told him I got you into this and I felt the responsibility to tell you what had happened."

"He accepted that?"

"He wasn't happy. Skye, he cancelled his part of the Vincent contract. Since I've been acting as the agent in this case, he told me to tell Vincent it's all or nothing, that he accepts the works in pairs—both glass and paintings, as contracted—or he gets nothing at all."

It was some comfort to hear how Pete had stood by her, but it hurt too when she realized how losing the whole contract would impact their long-term plans. She appreciated Pete's support, but worried about what that support would cost. "We've been counting on this contract."

"I know. I've been excited for the two of you. You're a great couple and I expect you'll soar as artists, even after this."

"I don't know about that. What are we going—" And Skye broke down. She couldn't help it; the sobs just came. She didn't resist when Vickie Weems, not knowing better, poured wine in her glass and lifted it toward her.

"Here. This should help," her professor said, and Skye drank, eager for the blunting effect the drink could bring. She didn't complain when Dr. Weems refilled her glass, either. She refused the offer of dinner, but she didn't stop drinking until two empty bottles sat on the table.

PETE POUNDED on the door of Skye's apartment, growing more frightened by the minute. "Skye, let me in! Molly, are you there? Somebody, answer the door!"

He'd been calling and texting and trying to reach Skye ever since Vickie called him last evening. When Skye didn't answer his calls or reply to his texts, he'd driven to her apartment. He was determined not to leave until he saw her. "Molly! Let me in!"

A disheveled, unhappy Molly opened the door a few inches, keeping the chain on so Pete couldn't push through. "Skye says you need to go away. She doesn't want to talk to you."

"But she's here?"

"Yeah, she's here."

Pete set his jaw. "I'm coming in. You can take the chain off and let me in, or you can watch while I kick in the door. Up to you."

Molly took one look at Pete's face, meekly removed the chain, and stepped aside.

"Where is she?"

Molly pointed and Pete half-jogged down the hall. He found Skye huddled under the covers. As he hurried across the room, it occurred to him that he could have found her in any state of dress or undress, and he was lucky to arrive when she was fully covered in pajama pants and a t-shirt. Anything less would have made their situation even more awkward than it already was.

He smelled her before he saw her, and then Skye saw him. She gasped and shouted, "What are you doing here? Molly! Get him out!"

"Don't blame her. I wasn't about to take 'no' for an answer." He sat at the edge of her bed and began gathering her into his arms.

She fought him, struggling to get loose. "Let me go, Pete! I mean it, let go of me!"

Reluctantly, he let her go. "Okay, but I'm not leaving. I love you, Skye. I should have known better than to leave you with Vickie."

"It wasn't her fault. I never told her—you know, about AA. I'm the one who should have known better. Oh, Pete!" Her tears began in earnest. "I drank, Pete. I completely relapsed. I finished off two bottles at the restaurant and stopped at the liquor store on the way home. I've crashed. I've burned. I've failed. Oh Pete, I've failed completely!"

He reached toward her again. When she didn't resist, he gently took her in his arms, slowly, letting her accept his embrace. "You haven't failed." He kissed the curls around her face. "You had a relapse. Relapses happen."

"Not to me! You don't understand—"

"What do you mean, I don't understand?" He allowed his voice to grow harder. "When I heard the news in Vickie's office yesterday, the first thing I wanted was a drink."

"But you didn't take one. I did!"

"If someone had been there pouring a glass of wine for me, I expect I'd have swallowed it too." He stroked her hair. "I talked to Vickie. I told her you're recovering. She feels awful about this, but I assured her that none of it is her fault—not the broken contract and not the…not the rest of it either." He stroked Skye's face and shoulders, kissed her cheeks and forehead.

"Skye, I love you. I plan to make my future with you if you'll have me. If you have a broken contract with some weird collector, I want to break my half of it too. If you have a relapse, I want to pick you up and get you back into recovery. I want to be here for you, Skye, any time you need me, and I hope you'll do the same when I need you."

"But I'm such a hypocrite! I broke up with two different men because they relapsed, and here I am now—"

"I'm so glad you broke it off with those men." He kissed her lips, just a quick kiss, meant to reassure. "If you hadn't, you wouldn't have been here for me to love. I feel sorry for those dudes, but I'm glad they're gone."

"But they relapsed, I broke up with them because of it, and now I've relapsed, and… How can you even look at me?"

"Skye. Sweet, wonderful Skye." He held her while she cried, kissed her hair, her face, her ear, stroked her shoulder and her back, soothed her until she'd cried it out.

"There," he said after a time. "How do you feel?"

"Horrible." She put a hand to her head.

"I don't doubt it. You have a hangover. Your body has gone alcohol free long enough that even a little is too much."

"And I'm afraid that wasn't just a little." She looked to her night table where a nearly empty liquor bottle perched.

"Okay, so you binged. Today is day one of your new sobriety." He lifted her chin. "Here's the deal. I'm not letting you out of my sight until you're feeling better. Well, maybe for a few minutes while you have a shower, 'cause, well, you really need one."

"I'm sorry. I—"

He put a finger to her lips. "Stop apologizing. It's time to stop the regrets and start new. Go get your shower, then come out dressed to stay in—clean pajamas if you have them. I'll order some lunch and have it delivered. Later today, you may feel up to going out. We'll get some dinner when it's time. Then you can get dressed to see people. It's Thursday, remember? We'll go to AA. You can share what happened if you feel up to it. Other people may take heart when they realize that even stone hard Skye can slip."

"Oh no! Whatever else I do, I can't share at AA. I don't even want to go."

"You need to, love. You need to get right back up on that wagon and back into recovery. I'll stay with you through it all. Promise."

She looked at him, and what he saw in her face was raw anguish. "How can you still love me? Really, Pete. How can you?"

"I love you. That's all there is to it. I love you because you're wonderful and because I love you, and I want to be here for you when you need me."

She swallowed hard. "I love you, too. So much. I want to be good enough for you."

"Oh Skye! You're the best part of us, always have been, and I know now that I will love you forever. Now come on and get cleaned up. We have work to do."

Skye discovered he meant it, too. Pete was there for her, just as he'd promised, bringing hope back into her world. He was there at the AA meeting that evening, holding her hand when the sharing period passed and she said nothing, and he was there the next week when she spoke during sharing and sobbed her way through the story of her relapse. As he'd predicted, several people thanked her for telling her truth and helping them deal with their own relapses.

He was there in Vickie Weems's office the next week when, after days of negotiations, Arthur Vincent called to say he'd had a change of heart. He was accepting the whole shipment just as it had come to him and requesting both artists to appear at his event.

"I don't know whether we should go through with this," Pete said when he saw the look on Skye's face. "After the way he treated you—"

"We need to go through with it." Skye offered a genuine smile, calmer and more serene than she'd felt in days. "We plan to make our lives this way, Pete. We need to be professional about it and not let emotions get in the way of a good paycheck."

He squeezed her hand. "You're right. So we'll tell the guy yes. Once he sends the money for the work, we can accept the extra cash to show up at his party."

Dr. Weems seemed pleased with their choice. "I'm glad you made that decision. Being professional about your work means putting all the emotion into the art and leaving it out of your business negotiations. You two are well on your way."

Skye thanked Dr. Weems, Pete did the same, and Skye proudly announced that their future negotiations would be handled by their new agent. Pete told Vickie their agent's name, and their mentor could not have been more impressed. "You're starting at the top," she told them.

Pete was there for Skye in Destiny when she showed her family her new diamond ring and asked them what they thought of a wedding on the fourth of July. Olivia was the first to comment: "You're declaring interdependence on Independence Day?"

Pete said, "That's the idea."

"Good," Olivia said. "I like it."

Enrique said, *"También*. Me too," his grin wide and welcoming.

Skye answered, "That's it, then. We'll plan for the Fourth."

Pete added, "Honestly, I just like the idea of the whole nation celebrating our anniversary every year. Fireworks and the whole deal." He pulled Skye close.

Olivia added, "We always love that holiday, and a wedding will be a good excuse to gather the family for the first annual Reyes Reunion."

Pete said, "Great! Just don't expect us to spend every anniversary with the whole clan."

"Deal," Olivia said, and they sealed it with a high five.

Pete was there for Skye while she fought through the cravings after her relapse, and when she broke down and told the story in a different AA meeting, invited at the request of their group leader, then again the next week when she spoke to still another group. She laughed with Pete about it, calling herself a poster child for post-relapse recovery. He held her, kissed the curls at her temple, and declared she was a marvel and a great example for anyone.

Pete sat with her when they signed contracts to buy a comfortable family home in Destiny and when they hired a local firm to build their workshop, complete with a small glass forge, a metals forge, a paint studio, and all the equipment they'd need to grow their business and their reputations in the art world.

He was there to watch her walk across the stage when she got her diploma, to see her sell her women's sculpture series to a nationally known gallery in Los Angeles, and to watch her sign her first contract for a single-artist exhibition there.

Skye was also there for Pete when he graduated with his master's degree, accepted a teaching job at a junior college in the foothills, and signed for a solo exhibition in a prestigious San Francisco gallery.

Most importantly, they were there together, side by side, in Destiny's old stone church on the Fourth of July when the Reyes family and friends gathered for their wedding. When the minister asked Pete if he'd take Skye as his wife, he squeezed her hand as he said, "I do."

Skye looked at Pete and saw the man she'd dreamed of. He smiled as though lit from within and she knew she had found him—her ideal partner, her heart's home.

The minister announced it was time for the couple to kiss for the first time as husband and wife. Pete leaned closer and whispered, "We belong together, love. I'll be here for you as long as I live." The kiss that followed was sweet, filled with tenderness and promise.

Epilogue

The Fourth of July had come again in Destiny, and the townspeople gathered for their annual picnic in the park, *not* preceded this year by a wedding. Mrs. Burnett, the principal at the elementary school, asked volunteer children from the primary grades to present a patriotic tableau in front of a backdrop hand painted by Mr. and Mrs. Koury, local artists who were now celebrating their first anniversary. Max Burnett kept an eye on the Burnett twins and held tight to the baby while Amber and Mrs. Nguyen guided the children through their play.

Mr. Winston, who taught math at the junior high school, challenged all comers to a running-jumping game based on a logic puzzle. Only his two sons and his wife, who still went by Ms. Kerr, could keep up with him, though most of their math students made a valiant effort.

Sunny and Evan Millett came up from the valley for the weekend, Sunny radiant with her new condition, the two of them steeped in the secret they had shared only with family, but which most of the women in Destiny had already guessed.

Mr. Frantz, the high school principal, was clearly making an effort, trying to greet every one of his students and speak to each of their families. No one blamed him for being distracted, considering his wife was now four days past due. Every time she moved or made a sound, he was beside her, asking, "Is it time?" Meanwhile, people around them placed bets in the pool Mrs. Bailey had created. No one knew yet that the winner would be Liza, the office assistant from the elementary school, who had placed her bet on "boy, between noon and one p.m. on July 5."

In the midst of the joyful chaos, Skye spoke to the man she loved, the one who had stuck by her when she had even given up on herself.

217

"I can see you watching all the families with children. Maybe you'd better tell me what you're thinking."

"Look at them," Pete said, his gaze taking in the whole community. "This is what family and friends are meant to be. I always thought this stuff was just on movies and TV, you know? Like it couldn't be real."

"You're right," Skye answered. "It does seem too good to be real, but real it is, even if family life doesn't look like this as often as it should. I'm afraid we've learned that the hard way." She knew Pete still hurt over his father's refusal to attend their wedding the year before. She appreciated that his mother and brother had come, although they'd barely stayed long enough to get through the ceremony.

Pete would find healing here—just as she had, just as so many of her friends and family had. They'd build their destiny here just as the first prospectors had predicted for themselves, and that led her to the words she'd been hunting. "This is what family and friends should be, but what I'm talking about, dear husband, is the way you're watching the children."

"I've been thinking about it. You know how we decided we didn't want to complicate our lives with a child for a while? How we wanted to get established as artists before we added a baby to the mix?"

"Yes, I remember."

"It seems we're both pretty well established. We have a great agent and we've been getting some amazing offers and commissions. I have the job at the junior college that pays the bills between commissions and covers health insurance, even maternity. I'm wondering if maybe we aren't getting there, you know? I mean getting ready to have—"

"A baby?" Skye smiled, and, as she had intended, there was something in her small, secret smile that caught his interest. As understanding dawned on his face, Skye laid a gentle hand on her belly.

His eyes grew wide. "Skye, are you— Are we—?"

"Late February," she said. "I didn't plan it either, but it seems someone is eager to join us."

He whooped, kissed her, and lifted her off her feet.

When she touched earth again, she asked, "It seems safe to say you're okay with this."

"Much more than okay," he answered. "But how are you? Are you feeling okay? I mean, I hear guys talking. I know it can be tough in the beginning, morning sickness and all—"

"I'm fine." She put her hands on his arms. "I can't guarantee I will stay that way, but so far, I'm feeling great. I will need to be careful around the workshop, though. The paint fumes and other chemicals can be—"

"Of course. We'll see to it that you get all the ventilation you need. That you get everything you need. You can even quit working for a while if you need to or want to. We'll manage. I'm here for you…all the way. I'm always here for you, and I'll be here for our baby, too."

"I know," she said simply, standing on tiptoes to give him a soft kiss. When she pulled back, she saw her love reflected in his beautiful dark eyes. "Thanks for sticking by me."

"My love," he said, "it's the happiest thing I've ever done."

A Message to YOU from the town of Destiny

I hope you enjoyed *Winter Skye,* the fourth and final book in the Seasons of Destiny Series. Please consider rating and/or reviewing it. For more heartwarming, small-town romances please check out my Christmas Town Romance Series and my Rainbow Rock Romance Series. If you'd like to stay up to date on my books and find out about upcoming releases, contests, giveaways, and more, please sign up for my newsletter at www.susanaylworthauthor.com. Thanks for reading. May you find your own Happily Ever After.

Warmly,
    Susan

Books by
Susan Aylworth

Visit **susanaylworthauthor.com** to get any of the books listed here.

The Rainbow Rock Romance Series [available in eBook]:
Welcome to Rainbow Rock, Arizona, a quaint small town nestled in the
striped hills of the Painted Desert region, where every rainstorm brings
a rainbow and every heart is filled with hope and love. Meet the
McAllister family—brothers Jim, Kurt, Chris, sister Joan, and their
beloved widowed mom, Kate. Follow each of their stories as they find
love under the high desert stars. Get to know the McAllisters' friends
and neighbors in Rainbow Rock and enjoy more heartwarming
romances in this wonderful and memorable close-knit community.
Each story may be read separately but there is great enjoyment in
reading them in order.

Over the Rainbow: **Prequel**
Joan McAllister never imagined a world without her larger-than-life
father. After his sudden death, she is overwhelmed with sorrow,
harrowed up by guilt, and coping with her father's dying wish:
helping her mother run the family farm and care for her three younger
brothers. To complicate matters, Joan is attracted to a man she met at
her father's funeral. How can she be thinking of romance when her life
is in turmoil?
Bob Riley sees in Joan the woman he has always wanted. Even though
they met under somber circumstances, there's nothing somber about
his feelings. Bob knows he and Joan have much in common, and he's
pretty sure she's attracted to him, so why does she keep pulling
away? Come to Rainbow Rock, Arizona, and learn what awaits Bob,
Joan, and the rest of the McAllister clan in *Over the Rainbow.*

Ride the Rainbow Home: **Book 1**

In time for her ten-year class reunion, Meg Taylor is lured back to the tiny town in northeastern Arizona where she suffered through high school. Overweight, step-daughter to the principal, she was anything but popular. Now she's slim, attractive, and accomplished—and still wary of all she knew then.

Except for Jim. "Little Jimmy" McAllister was one of her two best friends. Ten years have changed him, too. (No one calls him "little" anymore!) He always cared about Meg and seeing her again only enhances those feelings. He wants her to stay, permanently, but Meg, the daughter of a serial-marrying mom, can't imagine herself in "happily ever after." What will it take to change her mind and bind her heart to his?

At the Rainbow's End: **Book 2**

Alexa Babbidge is about to hit it big as a Hollywood scriptwriter—if only her car will cooperate. Stranded near Rainbow Rock, Arizona, she is rescued by Mr. Could-Be-Right. Too bad she isn't looking for romance! But she is looking for a job, at least until she can reschedule her meeting in movieland.

Kurt McAllister is looking for a scriptwriter, not a wife. But Alexa fits easily into his video production company, and almost as easily into his life. As they work together, taping a documentary about Navajo weaving, he longs to persuade her to stay.

Gold beckons at the end of the rainbow, and Alexa, who has seen too much of poverty, can't resist its pull. Kurt longs to hold her, but at what price? As their time together draws to a close, each must decide whether it is wealth and fame or love and family that await them *At the Rainbow's End.*

Don't Promise Me Rainbows: **Book 3**

When faced with a birthing emergency in his prized breeding stock, pig farmer Chris McAllister calls the local veterinarian for help. He expects the wiry, middle-aged man his family has long trusted, not a petite but tough young woman whose edgy personality could qualify her as an Amazon queen from Greek mythology. Even so, he can't avoid a magnetic attraction to the pretty, red-haired vet.

Beneath her composure and stiff professional demeanor, Sarah McGill hides deeply painful secrets. She's only returned to Rainbow Rock for a short time, filling in for her dad while he recovers from a nasty knee injury. The last thing she needs is some cute cowboy stirring up trouble, digging for answers, making her feel emotions she hoped never to feel again.

When a project for the Navajo Nation throws them together, Chris and Sarah must decide whether they can risk their hearts to promises that come without guarantees.

A Little Night Rainbow: **Book 4**

Max Carmody was married once. It wasn't pretty. Now he finds himself stuck for the summer with a thirteen-year-old daughter he barely knows and a sister who will take her in, but not unless he comes with her. Marcie tells her dad she wants him to marry again, but the last thing this Mozart-loving-car-parts manufacturer needs is romance. In fact, his ever marrying again is about as likely as finding a rainbow in the night sky.

Cretia Sherwood was married too, and it definitely wasn't pretty. She is finally healing and regaining some independence after years of struggling to raise her kids on her own. Now that her daughter Lydia is thirteen and her son Danny is eleven, Cretia can take a breath and focus on making sure she can give her kids everything she didn't have growing up. The last thing this Mozart-loving mom needs is to lose her new-found independence to a man. When her daughter asks her if she would ever consider remarrying, Cretia replies—when she sees a night rainbow in the sky.

When love brings them a rainbow, both Max and Cretia have to choose between the security and safe routines of their present lives or a leap of faith, betting on the future.

Note: This book introduces thirteen-year-old Lydia Sherwood whom you'll meet again in *Always a Rainbow* (Book 7); thirteen-year-old Marcie Carmody whom you will meet again in *The Promise of Rainbows*

(Book 8), and eleven-year-old Danny Sherwood whom you will meet again in *Once in a Rainbow (Book 9).*

A Rainbow in Paradise: **Book 5**
Eden Grant vowed never to go back home. A painful childhood growing up in Rainbow Rock made Eden swear off marriage and a family of her own. With a successful childcare business in Phoenix, Eden can lavish all the love she has on the children of others. But when her best friend, Sarah McGill, asks her to be her maid of honor, Eden makes the trip home to Rainbow Rock for Sarah's wedding. What Eden doesn't count on is her immediate attraction to the best man. Logan Redhorse might be the best man at his friend Chris's fairy-tale wedding but holding Eden in his arms feels like his very own paradise. How can Logan reconcile his immediate attraction to Eden with the promise he made? An attorney for the Navajo Nation, Logan vowed to his ancestors and descendants that he will marry a desert child, a daughter of *Dinehtah.*
How can Eden and Logan reconcile their differences to embrace a future that could bring them both a love beyond paradise?

The Trouble with Rainbows: **Book 6**
Joe Vanetti was deeply in love with his late wife, Roberta. Even thinking of another woman feels disloyal. Although his romantic life ended with Roberta's death, he still has their children to raise. He's returned to Rainbow Rock so they can grow up close to his family. The last thing he's thinking about is dating, but when Joe runs into Angelica DeForest, the former "Ice Queen" from high school, he can't help but wonder at the change in her.
Despite a successful career as a violist, Angelica DeForest lives a lonely life. Painfully awkward and socially inept, she's spent her adult years caring for aging, bitter relatives. She promises herself she will try to be bolder, to reach out to others and maybe even (gasp!) socialize. She certainly doesn't intend to begin with Joe Vanetti, the high school Golden Boy who was always so perfect, so far above her, no matter that he's even more handsome now than back in high school.

A promising future beckons, if they have the courage to banish the ghosts of their past.

Always a Rainbow: **Book 7** (New to the series)
When a handsome Air Force pilot comes to her rescue in a tricky situation, Lydia Sherwood never expects to see him again—and certainly not on the operating table where she's about to assist in emergency surgery. He's come to the rescue again, hailed as a hero, but has suffered life-threatening injuries as a result. Lydia's admiration for pilot is almost as great as her attraction.
Drake Westcott is riding high—literally. Near the top of his class at the Air Force Academy and a standout in pilot training, he's flown some of the nation's fastest, highest-soaring airplanes. Only the U-2 remains, and Drake has sworn to fly "the dragon lady." Now that dream is gone, as is the life he had planned.
Lydia and Drake are on different trajectories with a world of obstacles ahead. Their mutual attraction is strong, but how can it overcome all that separates them?

The Promise of Rainbows: **Book 8** (Formerly: *Return to Rainbow Rock*)
Eleven years have passed since Marcie Carmody left Rainbow Rock for the big city, starry-eyed and eager to build her future. She found love with a struggling law student—or thought she had. When her boyfriend's rejection also leads to the end of her job, she limps home, dejected and ashamed, fearing harsh judgment from her family and community. Finding unexpected acceptance, Marcie also lands a new job in the law offices of Logan Redhorse, working with a new associate. On hyper-alert to make sure she exceeds expectations, she calls the police the moment she sees a man in a hoodie rifling through Logan's files.
Ryan Fields needs a new start. His wife has left him for a man she met in an online role-playing game and has taken his sons with her. Ryan is experienced in native law, having practiced with a Sacramento firm, and the position with Redhorse sounds like a perfect fit. He does not expect to be picked up as a burglar on his first visit to the office, thanks to a nosy redhead. No way does he want *her* as a legal assistant!

But Marcie's apologies and her office skills are real, and Ryan decides to give her a try, firmly ignoring the glimmer of attraction that hovers any time she draws near. Both Marcie and Ryan have wounds to heal and obstacles to overcome. Surely, they aren't ready to find new love, but Fate, and Love, may have other plans.

Once in a Rainbow: **Book 9** (Formerly: *Danny's Girl*)
Running from a man who has threatened her life, Manon DuPre fears even slowing down, let alone stopping, but the Arizona Highway Patrol disapproves of her speed. How can she persuade the handsome trooper that she needs his help, not an arrest?
Raised by a drunken abuser and a terrified mother, young Danny Sherwood grew up to be a protector. Maybe that's why he's such a dedicated patrol officer. When he stops a dangerous speeder on the Interstate, he doesn't expect a beautiful, terrified woman, who claims to be fleeing a killer.
As the community of Rainbow Rock rallies to help, how can Manon and Danny embrace a joyful future when they still must face their difficult pasts, and a potentially lethal threat?

Chasing Rainbows: **Book 10** (Formerly: *Roman's Holiday*)
Roman Kincaid has it all: a meteoric rise to fame and fortune as a country-pop performer and now, as an A-list Hollywood celebrity. He also has a demanding agent driving him to exhaustion. Depleted and dispirited, Roman takes an impromptu holiday, disappearing into Arizona's high desert. A chance encounter leads him to Lottie Beale's café and pie shop.
Lottie Beale is humming along to one of Roman's new releases when the man himself walks through her door. Keeping her cool, she serves him as she would any customer, but his presence fills her with happy thrills—and terribly unhappy memories. She has her own reasons to hide.
Roman's offer to travel with Lottie as his guide sounds like an awkward come-on when Lottie first hears it, but he swears he'll be the perfect gentleman and she easily reads his need for friendly, undemanding companionship—a need she understands too well. Their

road trip takes them to well-known places like Mesa Verde and the Four Corners monument, and to less famous sites only the locals know.

It also takes them on a journey of self-discovery as each comes to terms with where they've been and where they want to go. Can a famous star and a small-town pie maker find common ground? Anything is possible in Rainbow Rock, romance capital of the great Southwest.

An Unexpected Rainbow: **Book 11 (Formerly:** *A Monumental Love***)**
An unexpected romance might have the power to heal the past. Roxelle McCann is eager to meet the family of her roommate and "frenemy," Kyra Redhouse, so she takes a mini vacation to the Navajo Nation. Roxelle expects to find out more about Navajo language and customs and to be awed by the beauty of Monument Valley. She does not expect to find love among the monuments. The man she meets offers both a tender reminder of the past and a surprising possible future.

SEASONS OF DESTINY ROMANCE SERIES [in eBook and paperback]

Welcome to the small town of Destiny, California, where love blooms all year and the bonds of family and friendship last forever. The Seasons of Destiny series features four sweet and clean romances that will warm your heart based in a former Gold Rush community that you'll want to visit again and again.
Each story may be read separately, but there is great enjoyment in reading them in order.

Paris in the Springtime: **Book 1**
After false accusations lead to the loss of her job, Paris Cutler returns to the small mountain town of Destiny, CA to crash and regroup at her grandmother's. When she runs into her former high school crush, Greg Frantz, Paris begins to feel like a smitten kitten. Greg can't get Paris out of his mind. How can he convince her to make Destiny hers?

Sunny's Summer: **Book 2**
Sunny Ray arrives in the small town of Paradise to document the survivor stories of the Camp Fire, the deadliest in California history, for her graduate thesis. Her empathy enables her to connect with the community and to help the survivors heal, except for Deputy Sheriff Evan Millett. Evan's anger and pain run deep and Sunny is determined to find out why.

Amber in Autumn: **Book 3**
Amber Reyes loves her job as the elementary school principal in Destiny, California. When two new kids begin struggling, Amber steps in, not realizing their father is her childhood neighbor, Max Burnett. Max is also suffering, wounded by a disastrous marriage. How can Amber help Max's troubled twins and heal Max's heart so he can love again?

Winter Skye: **Book 4**
Skye Ray and Peter Koury are drawn together by their joint love of art and a determination to turn pro after they graduate from college. But it's their shared education from the school of hard knocks that threatens to shatter their dreams. With Christmas break around the corner, can they mend the broken pieces of the past and build a bright future together?

CHRISTMAS TOWN ROMANCE SERIES [available in eBook]:

Welcome to Christmas Town, officially known as Bedford Falls, CA—where the spirit of holidays are celebrated all year long, and where a wholesome romance is just around the corner. This sweet and clean small-town romance series will make you want to curl up by a cozy fire with a mug of hot chocolate and a plate of freshly baked gingerbread cookies. Enjoy Christmas year round and make Christmas Town your destination for Holiday romance reads.
Each story may be read separately but there is great enjoyment in reading them in order.

A Joyful Eve in Christmas Town: **Book 1 (formerly** *Joy Comes to Bedford Falls)*

A new job brings Claire Reiser to Bedford Falls, California, a Sierra resort village widely known as Christmas Town because it celebrates the Holiday Season year-round. Claire arrives just days before Christmas, reconciled to spending the holiday alone.

Ben Scarge is also new in town, whisked in to manage the estate of his late Uncle Simon, a curmudgeonly miser who puts Scrooge to shame. Like Claire, Ben knows no one and anticipates a lonely holiday. Then a furry visitor delivers a gift neither Claire nor Ben will ever forget.

St. Nick Comes to Christmas Town: **Book 2**

Kiley Ross postponed her dreams of a university degree for many years, but she's ready to tackle it now, including the newswriting lab class taught by grad student Nick Santino. Nick's class challenges Kiley in every way. Trouble is, Kiley can't seem to stop thinking about her movie star look-alike teacher outside the classroom.

Nick Santino knows better than to become involved with a student, especially in his first class as a teaching assistant, but he can't help his attraction to Kiley; she captured his attention on Day One.

Kiley and Nick are coping with the rules and getting through the term. When circumstances throw them for a loop, how will they deal with the fall-out?

Kisses and Kittens in Christmas Town: **Book 3**

Amanda Velasquez is weary of attending her girlfriends' weddings when she can't even get a date. Is it her fault she's tall and built more like her linebacker dad than her runway model mom? Marco Fuentes admires the striking woman whose quest for good health brings her to the gym where he lifts weights. A mutual attraction draws them together, but their pride and prejudices keep tripping them up. Can a basketful of abandoned kittens help them choose snuggling over sparring?

Mischief and Mistletoe in Christmas Town: **Book 4**

Emily Draper and Carl Fuentes can't possibly fall in love. New career opportunities have them both contemplating major changes, and they both know the odds for long-distance relationships. How can the magic of Christmas and a cute kitten called Mischief make their future warm and bright?

Holly and Hearts in Christmas Town: Book 5
Bethany Sheridan has created a comfortable life for herself and her disabled daughter, Gracie. But with the daily demands of her work, her pet fostering, and caring for Grace, Bethany has no time to date let alone fall in love. Richard Hale has just landed a new job with a load of responsibility. He has always relied on a stable routine to manage his severe stutter. But his life turns upside down when he meets the lovely Bethany. How can a wheelchair-bound Cupid, a sweet-but-confused service dog, and an adorable puppy called Holly turn their awkward meeting into a second chance romance?

About the Author

Susan loves people (and most other mammals), words in virtually all polite forms, and perfect raspberry jam. Her love of story began at an early age. "My parents, both teachers, read to me almost from the time I was born. They said I could recite every word of The Tawny, Scrawny Lion." She wrote her first book, "an eight-page shameless rip-off of Black Beauty," when she was nine. At her fifth-grade career day, she declared her goal to become a rich and famous author. Years later, she is pleased to have achieved the "author" part of that goal.

She loves research. "I know that sounds suspiciously like homework, but I love learning about backgrounds and careers for the characters in my novels. It's one way to live many lives at once."

Researching locations dovetails with her love of travel. She has stepped onto every continent except Antarctica, and hopes one day to visit there. She draws much of her inspiration from beautiful northern California, where she lives with her husband of fifty years, Roger, who is also a writer. They have also lived on the East Coast and in the Navajo Nation, the setting for several of her novels. Like most women of her generation, she wishes the kids would visit more often. When they're not around, "I hang with my imaginary friends," her characters, who take her on all kinds of adventures.

Susan loves hearing from readers. If you want to get in touch with Susan or join "Susan's Sweet Team" and get free books and other fun perks you can email Susan at susan@susanaylworthauthor.com.

You can also sign up for Susan's Wholesome Heart Newsletter and get a FREE book. Follow Susan on BookBub for updates on new releases and on Twitter @SusanAylworth or "like" her Facebook author page and follow her on Pinterest.